Slay Me Tender

An Aubrey Lyle Mystery by
Jenny Scholten

New Victoria Publishers

Norwich, Vermont

Published by New Victoria Publishers Inc., PO Box 27 Norwich, Vermont 05055 A Feminist Literary and Cultural Organization founded in 1976

Cover Art by Jack Pabis

Printed and bound in Canada
1   2   3   4   2004   2003   2002   2001

Library of Congress Cataloging-in-Publication Data

Scholten, Jenny,1968-
    Slay me tender : an Aubrey Lyle mystery / by Jenny Scholten
      p cm.
    ISBN 1-892281-15-5
    1. Stripteasers--Fiction. 2. San Francisco (Calif.) Fiction. I Title.

PS3569.C52547 S58 2001
813'.6--dc21

                        2001030570

For Grace who wouldn't approve.

Chapter One

Micki bent at one of my breasts, Maude at the other, each rubbing a nipple.

"They won't stand up," Micki complained, and Maude shook her head in exasperation, as the two strippers worked to improve the shape of my 34-Cs under the sheer garment that I was about to flounce in down Naughtyland's stage. They were my coworkers. The garment was a bikini that I'd put a hem of four-inch buckskin fringe on for my cowgirl number. The leather fringe danced back and forth over my rib cage as the two girls worked. I was starting to understand the appeal that the attentions of eager-to-please girls had to our strip club's customers.

"Better," said Maude, and they spun me toward the full-length mirror by the stage entrance. The mirror was always the last stop for us strippers before our show, to make sure strategic points were clean and covered, however temporarily. Our boss Mose Junior wasn't one for splurging on interior decoration, and the mirror warped our images with cheap glass. My reflected hips puddled into my shorter attendants' scrunched up abdomens. My green eyes and their brown ones, punched up with stripes of dark eyeshadow and black liner, were squeezed too far above lipstick mouths. My unruly reddish-brown hair warped even bigger, but my breasts remained sadly deflated. Micki and Maude turned from the distorted image to look directly at my disappointing chest.

They had a short conversation in Thai. Maude gave me the verdict. "Still droopy."

"It's so hot in here, that's why. Wait a minute." Micki spike-heeled over to the water cooler, our one backstage luxury. Cleaned-and-pressed spring water arrived weekly in five-gallon kegs, delivered by a gawking teenage boy whom I suspected may have forgiven the charges in exchange for peeks at the backstage scenery. Micki filled a paper cup with the sanitized water, demonstrably clean from its faint blue shade, like the rinse water after my Granny Leann had finished with the whites.

"No way. No cold water. These people aren't worth me catching pneumonia," I said, but I wasn't heard. "Master and Servant" by Depeche Mode had picked up where "Like A Prayer" by Madonna had left off, seconds before. Naughtyland's sound system was concussive. Bass notes shocked like sledgehammers.

We dancers had to scream at each other backstage.

"Master and Servant" was the fifth and final song of Naughtyland's featured performer of the week, Plushious Velvett, and also my cue. When the Depeche Mode tune ended, it would be my turn to go onstage.

"No, I like them saggy, really," I said to Micki. She now stood inches away and aimed the full Dixie cup at my bustline. Maybe I should let her do it, I thought. I was merely a professional stripper from Dayton, Ohio, surgically unaltered, a couple of years in the biz working out of this seedy Tenderloin club, my knees and my attitude corrupting in proportion to the months my career stretched on. Like all Mose Junior's featured performers, Plushious Velvett was a genuine Hollywood movie star, even if it was porno movies that she starred in. The night before I'd watched her gymnastics, watched her dildo show and watched her pluck twenty-dollar bills off the bridge of men's noses with her breasts. My appearance onstage would be a decided anti-climax for the crowd. I might need all the help I could get to coax one dollar tips from the porn-dazzled supplicants shipwrecked against the stage. I thought of the slack-jawed, though not unappreciative, stares that always greeted my entrance, then remembered that Naughtyland's customers weren't worth risking pneumonia for.

I caught Micki's wrist. I was about to point out that my boobs had grown in droopy the summer before junior high. My Momma had threatened that I'd look like one of those carved African statues whose nipples point straight to the ground if I didn't get myself a bra immediately. Some boobs were just meant to sag. Before I could speak, evidence to the contrary tore through the opening in the black curtain that serves as our stage entrance.

Nothing on her naked body jiggled as Plushious Velvett, breathing fast and shallowly as only an exercising smoker can, stomped between myself and Micki, broke my hold on Micki's wrist and tackled the outstretched Dixie cup. The water meant to perk my breasts smacked into the wall behind the ashtray.

The porn star dug in her spike heels where her Camel, its filter kissed red, still smoldered. She snatched up the butt and gave it a deep drag. The end of the cigarette blazed. Plushious Velvett's dilated pupils reflected the flare. She looked like a horse about to rear. Micki and Maude fled, their rear-ends, each bisected by a rubber band of lycra, disappeared into the dressing room.

Plushious Velvett pursed her lips as if to say something in the instant she paused between drags. Apparently there wasn't time. "Master and Servant" continued to deafen the audience, now looking at a bare stage and wondering where their genuine Hollywood porn star had gone.

The movie actresses were hired to perform nightly for half an hour starting at midnight. A new one rotated in every week. They were Mose Junior's latest scheme to crank yet more profit out of the ephemeral concept of a strip club. When one's only product is a fleeting glimpse of pussy, or for an extra twenty, a short dry-humping session euphemistically called a lap dance, one might think that diversifying would be the only way to keep customers coming back.

But Mose Junior needn't have worried. He had the laws of economics on his side. The nightly press of oglers into Naughtyland was proof enough that its particular commodity, though owned by half the population, was nevertheless in short supply.

I watched Plushious Velvett tremble the Camel butt to the end of a half-smoked but serviceable Marlboro that she'd salvaged from the ashtray. Even the tufts of blonde that perming and bleaching had left on her head seemed active with indignation. Plushious Velvett's brick-like calf muscles convulsed. The porn star's tall, lithe body was little more than a tanned support system, a string of bone struts and muscle joists, knit together to fly aloft the colossal domed architecture of her breasts. All Mose Junior's features had breasts like moored zeppelins, out of scale and tugging for altitude. When the porn stars had first begun to come through Naughtyland, a few months before, their amazing breasts had fed weeks of dressing room gossip.

"Got to go to Switzerland to buy those. They won't sell them here. Anything over a liter is FDA-banned," Plantagena had said. She should know. Naughtyland's popular thirty-four double D had gotten her relatively understated bosom installed by the third-best plastic surgeon in LA.

Words were percolating in my companion. The deep drags slowed in frequency to every second breath. Plushious Velvett dropped the Marlboro back into the ashtray. Its previous user had worn a cheerier shade of lipstick. The butt was striped plum and red. The porn star spat her gum into her hand with the force of an airgun.

"Fucker touched my pussy." Her eyes, bloodshot from nicotine, skittered over my face.

"I'm sorry," I answered. So that was the cause of her fit. I found it hard to believe she couldn't handle this turn of events.

Plushious Velvett hadn't seemed squeamish. And she was hardly new to the business, though it was impossible to tell anything about her age except that she was clever at disguising it. Customers weren't allowed to touch the parts of us they were most interested in, since in the eyes of the San Francisco vice squad, physical contact with our "private" parts pushed us dancers over the thin line to whore and moved Mose Junior from friendly neighborhood small-business owner to pimp. Nevertheless, the odd enthusiastic customer completed a desperate grope before one of our bouncers could get to him. The show usually went right on while the offender was eighty-sixed. I'd seen Plushious Velvett's stage show, the tamest part of which involved a phallic tower of shaving cream that she sculpted, plonked onto a customer's head, then sat on, buck naked. Many volunteered for the messy privilege of being crowned with a shaving-cream dildo.

"Sorry, well," she flung the gumwad into the ashtray, "that's it." The porn star bent over, back muscles popping against the pendulum force of her chest, and began clawing at the pile of custom-made costumes strewn about the floor. Like the other featured performers, she'd brought along an array of bedazzling, skimpy outfits that either skewered the viewers' eyes with the reflected points of ten thousand sequins, or burned enduring after-images onto their retinas in the color complement to some neon shade. I don't know how her audience avoided eyestrain.

"This is a horrible city." Plushious Velvett was flicking a series of bras with structure worthy of the Army Corps of Engineers over a slender forearm. "This is a horrible place. The customers are cheap and this neighborhood sucks." She made a mush of several sequined evening gowns and clamped them under an arm. "Your boss is too cheap to put me up in a real hotel. I can't sleep for worrying some street person is going to break in and kill me. I've got cash, you know. Lots of cash. That's what these are for, to bring in more cash. They were supposed to improve my life." She slapped her breasts. Shiny stretch marks stitched the orbs to her thin chest. A circle of wrinkles had bloomed around each nipple where flesh fell from the gravity-defiant implants. She faced me again, seized my hand, clapped it to one of them.

"Feel that," she said. "I'm gonna need new ones. Feel those lumps?" She steered my hand around various nooks and crannies. The breast had a viscous feel, heavier, denser than flesh. It responded slowly to my touch, like a done cake releasing a poke. "It'll cost me another eight thousand bucks to fix them. Can you believe that shit? Can you fucking believe that?" She flung my hand away. Spread out, fingers wide, my hand hadn't spanned even a quadrant of her breast. Plushious Velvett smashed a welling tear back into her eye.

I mumbled 'that's awful, I'm sorry' type things. She ignored me. She was collecting the bouquet of gowns and bras and the crowning garment of her show, a black satin cinched-waisted robe, embroidered in metallics and edged with a blue feather boa, that gaped to accommodate the cubic yardage of her chest even as it fell limply over her arm. It must have had an internal frame. Her eyes contradicted the blue powders and plucked arches that created an innocent expression in them. "Improve my life so I wouldn't be living in shit," she continued, not to me. "I'm alone, right? No one's paying my way. I won't be treated like this. I'm going to get the guy who did this to me. Then I'm going back to Oklahoma."

The porn star stalked off to the dressing room, dropping several g-strings behind her. Her ass, hard and brown as two hazelnuts, didn't move a millimeter as she went. I watched her go, sympathetic. We had a difficult job. And sadly, her threats were idle. Whoever had groped her would be long gone, evicted by the bouncers, but free to take his wandering hands to any of the twenty strip clubs in town, or to the peep shows, or to the prostitutes, or to the massage parlors. He would never have to learn respect. And porn stars don't earn much money if they go back to Oklahoma.

"What happened to my Marlboro?" Secrecia, a college student whom Mose Junior had recently hired despite hating her tattoos, her bitten nails and dyed-black, chopped off hair, searched the ashtray behind me.

"I think the feature just smoked it." Depeche Mode's synthesizer wheezed the song's final notes. I tugged a western-style negligee over my bikini. It helped to have a couple of layers to take off, to increase the small amount of voyeuristic tension in the strip show. By house rule, we had to show our breasts by the second song of our set and be completely naked by our third and final song. The negligee's white mesh laddered upward over my backside, seeking the looser fit of my waist.

"My last smoke. That wasn't very sisterly. She needed it though. Tense! Something's going on with girlfriend; she throws up before every show. And she keeps making everyone feel her implants and agree with her on how gross they are."

"Really? I guess I wasn't special. Anyway I think she just quit." I flexed my feet to stretch them inside the high-heeled cowboy boots that gave girth to my thin ankles. The first notes of "Girls with Guitars" by Wynnona were my cue. "I don't think we'll be seeing her again after tonight."

My words to Secrecia were to prove prophetic. But that night, innocent of the future, I strutted onstage to confront Plushious Velvett's shaving cream bathed fans.

My stage strut had been a couple of years in the making. Two years before, I'd come to San Francisco with a bachelor's in history and little idea how much it cost to live on a small earthquake-prone peninsula where apartment buildings couldn't rise more than a few stories. I'd already formed an idea of how cheap my second step-father Eb was, and was looking for work that would pay enough for me to help Momma out. Her job at the beauty shop didn't pay much. She had medical bills. I'd tried the temp agencies, but couldn't afford the wardrobe they expected on the salary they offered. I'd managed to find a job without that pesky "professional dress" requirement.

My shoulder muscles tensed into bulbs as I jumped into a soft spin around the metallic pole that pierced Naughtyland's stage. The soles of my boots clanked the metal. A whirlwind pushed tendrils of cowgirl fringe to the side. Heads and shoulders of the several men at the chest-high stage were a blur to me—a workshirt blending into the neighboring lapels and tie—someone's glasses and someone else's bald head reflecting the colored lights that spun through the dark club. The red-lit stage jutted long and narrow between the barstools the men sat on. None of their faces were more than five feet from me.

I twirled lower down on the pole than the point where I could step off. A decision had to be made. Take it on the knees and collide with the thinly carpeted hardwood? That would cause a grimace fierce enough to crack my fake smile. I opted for ass, shooting both legs forward with a pinch of my abs. From the landing I went straight into a spread-eagle almost naturally. I hauled my legs toward the ceiling. I'd never been athletic, but after a few weeks of stripping my thigh muscles had swelled like rising loaves. Through the V of my legs, I watched dollar bills plunk onto the rim of the stage.

One customer actually seemed to be making eye contact from between his bushy mustache and the brim of his baseball cap. I winked at him. When my set was over, I'd ask him for a lap dance.

The stage was the center of attention in the small interior of Naughtyland. It was the only area directly lit, the only area of movement. The ceiling, the tables and chairs, the extremities of the club, were done in black, lit only by quickly passing searchlights, refracted by the disco ball. Black curtains walled off the street door, the dressing room door, the stage door and twenty or so closet-sized cubicles hedged against the walls.

"Ah, behind the arras," said the thirty-something white man, taking a seat in the one armless chair, the only furnishing in any of the cubicles. "Splendid." He gave me the usual head-to-toe appraisal, which I gave right back. Preppies were one subset of my typical customers. Businessman types of all colors went for me too, and the occasional Asian man. Most Asian and Latino men went for busty blondes; black men seemed to choose either blondes or black women; white men skirting middle age made the many Asian women I worked with the most successful lap-dancers of us all. It was nothing personal.

"I'm Kent." Kent molted his tweed jacket, snuffled to adjust his glasses, reached for his wallet.

"I'm Aisling." I held out my hand for his twenty. It was taking him awhile to find it in the near total darkness of the cubicle.

The mustachioed baseball-cap wearer had been the first of a steady stream of customers that was typical for the last two hours of a night shift. Naughtyland's patrons tended to wait, holding onto their wallets as tightly as to their non-alcoholic beers, until we were about to close before paying for the private dances that were how we strippers made most of our money. This could be a tense dynamic. Women who hadn't made a stack of twenties by midnight were anxious that they would come up short of the hefty fee we paid Mose Junior for every shift we worked. A rush at the end was draining, demanding exertion from a body that craved rest. This man, I thought as I straddled Kent and ground into his scratchy pantlegs, will be my last customer of the night.

"Hmm," Kent latched onto the cups of my black wonderbra. "Very nice."

"Great. But you can't touch there, hon."

"Come on. You've been here since, what, five? You've got to be horny after working all day. Lucky you. You got the greatest job."

Kent wore a collared shirt of the kind that come wrapped in cello-phane and around cardboard. I batted his creased sleeves away from my tits, moved my cleavage up to his stubbly chin. That ought to keep him quiet and he couldn't see my face; I could stop smiling. I didn't bother to answer Kent. He seemed the sort who thought it would be great fun to gird oneself with tacky underclothes and flash strangers all day. Such activity would definitely make them horny. As I lapdanced Kent, I pondered which stereotype was more annoying: 'you strippers must get so horny' versus 'porn isn't work, it's fun'

Secrecia was onstage. She was one of a newer crop of dancers, a group that really was in college and not just saying it, stripping for the experience, they said, as much as for the money. They considered performing at Naughtyland, incredibly, part of their artistic trajectory. They inevitably danced to long, intellectual songs. Sorority's PJ Harvey tune had just begun, and Kent had paid to be sat on until the end of it.

He moved his hands to my ass. I slapped them away when he tugged at my thong underwear. I'd definitely gotten a groper. I was tiring fast, fig-uring on another few gyrations against the man's groin before my burning quads gave out and I'd have to change position, thinking about my futon and the heaviness of my quilt and how I couldn't wait to crawl between them. I was tired. I was grumpy. Perhaps I overreacted to what happened next. I felt cold noodle fingers on my breasts. Kent had made a sudden move. I looked down as the man's gold wedding ring, and then chunky class ring, disappeared into my bra. No doubt stymied, like so many by the intricacies of bra closures, Kent had gone the direct route and in an instant my breasts were bared, falling from the few square inches of black eyelet cloth that had covered them. Smiling goonily, Kent flicked his tongue at my left nipple.

Before his slobbery tongue could reach me, I grabbed him by the throat and slammed his head backwards against the wall.

Kent's glasses were knocked down his nose and he gargled something about a misunderstanding. He was careful to remain still, since I had a knee to his groin. I'd also pinned his sternum with an elbow.

He was wearing a nice silk tie, slippery and cool in my hands as I wrapped it around his neck. "What's so hard to understand about keep your hands off my—"

A stirring of air chilled my bare back and bubbles of light swept the walls and floor of the cubicle.

Shit. Someone had opened the curtain that had walled us off from view. I couldn't afford to get caught 'assaulting' a customer again. If it were Mose Junior standing behind us, it would mean my job this time. I let go of Kent's tie. From the viewpoint of whoever stood at the curtain, perhaps what was happening would seem to be merely a lapdance. Leg to groin, chest to chin, red-faced client. Lapdance.

"Um, trouble here?" The voice was a slow cadence. Dallas, the bouncer Mose Junior had most recently hired. Being new, Dallas didn't know of my past history, rumor or fact.

"He grabbed my tits." I plucked myself off Kent and snapped bra cloth into place.

"You okay?" Dallas looked at me, then Kent, running a hand through his dirty blond layers. Like us dancers, the bouncer had been hired for his body type. He was big and square.

"I'll live," I said. "But he should go."

Kent, deflated by the presence of an intruding male, meekly put on his coat.

Dallas' faded Levis followed Kent's tweeds out. I sighed and headed, finally, backstage to get dressed.

Chapter Two

"Bodyguards," said Mose Junior. "From now on, they've got to come with their own bodyguards. Someone touch her pussy, she quit. What am I supposed to do now? Her picture is in the paper; here all week, it says. Show at midnight, Wednesday through Sunday. Today is only Friday. What can I do?"

It was two a.m. and Mose Junior had to tune his whine sharp to be heard over the barks of locker doors slamming in the dressing room. He rarely ventured into the fetid mirror-and-locker-lined room where as many as forty girls sweated in various stages of undress. When he did join us, a long linen suit flapping among bare skins, he was careful to avert his eyes. Since Mose Junior had bought Naughtyland a couple months previously, he'd become even more paranoid about lawsuits. To avoid sexual harassment charges, he barely looked at us dancers even when our clothes were on, and had instructed the male bouncers to behave the same way.

"Which one of you can be feature? I don't pay, but no fee to work." Our boss rocked his brown Italian loafers back and forth, the leather too buttery to retain a crease.

"None of us are porn stars," said Cameron, peeling off her false eyelashes in the dance-school-sized mirror that covered an entire wall of the dressing room.

"You all stars. All." Mose Junior aimed his head slightly upward and appeared to cross his deep-set eyes.

I turned back to my locker to pull out my leather jacket. A stencil of 'Aisling' in black block letters differentiated my slice of gray from Mahogany's and Moana's. Mahogany tissued off lipstick, bending to see her reflection around a picture of her son in his Cub Scout uniform that she'd taped to her locker door mirror. She groaned as her posture stretched her hamstrings. Moana was asking me if she could borrow my silver shoes and what size was I. I stood behind Mahogany, catching a glimpse of myself in her mirror, and admiring the effect of my jacket's black leather over the blue geometry of my polyester men's shirt. My roommate Hugh had brought the shirt home for me from his job at the thrift store. The leather jacket was my favorite wardrobe item. I wore it every day. It made any outfit look good.

Mahogany swung her locker door closed, and the mirror caught reflections of Cameron squeezing her thick blonde hair into a ponytail, Plantagena squeezing her plump arms into a fitted pink t-shirt, and Salamé's snake tattoo uncoiling along her spine as she bent down to undo the strap of her platform shoe. Meanwhile Mose Junior's image bounced between mirrors around the room, so it appeared that several gaunt men were barely propping up their suits. In another mirror I could see Farrah, Salamé's girlfriend, tying a blue cotton bra around her pale chest. Then, wait a minute—mirrors don't lie. I reached around Mahogany and swatted her locker door open until her mirror reflected Mose Junior again. I'd been right. The apparent legion of besuited men had been looking at me.

He looked away quickly, searching for an unoccupied focal point.

"No way. I don't have breasts that you pay at the pump for. Forget it, Mose." A half-hour show every night for a week for no pay, even if our $120 stage fee were waived, was no bargain. I couldn't see myself wallowing naked in shaving cream for one-dollar tips.

"I let you keep your job here, even after you make trouble," said Mose to his focal point, which seemed to hover several feet behind the water-stained wall. "I can fire you. Then you will be back to job at Kentucky Fried Chicken." The comment was indicative of Mose's thought pattern. He grouped Americans by the going stereotypes, and my Southern drawl, though faded as a result of ridicule, college, and California, branded me a chicken-fryer. Seeing no employment alternatives other than fast food for us strippers, Mose Junior threatened the Latinas with Taco Bell and the Asian women with Panda House to keep us in line. It was one of his charming characteristics.

"I don't owe you one, and I'm not going to be your feature." Ever since I had 'made trouble' by investigating the murder of a former Naughtyland employee, Mose Junior suspected me of some kind of clandestine activity. He wasn't sure what, and I brought in business with my regulars, so he hadn't gotten it together to fire me yet. I think he suspected I had a brain. He wasn't sure what to do with the information.

"I'll do it," Mahogany turned from her locker and tossed her long braids along with the strap of her leather bag over one shoulder. "I could use the break this week, with Boy Scout camp coming on. James is wanting to go." She moved her hands to her bodysuited hips. Her lacquered fingernails were almost long enough to meet at her navel.

Mose Junior struggled with his focal point. "You don't have the right look."

Motion slowed or stopped among the dancers who were struggling into or out of clothes. We all knew what 'the right look' meant. No one spoke about the racial tensions at Naughtyland. These were powerful. In this place our ethnicities were part of what we were selling. Strippers hung together by race. Money kept score between us. Black women were as discriminated against in the sex industry as anyplace else.

Mahogany tapped the shined stacked-heel engineer boot that loomed from below her fashionably ripped jeans. "Figured you'd say that. Don't you know discrimination based on race is illegal in this country?" She did not have to raise her voice; the low rhythmic hum of chatter in the room had stopped.

Mose put manicured hands to his stack of hair, bunching his suit around his neck into a puppy scruff. He squinted against the glare, or perhaps to avoid the problem of eyes contacting with potentially litigious girls. "I never say anything like that, right? You are the new feature. Start tomorrow, midnight."

Mahogany was high-fiving all around when Mose Junior brushed passed us to make his exit. "Ashleen," he gave my stage name the authentic Irish pronunciation, though no doubt inadvertently. "You come to my office."

"Now? It's two a.m."

"I pay for you a cab home."

I followed him upstairs.

"Can she sue me?" My boss hadn't even taken the time to assume the power position, seated behind a desk and not offering the employee a chair. Since Mose Junior's desk was a battered aluminum-and-particle board concoction, and the chair behind it as rickety as the man who sat in it, it was just as well that he leaned against his office's wood paneling. He assumed the hair-wringing posture once again, framing the bared-breast and processed-hair sections of a brunette in the triangle of his bent arm. His office was decorated with promotional posters of his beloved features. I'd met Wanda Watermelons, the Mose-framed brunette, several weeks before.

"How should I know? I'm calling a cab." I rubbed my eyes. They stung from fatigue and mascara. My knees were beginning the complaints they seemed to have after every eight-hour shift of dancing. I didn't feel like being a legal advisor, even had I been qualified.

"You are with a union, right? It's okay, I do not wish to fire you. Just tell me if I can be sued."

"I'm not with any union!" I picked up the office phone to dial Veteran's Cab. "Where do you get these ideas?" The phone sat on the desk next to a creased copy of "Big Honkin Tits." A blonde who squatted and dribbled her breasts together was the magazine's covergirl. I recognized Plushious Velvett. The magazine was from 1989. Plushious Velvett's investments had grown considerably since then. I asked the inquiring female voice for a cab at Naughtyland. "Ten minutes," answered the dispatcher. She didn't ask for directions to the club before hanging up on me.

"Well, I'm outta here. Goodnight." Mose Junior's cologne had invaded my sinuses in the close space of his office and a headache was beginning.

"Wait! You didn't answer my question."

I looked at my boss. Mose Senior had bought the strip club for his boy in June when its previous owner, Whitmore Grady, had decided to run for mayor and found it prudent to sell. Yet Mose Junior wasn't new at running the place. He'd managed the club for Grady for years. You'd think he'd have studied the details of anti-discrimination laws long before. Perhaps not. I'd noticed that there weren't many black women offered auditions at the club.

"I don't know, but I'd watch out if I were you. You don't want to keep pissing these women off. Plushious Velvett said you've been putting up the features in some slum. They're used to luxury. They're from LA. Treating people right can go a long way."

"I treat them right! I rent a whole apartment for them, close to work, they can walk. I even put in some food in the freezer there. What more can I do?"

I yawned. "Oh spoil them. Put them up in a neighborhood where they won't be woken by knife fights and a morning of bring-out-your-dead, and your features might stick out the week."

Naughtyland was located deep within the Tenderloin, San Francisco's aptly-named red-light district. If the apartment in question was close by, it was in the lively thick of strip joints, adult book stores, flophouses, liquor stores, bars, and massage parlors that gave the area its dubious character. Asian restaurants thrived in the neighborhood, too, and a few trendy hotels sparkled over a steam-cleaned stripe of sidewalk. But, for the most part, the Tenderloin was left to porn patrons and to the poor who lived there, their neighborhood as worn as the old pennies in their pockets.

Mose Junior put a slender hand to the lapel of his suit, his skin pale against the linen's summery color of shark-gray. "Do you think," he asked, "that's why she left?" He moved to his desk, touched fingerpads to his copy of "Big Honkin Tits", and made a spider motion with his fingers.

"Well, she did mention being scared to go to sleep at night. Where are you keeping them, anyway?"

He looked down at the magazine. Mose Junior's beloved, genuine porn star must have been propped up somehow to maintain that spread-eagle squat on the cover. His fingers stopped moving. "What neighborhood do you live in?"

"Lower Haight. Why?"

"Nice?"

"I don't know. It's got a lot of coffee houses and people dressed in black walking between them."

"What kind of people?"

"What are you getting at? Coffee-loving people."

"Features staying at your house," said my boss. "You live nice, right? You are nice girl. Nice neighborhood."

"What! Just because poor people can't afford it anymore, that makes it nice? I don't have an extra bedroom! Don't you know there's a housing crisis in this city? I already have four roommates! This is crazy." My repressed Southern accent was creeping up on me as it does when I get upset, or drunk. I shut up.

"Unless you want to be feature until I find new apartment." Mose Junior risked a look directly at me.

"This is blackmail or something."

"Only until I get a new place. Nice apartment for the girls. Until then you are good company for my girls. Like slumber party."

"Are you listening to me? I've got four roommates. My apartment is already a slumber party. And finding a place to live in San Francisco takes months, even if you've got money." I picked at my cuticles. It was notoriously difficult to find an apartment in San Francisco. That was why I had four roommates. It was impossible to find one for less per month than what had covered a season of mortgage payments back home.

Like many wealthy men, Mose Junior was cheap. We'd have porn star guests in the three-bedroom apartment over the ElQuake-O Taqueria forever. I couldn't accommodate them all on my futon. "I live in squalor. Really." What would Hugh, Geoffrey, Zan, and Vivian say? God.

"Squalor. I do not know this word. Remember, Kentucky Fried Chicken you make four dollars an hour. The new feature comes Sunday. I will send her to your house. Your cab is here."

I could hear the horn honking from Jones Street, though the office was in the back of the club, its one window facing an alleyway. Cab drivers aren't known for their patience.

"We only have one shower," I said.

Mose Junior opened the top drawer of his desk with a tiny key that he fished from his pocket. He unzipped a blue vinyl Bank of America bag. "How much do you pay rent?"

"Twelve-fifty."

"Altogether? What is your part?"

"Three-fifty." The bank bag bulged impressively. He deposited huge wads of cash every night, I knew, because Mose Junior started hassling each dancer for 'his money', the hundred-and-twenty dollars stage rent, an hour before closing. One day's take would have split the seams if the bag had been made of weaker stuff.

He counted eighteen twenties off the top of the inches-thick stack of bills. "Ten for cab."

I crumpled them into the pocket of my leather jacket and bit my lip before either an automatic 'Thank you', or an expression that would land me in the employment line at KFC, could come out.

As the taxicab gunned down Market Street toward the Lower Haight, I pondered how to break the news to my roommates that a very special guest would be showing up in two days, wheeling in a luggage set that would compete in volume with our furnishings, and scattering lingerie, spike heels, and backlog stock of her XXX videos around our already cluttered apartment.

"I'm not in a hurry," I said. The cab driver had just run the red light at the Van Ness intersection.

"No problem." He didn't look at me as he moved another Nilla Wafer from the box beside him to his mouth.

Bending my legs exacerbated my knee pain so I straightened them by resting my calves against the back of the driver's bench seat. My platform soles grazed the cab's ceiling. I slumped into the stratum of odors that the sedan claimed for itself: gasoline, rubber. Up higher the smell of his meal preceding Nilla Wafers lingered: sausage pizza. For a moment the car window seized the Libertarian Bookstore out of the foggy August night. I cracked the window. I was starting to feel queasy.

The driver stopped for the light at Market and Duboce. In the plate glass window of Hot N' Chunky Burgers, the cab was the only shadow.

The red spotlight held us there, alone, the silhouette of my upstretched legs oddly placed where a head should be. The driver's shadow loaded another Nilla Wafer. He waited for the light to change. I was almost home. My roommates were all nocturnal; they would still be up.

We always seemed to have houseguests. Our most recent, Peter and Rainbow, had left a few weeks before. They'd hitched north, planning to fight the forest fires that ignite much of California predictably enough to create dependable summer jobs. They'd been good, unobtrusive house-guests, except for when their dog had given birth to thirteen puppies on our kitchen floor. Surely a short succession of porn stars wouldn't be as disruptive to our household as that had been. I hadn't been able to use the kitchen for a week.

I picked my cuticles as the cab turned right onto Church and I told the driver to stop at the corner. I'd pitch Mose Junior's imposition to Vivian and Zan as an experience in diversity. Hugh, I could convince of anything. It was Geoffrey's reaction to the news that enormously busty porn actresses would soon be picking at their Lean Cuisines over his Formica kitchen table and soaking their corns in his shaving sink that I most worried about. Whether pro or con, Geoffrey's reaction would be loud.

Chapter Three

"Wake up, Aubrey, dear. She's gone, and her little dogs, too. I sent her to Chamfon down at Atlas and Memphis, and I hope he can do something with that miserable frizzyperm. I know it's early, but that was an emergency. They say people will look like their dogs, but you're not waking up!" Geoffrey's high cheekbones and blue eyes dangled over me, puzzle pieces that I couldn't quite put together. In groggy confusion I reached up to bat my roommate's head away.

"You missed." Geoffrey shook me again, with enough force to rock my ribs against the bones of the green couch that, along with a thirteen-inch television, furnished our living room. The couch's cushions had flattened. I slept supported in slices by the couch's wooden frame at my chest, hips, and knees. It wasn't comfortable.

"I'm not waking up because I didn't get any sleep. Go away." I rolled toward the wall, pulled my quilt over my head. The polyester pieces that locked together into the quilt's 'log cabin' pattern sealed out oxygen as effectively as a plastic bag. My Granny Leann had been an enthusiastic promoter of polyester, and had reluctantly cut up her decades-outmoded pantsuits to piece quilts that never died.

"Aubrey, it's time to face reality. We're here to help you do that. Come into the kitchen when you're ready, which will be in the next five minutes. Zan's making your tea." Geoffrey left, complaining about the weight of double knit as he dragged my blanket along behind him. He came back a moment later to throw Hodge onto my back. As the cat kneaded my vertebrae I heard a soundbite of conversation from the kitchen, then quiet after the door swung shut.

"Can't take it," Zan had been saying. What a newsflash.

"Aaaaah," I said, wincing in pain as Hodge clawed through the thin fabric of the aged cotton shirt I wore, another rescue from the men's department of Hugh's thrift store. I'd slept in my clothes. Vanessa Sassy had beaten me home by hours the night before, and I hadn't wanted to disturb her beauty sleep to fetch the t-shirt and sweats I usually slept in. I especially didn't want to disturb her two terriers. Champagne and Caviar, once they got started, seemed to compete for endurance in the yap department. I winced again, thinking of the smell of dog that was surely beginning to permeate my futon. As the only roommate with my own bedroom, I'd handed it over to "my" houseguest upon her arrival the night before last.

Hodge jumped lightly to the carpet as I sat up, and followed me into the kitchen.

Zan was pouring a column of steaming water into an oversized plastic mug writ with a guarantee to give its bearer free coffee refills forever at Mr. Mike's Convenience Store when Hodge and I pushed into the crowded room. Kitchens in old San Francisco apartments seem to often be converted hallways; bathrooms, former linen closets. The building my four roommates and I shared with the ElQuake-O Taqueria was a cube with no architectural style amid a neighborhood of Victorians. Like its prettier neighbors, it had been constructed when indoor plumbing was just a curiosity.

"Here's your tea," Zan nudged the mug toward me. She proceeded to fill up several other mugs from our eclectic dishware collection, all arranged on the considerable whitespace of our antique stove.

"I'll get you some milk," said Hugh. It was impractical for me to try to push my way between Zan at the stove and the edge of our kitchen table to reach the refrigerator. Geoffrey and Vivian sat at the formica table, using the two chairs. Hugh set the small carton of milk on the table and resumed his position, leaning against the voluminous curves of our rusting sink.

"You look like hell," said Geoffrey, as I poured a half-inch of milk into my Earl Grey.

"Thanks, precious." To my annoyance, I couldn't say the same about him. Geoffrey's angular face, a beveled frame for his dark-lashed blue eyes, prettily withstood any morning after. His current crisis was that his brown hair had receded a millimeter over the summer. He was dealing with that fact through a series of collages, using photos of parts of his face, that were currently decorating our living room wall.

I took a swallow of the steaming tea, and was rewarded with a watery brew weak as spit. I set the mug down on the table and fell hard onto Vivian's lap.

"Ouch!"

"Well why did you get me up so early?"

21

Vivian slicked her chin-length bob straight back with handfuls of coconut oil. On better days I liked her beachy smell. At that moment I was reminded of a bout with a pitcher of Piña Coladas that I'd had five or six years before, and my stomach tensed a few inches upward and quivered there. Funny how smells rivet you to another time and place.

"I didn't!" Vivian pushed me. "Go jump on Geoffrey."

"Ug," I said.

And Geoffrey said, "No you aren't going to muss my clothes. Today I have an appointment."

"An appointment?" He had plenty of dates, but Geoffrey never had appointments. He was a construction paper artist who worked, mostly at night, out of his bedroom and occasionally out of our living room. As far as I knew, no one outside of those two places had ever taken note of his work.

"Yes, and that's the reason I got you up. We have to talk about Vanessa Sassy before I go."

Shit. Here it came. I took a sip of my strengthening tea.

Vanessa Sassy, Naughtyland's featured performer of the week, had shown up Sunday night at the other side of the iron door grille that screened out the neighborhood, both her hands braceleted with leather straps. Most of the straps were attached to suitcases, but two were fastened to a pair of terriers so alike that I wondered for a moment if dogs had identical twins as I carried several pieces of her Samsonite set up the flight of stairs that led directly into our living room. I was determined to do all the work myself since my roommates were being such good sports. When I had broken the news to them about our impending houseguests during a commercial break in the Late Movie, poor Zan had begun to chew the end of her blonde braid, but that was probably because of Vivian's whoops and applause at the announcement. Vivian could run roughshod over her girlfriend at times. Hugh had pushed his glasses back up to where they lifted his bangs and inquired how long could he expect the company. I knew he would be uncomfortable moving through the small spaces of our apartment with a vast prow of bustline to avoid, but he was too gentlemanly to say so. Geoffrey had shrieked with laughter until Doña Rosa, ElQuake-O's proprietress and our downstairs neighbor, banged the ceiling with her mop. He promised to get his father to send him money for a VCR so we could watch all of our new friends show off their acting skills. But since Vanessa's arrival, all four of them had been great. Friendly, but not overbearing. If Hugh wasn't exactly friendly, well, it was obvious to everybody that he was shy. Things had been going well, I'd thought. I gulped some more tea, aware of being stared at by four pairs of eyes.

"Sit down and stop looking so guilty." Viv gave up her chair for me.

"Look, you all, it's only until Mose Junior finds a place to put them. Probably a couple weeks, tops."

Geoffrey cut me off. "Y'all! Did y'all hear a y'all? How 'bout that."

Whenever a note of melody crept into my voice, my California roommates never failed to point it out. Hugh was my only fellow Easterner, from New England. Though I had grown up in a suburb of Dayton, my linguistic inheritance was my Momma's Kentucky drawl, an undistinguished Southern accent featuring vowels at thirty-three rpm and first-syllable stresses: *um*-brella, *tee*-vee, *Dee*-troit, *co*-caine.

"Hugh, what's up? You can't deal with Vanessa?" I looked up at Hugh. His fingers crowded the handle of a china cup. He splashed tea as he clattered it onto the pile of dishes in the sink. Hugh drank camomile to calm himself down.

"There's been discussion that you should ask your boss to reconsider," he said.

"Reconsider? Why didn't you tell me before there was a problem?"

Jostling his foot, Hugh's Nike began to toss ripples up the leg of his brown stovepipe pants. So much for the camomile. "Well, to put it diplomatically–"

"You're a nervous wreck. We can't stand you catering to her every whim so we won't be annoyed; it's annoying. You aren't getting any sleep, and you're the one who hates dogs. As much as we like Vanessa, and she's great—did you get a taste of that pasta she whipped up last night?—you're more important. She has to go." Geoffrey stood up at the end of his speech and smoothed his ribbed t-shirt over his abs. It was tucked in to his belted 501's neatly as a wrapped present.

"What?"

"It's not her, it's you, is what Geoffrey is trying to say." Zan's voice was always kindly. "We're worried about you."

"Look at yourself, you're a stress case." Vivian picked my hand up off the table. "And picking your fingernails again."

"You need your sleep," Hugh added.

"So you're to go on and tell your boss, Jesus, Moses, or whatever his name is, that he's just going to have to find another place to warehouse his triple X porn stars, lovely as it is to host them. Now, tell me how I look? This appointment could be important to my future life." Geoffrey posed in profile, pretending to hold a cigarette in one hand, lifting aloft his tea with the other. His mug read "World's Best Grandma."

"Your wife-beater's a little low-cut." Vivian moved to yank upward the u-necked sleeveless undershirt that was Geoffrey's everyday apparel. He had one in every color of the rainbow. Today's was violet.

Yaps on the stairs interrupted my next swallow of tea. "Move, Vivian, I have got to see how she turned out! I hope Chamfon was thinking silhouette, because what she had going on before was Jabba the Hutt." Geoffrey pushed through the door that divided the kitchen from the living room. Viv practically dropped her tea to follow him, and Zan propped the swinging door open with her hiking boot so she could keep an eye on the proceedings from her post at the stove. A terrier trailing his leash scurried in and out of the kitchen; Geoffrey was saying things like it really accents your bustline at that shorter length; Vivian was asking questions about hair products; and Vanessa Sassy was answering, "Thank you" and "Here, honey, let me give you some of these shampoo samples." Like her bustline needed accenting, and since when was Viv interested in washing her hair? I sighed and leaned into my hand. Hugh sat down reaching across the table to pat me on the head.

"What do you mean, not working out? Jimsy, push the truck, don't throw." Moses whined.

I winced in pain, rubbed the tender spot on my knee that had just been in the way of Jimsy's Matchbox truck's trajectory. Again I regretted my decision to visit Mose Junior in his stale-smoke-scented office before the day shift even got started. My boss' young son pushed the small toy underneath his father's desk. Following it, Jimsy head-butted a new dent into the desk's metal front and started to cry.

"We just don't have enough space. I'm sleeping on the couch." Wasn't he going to do something about that crying kid?

"What can I do? Feature needs nice place, you told me, right?" My boss raised his hands in his accustomed gesture of helplessness. Rings that had caught at the knotty knuckles of his thin fingers fell back into place. He picked his cigarette out of the ashtray on his desk, inhaled, then aimed the smoke toward one of his girlie posters. The gray cloud obscured Steel Buns Magnolia's upthrust bosom.

"I'm trying to tell you, I live in a slum. My place isn't nice. There's decades of lost small items in the shag carpet. The appliances have been there since the Great Depression. We got our furniture off the street. We live above a restaurant, and the place always smells like burnt lard. They don't turn off their jukebox until three a.m., and it's all Mariachi music."

"No cockroaches, no mice?"

Jimsy's screams had turned to hopeless snuffles in the absence of any response. I had a feeling it would be a short reprieve.

"No." I should have lied. Thanks to Geoffrey's sniper-like assassinations of anything that crawled in the kitchen, we hadn't seen a roach in years. Vermin didn't infest San Francisco as efficiently as they had Dayton, the city was too dry, or too new.

Jimsy stuck a pudgy hand beneath the desk. His face screwed inward. One second later the inhuman shrieking resumed. At the same instant, the show started downstairs with bone-jarring Black Crowes guitar chords.

"Aren't you going to do something about your kid?" I had to scream to be heard.

Mose Junior was no doubt waiting for the nearest female to take care of the toddler. He unfolded himself from his desk chair and followed his exhalations of Marlboro smoke around to his son. He scooped him up with one hand. Jimsy quieted, perhaps from the sensation of being perched high in a leafless, sap-starved tree. Mose Junior looked admiringly at his red-faced son. My boss had daughters, too, probably quiet ones, probably at home being quiet with their mothers. But Jimsy was the kid he showed off.

"This is my son."

"I know. We've met."

Mose waved Jimsy's hand at me, so it appeared that the child, too, had a Marlboro as a sixth digit. Just then the phone rang, the noise barely audible above the rock music that pounded upward from downstairs.

"Hello?" My boss answered. "Plushious? She is not here. Who is this?"

Jimsy started to fuss again. Without a hip to prop him on, Mose had a hard time balancing child, phone, and cigarette, and his son was slipping down the shiny gray fabric of his suit jacket. "She left last Friday. Two days before contract ran out." He turned to slide Jimsy onto the desk. Mose Junior continued to bark unhelpful answers into the receiver. "I don't know. No, she did not leave number. I think maybe L.A. Okay." He hung up.

Jimsy's squat body slithered dangerously among the glossy porn magazines that covered his father's desk.

"What, Plushious Velvett didn't make her next gig?" I'd figured her fit the previous Friday night had been a routine venting. We're always threatening to give up the biz. But what else pays so well? Stripping kept me independent of a man's income and far from Dayton. My definition of success.

My boss shrugged. "Some club in Texas. She scheduled to work there

25

this week. Broke her contract with them, just like with me."

"Broke her contract? Did she show up at all?"

He shook his head. "Not professional." A shriek interrupted. Pushed away by a diapered bottom, a slippery stack of "Big Honkin Tits" fell to the floor. Jimsy wobbled sideways and once again bumped his head. This time my boss picked him up as soon as the screaming started.

"Look, you've just got to find somewhere else for the features." I rubbed my head. How could anyone endure this constant howling? Cigarette smoke filled my nasal passages. Every downbeat of "Hard to Handle" made it turbulent. "My roommates are complaining. It's the feature girls or me."

Mose Junior was gazing at the glossy poster of Vanessa Sassy. He'd moved it to the prime spot on the wall across from his desk. The shot was a soft focus of her torso. Above a knit stomach, silicon breasts drove her thin upper arms into permanent akimbo. Her arch of blonde hair had been frozen into waves. Her face figured small among these bionic accessories. Still, her lipstick glazed a genuine smile.

Before he could say something like, isn't she beautiful, I said, "Are you listening to me? I'm threatening to quit."

I stayed at Naughtyland, in spite of Mose Junior, because it was one of the few strip clubs in town with stage rent low enough that dancers could pay it without resorting to hand jobs. Mose Junior made sure of that—the last thing he wanted was jail time for pandering. While some of the other clubs in town were lax about prostitution laws, Naughtyland was clean and still lucrative. At times, it was very lucrative. My earnings fluctuated, but I averaged three hundred dollars a shift. With what other job could a history major without computer skills make three hundred dollars a day? I couldn't afford to quit. And I didn't want to quit. The money gave me independence, the lax schedule gave me freedom. Freedom and independence were all I asked of life. I only threatened to quit because I knew Mose Junior wouldn't fire me. I had a following of regular customers, I wasn't a drug addict or a black-clad depressive, I always had his fee by midnight. I qualified for employee of the month.

Jimsy, calmer now, was exploring his father's jutting cheekbones with chubby fingers. My boss leaned to stub out his cigarette. "Shouldn't smoke around the boy. Space your problem? Not enough space?"

"That's what I've been saying."

"I can give you the keys to the place they been staying. You can move there. Not the feature girl. If she's happy, I'm happy, right? Can't have her running out on me again." With a long arm, Mose Junior reached across his desk and slid open its top drawer. He pulled out a keyring. One key dangled from it, along with an enameled disc spelling LIBRA in purple glitter. "See, I treat you like a superstar. Fourteen-thirty-two Taylor. This is for security door. Ring number thirteen, the handyman. He has the apartment key."

The lobby of 1432 Taylor Street smelled of rot and metal, like cabbage cooking in an aluminum pan. I'd gone directly from Mose Junior and his loud son to look the place over. It really was close to work, one block east and three north, a five-minute walk. And it was in a section of the Tenderloin with quieter street activity, less litter, and fewer sex-related businesses than Naughtyland's. In this neighborhood—one not included in any guidebook to the city—the seediness factor fluctuated from block to block. I'd passed only one sex emporium on this particular block, and one massage parlor, named The Lotus Leaf, near the corner with Ellis Street. Unlike the flashy marquees and assertive barkers that gave strip clubs the street presence of a playground bully, massage parlor facades faded into the neighborhood's restaurants, liquor stores, cafes, cheap electronics shops, and foreign newsstands. The Lotus Leaf was boarded-up and blacked-out, with only a hand-scrawled cardboard advertising "Oriental Massage" to identify itself. Any patrons would undoubtedly be discreet, unlike the legions who roared forth from Naughtyland on weekend nights. Couldn't ask for a better neighbor, I thought, rocking on my stacked heels as I waited in the lobby. I buzzed number thirteen again.

Maybe me moving out temporarily would be the best solution to our apartment's overcrowding, I thought. The line at the bathroom would be shorter. And my roommates could only think it was the best thing for my perceived lapse in mental health.

The building's carpet was a former-glory red with a pattern of green and gold swirls, haphazardly vacuumed. Twelve gold mailboxes were lined up along the wall to my left, leaving me to puzzle about number thirteen. Its buzzer stood alone to the right of the mailboxes, obviously an afterthought. I reached over to push it again. Noontime sunlight penetrated the low canyon of cityscape on Taylor. It filtered through the grille behind me to make stripes on my black sleeve.

Still no answer.

Number 1432 itself was a wide, three-storied brick building, at least as old as the Victorians that populated newer, more outlying neighborhoods. The Tenderloin had no wooden structures. The neighborhood was reconstructed where the original city had burned and left residents skittish about building with flammables. Any building that touched another touched it with bricks. Number 1432 trundled upward into a flat corniced roof, both roof and body shedding an old coat of white paint. Drilled into the bricks over the security doors that defended its entrance was a gold plaque. This building had a name. The plaque read, in gold-plated cursive, 'The Tender Arms.'

A flannel-shirted shape slouched toward the glass door. Thick fingers worked at the sapling-sized deadbolt. The shape pulled the door open to smells of bad breath and rotten vegetables.

"Hi, I'm Aubrey Lyle. Mose Junior sent me over." I stuck my right hand out. He looked at it, made brief eye contact before settling his gaze on my chin. In my three-inch heels, we were about the same height.

"Clem." He pulled the door open enough to let me pass through it. We shook hands. The black hairs on the back of his had caught grains of coarse yellow dust. "Sorry, sawdust."

Clem continued to not look at me as I entered the building's foyer and looked around. The inner lobby of The Tender Arms was lit by wall sconces—fluted cups of yellow that fanned their low-wattage beams toward the ceiling. The wedges of light were broken by the shadows cast by insects fused to the bulbs. Velveteen fleurs de lys patterned the wall paper and, as the old wallpaper disintegrated, pollinated the air. It wasn't bright in there. I could barely make out Clem's features. His hair appeared tousled. He wore dark jeans or workpants. The toes of his boots shone in thick silver stripes where they'd been repaired with duct tape.

"Mose Junior has an apartment here?"

"That's right. Figured you were one of his girls. Upstairs. Come on, I'll show you."

One of his girls? My shirts didn't need interior frames. I smoothed the black clingy rayon of my front-buttoned blouse over my chest as I followed Clem past a stairwell. He was wrenching open a door-sized black grille that folded into the right side of a doorframe. A door behind the grille led to a small room. "Come on in—elevator." Clem twitched a hand toward the tiny interior.

If Momma hadn't been drugged numb through many of my formative years, she would have warned me about situations like this. As it was, I stepped into the small compartment with the total stranger. The building was only three stories. The trip couldn't be long enough for him to try anything. I secured the heavy door behind us. With a thick finger, Clem pushed the button marked 3, right below a red button labeled Stop.

With a knee-buckling jerk, the creak upward began. This is how a fish must feel on the line, I thought. At least I could get a better view of Clem under the raw bare bulb. He was younger than I had guessed; couldn't be more than thirty with thick brown hair that he cut himself and a brown stubble. His clothes were clean, the blue jeans pressed into a crease. He stood still, hands in his pockets, watching the floors paddle by through the porthole in the elevator door. By the time we reached the third floor, the elevator's vegetable smell had been beaten by the piney tang of Clem's deodorant.

"301. Best apartment in the place." Clem strained to haul the grille to the side. "This way."

I followed him past the stairwell which made u-turns up the middle of the building. I ran my left hand along its banister, a horseshoe-shaped white fence on this top floor, where the stairs ended. A snowstorm of paint flakes fell where I rubbed. I stifled a yelp as splinters bit into my palm.

"The door's tricky. Got to lift the knob like so, jiggle it to the left. This key goes in the doorknob, this one's for the deadbolt." Clem demonstrated. He pushed the door open. "Smells like they haven't taken the garbage out in a while."

He didn't have to tell me. A smell like the compost heap needed turning was evident as soon as he'd opened the door.

"Well, thanks. It's okay, I'll take care of it. Could I just get copies of the keys?"

Before he handed them to me, Clem had something else to say. I watched him cook it up. It took a few seconds. "Seems like Mose ought to have some keys. He gives the place out to enough girls."

I blew a stray strand of hair off my eyebrow. "He told me to get them from you."

"Lots of different girls here. The other tenants don't like it."

"Really? Well I'm the last. I won't be here long, just until Mose finds another place."

"He won't find another for this price. He's getting a bargain."

"What do you mean?"

"Pays four hundred rent here."

That was a bargain. Rent control was only effective in San Francisco if you never moved. Once an apartment was vacated, the price changed to whatever the landlord could get. With only seven square height-restricted miles to work with, San Francisco's landlords could name their outrageous price. The city had the highest rents in the country, and many desperate tenants. For 301, The Tender Arms, Mose Junior was paying about one-fourth of what a typical one bedroom would cost. "The place must be a real shithole then. If you'll excuse me, I've got to get moving into it."

Clem shook his head. "Rent control. One of the last rent control places in the city." His palms were rough, aggravating my new splinters as he slapped the two keys into my hand. "People would kill to score one of these. I've got the basement apartment if you need me."

"Right." I weighed the keys in my hand, waited in 301's doorway to acclimate to the stench. A genteel screech of the elevator grate, then the pneumatic hum pressed the super back toward the basement.

The apartment's door swung open through a good percentage of the living room. If this was the nicest apartment in the place, I'd hate to see the others. A thousand seating arrangements had clawed the living room's hardwood floor. A thousand high heels and chair legs had pricked it. The floor seemed to be worn a fraction in the middle, like a pastry board hollowed from a lifetime of getting crushed under a rolling pin. A bookcase and three drawers were built into one corner. Another corner gave access to the bedroom through a transomed door. A black love seat beside the bookcase clashed with a hotel-issue endtable next to it. Magazines cluttered the endtable: 'Big Honkin' Tits,' 'Redbook,' 'Ladies Home Journal,' 'Motor Trend.' Mose Junior must have combed his doctors' offices for those back issues.

The room faced the street through a generous window, four feet tall, wide as a single bed. Several unwatered plants shriveled to death on its wooden sill, but one plant thrived. Its thatch of muscular, upright leaves flung themselves tight against the glass as if desperate to escape the apartment. A similar one grew in Momma's beauty shop. She called it a snake plant, complained that it never would go on and die.

I took a step to the right and a peek into the apartment's other room. The bedroom was furnished only with fox-hunting scenes hung erratically on the walls. I looked behind one of them to find a gaping hole in the wallboard. Shards of whatever material predated sheetrock tinkled in a short shower as the print rocked back into place. Not even a bed. No wonder Plushious Velvett had complained. The bedroom did have a long closet though, against the far wall, which wasn't far at all in the small room. Plenty of storage space for g-strings, scaffold brassieres and high-high boots. Curiously, a few such items littered the floor, remaining where they'd been flung—a tumbleweed of thong panties, a purple gypsy scarf, an acrylic stiletto with a black strap that I thought I recognized as Plushious Velvett's. Why would she leave an eighty dollar shoe? Not to mention the black vinyl thigh highs, laddered with buckles, entwined and losing their plastic sheen to dust. Though made of vinyl, those boots cost a hundred dollars a pair. I knew, I'd recently bought similar boots myself. For that matter, I reminded myself, this clutter could have belonged to any of the apartment's porn star guests. That year all of us had invested in the latest stripper fashions: the acrylic stilettos, the metallic scarves, the thongs, the black thigh highs. Though the porn industry was perhaps the only arena where fishnets, bouffants, and blue eyeshadow would never go out of style, most of us strippers felt we couldn't afford to look out of date.

My feet had stirred several pages of notebook paper, crumpled and strewn across the floor like the rejected beginnings of a novel. I pieced two of the scraps together, matching up the ruled blue lines. This litter was less anonymous. "Plushious Velvett" was doodled in the margins in various scripts. The signature, rounded like a cheerleader's in a yearbook, was variously embellished by a pair of legs made out of the V and an outline of puckered lips dotting the I. Plushious Velvett's further literary output, scrawled down the middle of the page, reminded me why I'd never liked poetry.

In my dream he comes after me
with a knife,
aimed straight at my
tits.
Fucking Bastard!
Fuck him!
Fuck!
I Hate Him!

The poem finished with several other profanities. I let the pages fall back onto the floor. The bedroom mess could wait. I pushed my sleeves back up as I walked the four paces to the apartment's third roomlet and source of stench—the kitchen.

Tomatoes. Plushious Velvett must have had a thing for them. Tomato skins papered the cracking porcelain of the kitchen sink, their edges curling into scrolls, the middle parts of the scraps slicing into slime mold. The meat of the tomatoes festered in a cast iron skillet on the stove, mixed with green-furred bones of what might have been carrots. A swirl of pasta fossilized in a large pot, the white furrows plowed with green.

The first thing I did was open the window behind the kitchen sink and take a deep breath of slightly less fetid air. The window opened onto an airspace, a mere indentation drawn by a kindly architect to give tenement-dwellers kitchen windows. On that August afternoon, the space served as a vertical tunnel to convect the asphalt heat that had just beaten the summer morning fog. The duct also handed up the familiar urban smell of cooked piss. Across the airspace, the kitchen window of 302 framed my reflection, close as a bathroom mirror. I could see the fingerprints in the dust of its venetian blinds.

I found a pink plastic bag marked with Chinese characters to splat last week's spaghetti dinner into. Then I breathed again at the window and turned to face the two pots of glop. The tomato and carrot mixture thumped into the plastic as a semi-solid unit. Petrified pasta was heavier than I'd imagined. This was no diet portion of spaghetti. Plushious Velvett must have been expecting a crowd. I needed both hands to heft the stock pot over the trash bag propped open between my feet on the pre-World-War-Two linoleum.

The top layer of spaghetti cracked off, followed by a plug of white protoplasm. The protoplasm melted over the rest of the trash and away from a strange thick yolk. After a moment the yolk resolved into a shape. The shape, unmistakably, of a handgun.

Chapter Four

Shaken by my discovery of the pasta-dredged gun, I wiped it off with a tissue. It proved to be a small, elegant Smith & Wesson, familiar to me from clippings out of a gun enthusiasts' periodical that my Momma had sent. Her husband, though unwilling to part with more than a dollar for a waitress's tip, had been eager to make a present to me of a handgun, "For urban defensive carry." It was his way of saying, "We're worried sick about you honey, think what you're doing to your Momma, come on back home where we can protect you."

Finding a gun embedded in her uneaten meal and her wretched poem made me frightened for Plushious Velvett, genuine Los Angeles porn star. Why hadn't she shown up for her next gig?

Hugh was the only one home when I returned from Mose Junior's apartment, still unnerved. Hugh hadn't been enthusiastic after my announcement that I'd be spending the next week away, but he agreed to help me move, helped with my suitcase and agreed to feed Hodge. I left a note for the rest of my roommates explaining Mose.'s generous offer, reminding them that I'd get a good night's sleep at last, and that I'd still be home for meals. They weren't to worry.

We shared a cab back to The Tender Arms. Hugh wasn't talking. He looked out the window, upper body still, jitterbugging his left Nike. Once in a while he pushed up his black-framed glasses or finger-combed his blond bangs. The driver hurtled through the Tenderloin. Stores advertised liquor and diapers. Windows wrapped in brown paper didn't advertise whatever shady dealings were going on within. Windows postered with porn stars did. The tired businesses went on for blocks, badly fit together, unrelieved by greenery. Sidewalks soaked in filth joined them all together with a concrete seam.

I tried to break the ice with Hugh. "Remember those gun magazines Momma sent me, last spring after the accident?" The cab driver glanced at me in the rear-view.

Hugh grimaced. He didn't like to be reminded of a car wreck he'd been sort of responsible for. Hugh fainted at the sight of blood, and if he saw a drop of red while behind the wheel of a moving vehicle, well, same reaction. He'd survived the accident with only a superficial leg wound. Though my roommates and I had repeatedly asked him to show us the scar, he never would.

"I remember. They wanted to buy you a gun. You sent the magazines back, refusing to play into your mother and step-father's suburban paranoia about so-called inner cities."

"Right, well…," I suddenly realized that despite previous cynicism, I liked the idea of keeping this new-found gun around, for some reason that I was unwilling to explore.

"Why do you mention it?"

The cab came to a stop at a red light at Golden Gate and Gough Streets. The driver must have pressed a button. As we stopped, all four doors locked with a pneumatic thud.

"Nothing. Forget it." The last thing I wanted was Hugh worrying about me. He forgot to pry, since at that moment a prostitute scratching at him through the cab window provided a distraction. She leaned forward fetchingly, puddling her enhanced breasts into each other with a practiced squeeze of her shoulders. She was Asian, thin as a credit card, and seemed to have gotten dressed by spinning into an Ace bandage of red lycra. Hugh replied to her saucy smile with an awkward shake of his blond head. He sat paralyzed, staring forward as the young woman continued to tap on the window. She looked about fourteen.

I leaned over Hugh. "He's with me," I shouted loudly enough to be heard through the layer of glass.

"No English." She clattered her manicure against the cab. An overstrained inch-long red-lacquered nail tip snapped off. "Shit, goddamn it," she said, turning to look for it. A moment later she retrieved the nail tip from its landing place near the curb, rubbed it clean and put it into the transparent cube on a string that was serving as her purse. The cube was decorated with a cartoon kitten. It also contained a thin roll of bills. She straightened, tucked her long-layered black hair behind her ears, dragged on her cigarette and looked down the street. She was headed toward the car behind us as the light changed.

Hugh's face was as red as the broken nail so I decided to spare him the several teasing comments I had ready. I bit my lip to keep from laughing.

"Are we almost there?" Hugh didn't risk looking at me.

"Not too far, three or four blocks. Why?"

"Is this the best neighborhood, with um…all these sex workers around?"

"You mean hookers? What are you talking about?"

"Just asking—"

"Well don't ask! Do you realize what you're saying? Hugh, what do you think I do for a living? The same basic thing that these girls are doing. Face it! Same hustle. I probably get more money for it just because I'm not forced to walk the streets. Do I make any neighborhood I live in quote bad? I am these people Hugh. Watch the road!" The distracted cab driver swerved around another lycra-clad Asian teenager. The girl made an obscene gesture.

"Sorry. Sorry, right, I... No need for this tirade."

"Don't you get it Hugh? You're just like the customers, with all their what's-a-nice-girl-like-you-doing-here crap. In spite of the relentless 'close your legs' drill that girls get from infancy, I dance in public, buck naked, for strangers. I am not a nice girl! It's their own stupid justification for their sorry behavior! As if it's fine to pay to plunk their ass down two inches from a stranger's—Slow down! It's up here—pussy as long as she's a nice girl!"

The driver slammed on the brakes. "Here?"

"Not here here, up there. Just let us out at the corner." The bench seat caught our backs as the driver accelerated, too abruptly. Hugh held his stiff pose against the g-forces, legs crossed, eyes glassy, Nike stilled.

"I fail to see the connection you were speaking of," he said.

"It's not other people, it's us, is what I'm trying to say. Customers and sex workers make the industry happen. We're not too nice for it or too good for its neighborhood. We are it. I am it. Sex workers aren't other unfortunate degenerates, they're me."

"Okay. Point taken. But I'm not a customer."

Right. I'd given Hugh what he knew to be the worst insult in my vocabulary.

"I'm just upset because you're supposed to be one of the few who understands all this."

"I understand it, Aubrey." Hugh's eyes were brown and soft, and finally met mine. His glasses were thick enough to magnify them a little.

"Then what was all that neighborhood bashing about?"

"It's not about that."

"Stop! Here we are." We'd reached Taylor, half a block from The Tender Arms.

The driver had gathered enough speed to slam on the brakes again. It was a good thing I hadn't brought Hodge, I thought, getting out of the cab. My cat preferred life at his own pace. And at low volume.

I touched a hand to my flushed face. Hugh looked correspondingly pale. Of course he hadn't meant to piss me off. He was always good to me, wrestling, at that moment, with the giant suitcase I'd filled with the stretch pants and extra-large men's short sleeve shirts that were my summer wardrobe. The hard-shelled jumbo-sized suitcase had seen me out West. A frayed Greyhound ticket still fluttered from its handle, AUS TX to SF CA. I remembered getting off the bus that had smelled of putrefying baloney sandwiches, released into an August mercifully cooled by the Pacific, and thrilled by the absence of nuclear-hot winds that had suffocated me under all that big sky.

I should learn to be better at apologies.

I had also brought my sleeping bag and an air mattress of Geoffrey's. Hugh steadied them against his chest while I went through each key at each lock in the process of getting into the building. I've never been good with keys, or maybe it's locks I'm no good at.

"Smells like cabbage." Hugh pulled the suitcase through the inner door.

"Could be worse. Let's take the stairs. That elevator gives me the creeps."

We ascended the stairs, which wrapped upward in the shape of a paper clip.

"What floor did you say you were on?"

"Third."

The suitcase thumped every step.

"Watch the banister," I warned Hugh. "It'll give you splinters."

The apartment still stank. I'd have to ask Clem where to take out the trash.

Hugh looked around the living room, at the frightened plant, the clashing furniture, the eroded floor. Shards of dingy white paint had buckled off the wall around the hunting print that I had disturbed earlier. I closed the door behind us. A drywall icicle skittered down the wall and tinkled into pieces on the floor.

"Nice," Hugh said. "Victorian touches in the cornicing and built-ins. Looks like oak in the flooring."

Hugh moved off to explore the kitchen. I looked for the bathroom. I was planning on working the seven-to-close, and needed a shower.

My shower was so hot and so long that a square foot of ceiling plaster crumbled from humidity and joined the steaming water to drain away. I changed into a long-sleeved shirt and clean pants from the suitcase. I found Hugh stocking the dorm-room sized refrigerator with a six pack of Coke, Earl Grey tea, and a carton of milk tiny enough to fit in the door.

"I did some shopping for you."

"That's nice of you. Thanks. Nice to know there's a grocery store around here. The tea can go in the cabinet. Here," I opened one of the wooden doors for him. Poor Hugh sometimes missed out on common sense.

"Sure you'll be all right here?"

"Yes. Stop worrying about me. You know I can't stand that."

He examined my hair, wet and soaking the back of my shirt. "Okay."

"Good. I'm going to blow up that air mattress."

I'd unraveled the mattress and heaved several lungfuls into it before Hugh joined me in the living room.

"You won't need that," he said. I was panting like the loser of the four hundred yard dash, and the mattress was half full at best. I couldn't manage a 'why not?'

"Come look at this."

In the bedroom, Hugh had opened the doors to the closet that spanned almost the entire breadth of the small room's far wall. A metal bedframe fit upright inside of the closet, clamping a mattress whose underside was patterned with rust colored arcs jarred a bit northward of their corresponding steel springs.

"What is that contraption?"

"You've never seen one before?" Hugh pushed his glasses up his nose. "Murphy beds were quite common in apartments earlier this century. They were actually invented here in San Francisco, by a man who got tired of entertaining his dinner guests on his bed. He had no place else to receive them."

I took the few steps across the room, kicking aside hard shoes and soft lingerie. My finger came away from the antique bedframe covered in fine red dust. "So people have always lived packed together in squalor here in San Francisco?" I had somehow gotten the impression that in the old days, people had more elbow room.

"Sure. The original tenements were Victorian affairs built in the spirit of the times by middle-class reformers as housing for the working class."

"How very kind of them."

"And this place used to be a studio apartment. See how the wall there jams right over the molding? It's not original."

Hugh pointed to a thin strip of molded wood, painted white to blend in, that ran around three walls of the room at a height meant for picture hanging. The fourth wall, the one that divided the small bedroom from the only slightly larger living room, broke the line and had no corresponding strip.

"A later addition, to make the place a one-bedroom. Landlord must have thought that would be a selling point."

"Even though this one-bedroom is now smaller than the original studio."

"Right, it doesn't make spatial or aesthetic sense. It makes financial sense. One-bedrooms rent for a higher price. Let's try the bed."

"So to speak."

The black sleeve of Hugh's t-shirt covered his blush as he tugged at the black metal frame near its top, the bed's foot. I reached up to help on my side. The bed yawned open with a shriek of springs, gained momentum, finally slammed against the floor. Two flattened pillows bounced off the mattress. I winced, expecting Doña Rosa's retaliating broom-handle knock.

A blue chenille bedspread and a navy wool blanket, wound up like a candy-cane, meandered across the bed. A thin fitted sheet barely spanned the aged mattress. No flat sheet seemed to have been provided. I retrieved the pillow from the floor, plumped it up, whisked off the bedspread. Hugh snapped the wool blanket into the air to straighten it.

With a soft slither, Plushious Velvett's boa-trimmed black robe, its box-like bodice crushed, landed at my feet.

"Okay. The shoes, the underwear, they could have been anybody's. But that robe was the climax of Plushious Velvett's act. Something's happened to her."

"Right. She forgot it."

"She didn't show up for her next gig at some honky tonk in Texas."

"I wouldn't consider that evidence that something dire has happened to her."

Hugh and I were searching for a place to eat. We were hungry after moving, and I wasn't about to cook anything in that kitchen. Halfway around the block from The Tender Arms, we'd passed three liquor stores, several darkened bars, two XXX video places, a donut shop and a Middle Eastern deli. The deli's counter displayed trays of florescent-lit greenish glop. I was in the mood for something harder, preferably meat.

I wasn't planning to tell Hugh about the gun I'd found. He'd only worry.

"There are myriad possible reasons for her failure to arrive in Texas. As for the robe, people forget things." Hugh shrugged into his jacket. He was skinny enough to feel the cold as soon as fog rolled back over the city, several hours before summer sunsets.

"Not that thing. Things like that cost thousands of dollars. Did you see the chest on it? It was custom-made." I stopped to look into a storefront made promising by its steamed-over windows. It was a laundromat, crowded with chugging rows of washing machines and immensely bored patrons. "Something is definitely wrong. She didn't show up at her next scheduled gig. You can't walk for thirty seconds in any other part of this town without running into four restaurants, and at least one of those will be a taqueria. God."

"What about that place across the street." By this time, we were back around the block, standing in front of the Lotus Leaf Oriental Massage. Hugh pointed to a skinny storefront. Behind its window, a row of vinyl tables with orange chairs welded onto them shone under the florescent lights. We crossed to read its sign. Arranged over the doorway, reflective stick-on letters spelled "Massimo's."

"I smell meat. Let's try it."

"I hope it's heated."

"You can at least get coffee."

He got more than that. Hugh was as good an eater as I was, and even ordered a second greasy cheeseburger from the waiter, a bouncy young man in Converse tennis shoes and a black watchcap who went back to his copy of *Teach Yourself Visual Basic 5* after spinning the order kitchenward. We were his only customers.

Suddenly Hugh stood up with knee-cracking velocity. "Let's go," he said, and began to untangle his legs from the black tubes that connected the table and chairs.

"But you haven't gotten your other cheeseburger yet."

"Let's just go." Hugh's glasses were slipping down his nose, and he only lets them get ahead of him on desperate occasions.

Hugh had been facing the door, and I followed his gaze. A small-boned Asian man steered two women companions past the 'Please Wait to Be Seated' sign. He aimed them toward the one curved orange booth, in the restaurant's back corner. The women, who had attached themselves to the man's arms, towered over their escort in four-inch heels. Their fluttery clothing was a contrast to the man's dull casual style, peacocks to his pea-hen. The women, too, were Asian, and small-boned enough themselves to make their uniformly large breasts alarming. One of them was Hugh's teenaged tormentor of earlier. That fingernail hadn't been replaced. Her right hand looked oddly gapped, like bad teeth. Because of the heels it was a slow procession to the back booth, and by the time the trio got there, three Juice Squeezes, a basket of fries, and two small plates of salad were on the table. The waiter was looking busy behind the back counter, his book whisked out of sight.

"Oh, Hugh, she didn't even notice you. She's required to fawn over that guy. He's obviously her pimp. She won't be looking over here."

Hugh slumped back down. He tucked his head as if to hide behind his long blond bangs. "You don't think?"

"No way." Hugh couldn't see, but I could from my position across from him, the two young women take turns laying french fries onto their male companion's tongue. Our acquaintance was less skilled at hiding her boredom than the other Asian woman, who was dressed in black. When Missing Fingernail wasn't feeding the guy, she turned her head to the silent TV that propped up a few desiccated plants in the opposite corner, and watched the mute gapings of the six-o'clock news. "She's watching TV."

"I'm sorry but I don't think I'll be able to enjoy my cheeseburger under these circumstances. I'd really like to go."

"Okay. But at least let me get it wrapped up for you, you can take it with."

"I'll be waiting outside."

Hugh was going to have to get over this disappearing habit of his. I waited at the counter the few minutes I had to, drawing in deep breaths of the happy, summery smell of grilling meat. Our formerly relaxed waiter blustered around between the grill and the counter, baggy jeans and over-sized t-shirt flapping behind him, exploring all avenues of busywork, wiping clean things clean, resweeping, toying with the grilling burgers like a chef.

"Is one of them Massimo?" I indicated the trio as the waiter crumpled a paper bag containing Hugh's burger into my hand.

He shook his head. "Johnny," he whispered, and motioned for me to stay put as he flipped Johnny's burger. The waiter took advantage of the ensuing popping and sizzling to continue in a low voice. "Owns Lotus, across the street. We pay him a little monthly fee. We're run by Italians, but we don't want any trouble with the Asian gangs. They run this neighborhood. Got to grease a few palms around here if you're not already in with the Asians. Isn't it wild?" He widened his eyes conspiratorially.

"I see." I looked at Johnny, slurping at the girls' alternating fingers along with the French fries. He laughed like a little boy with a new toy firetruck. Not one of the trio looked old enough to be legal.

"Thank you." The waiter smiled pleasantly as he handed me my change.

Outside, I hailed a cab for Hugh, and packed him into it with his cheeseburger and a kiss on the cheek for all his help. It was time for me to get ready for work.

Chapter Five

Mose Junior couldn't remember what club it was that had called to ask about Plushious Velvett.

"Someplace in Texas. Why, you looking for a new job?" He didn't look up from his ledger-sized checkbook.

"I just wondered if she ever showed up."

My boss shrugged. By examining a long crack in the wood paneling on the wall behind me, he managed to take in my burgundy underwire-and-panties set with peripheral vision. "You look nice in that color. All the girls, they want to wear black. I say, put a little color onstage, prettier." He dropped the gold pen he was holding. "But I am not saying you're sexy, right? No harassment." He laughed nervously. "Right?"

"She never told you her real name? Are you sure she didn't leave an address, anything?"

"No, nothing. What am I, her secretary?" Mose thumbed the edge of his checkbook, stared at the photo cube that balanced crookedly on his pressed-board desk. It was crammed with photos of his various children. Next to the cube was an ashtray—the kind meant to be fitted into a stand. The gold metal was beaten out large as a soup bowl and filled to the brim with Marlboro butts.

"Well you must have paid her. Who'd you make the check out to?"

"Check is none of your business." Mose covered the open checkbook with two sprawls of his large hands.

I sighed. "Look, this could be very important. I have this robe of hers, remember the one that she ended her act with? It's got a thousand dollars' worth of sequins on it. Probably two thousand in feathers. She'll be very sad that she lost it. She might give other porn stars a bad impression about this place if she thinks someone at Naughtyland stole her best costume. Your darling features won't come all the way up here from L.A. to work in a den of thieves."

Mose looked at his posters as he lounged backward in his chair. He lit a Marlboro. After a long drag, he flipped backward through the tissue-sheets of the checkbook. It was the duplicate kind. An impression of every check was captured on the thin leaves. I noticed Dallas' unimpressive pay-check, and a check to Purissima Springs. Guess he did pay for those tubs of spring water. We dancers didn't get paychecks. We were supposed to license ourselves as a business, and also sign a waiver that swore nothing that might happen or had happened was or would ever be Mose Junior's fault. All of us signed, few licensed themselves. I refused. What would I put on the application—for nightly rental of nether bodily parts?

Because most of its employees were unpaid, Naughtyland's expenses were minimal. After flipping back three of the tissue pages, my boss stopped.

"Here we are." He leaned over the page and ran a finger under the words as he read them, "PV Incorporated."

"Let me see." Over his protests, I spun the checkbook around to con-firm Mose Junior's reading. PV, Inc. Of course. Anonymous, polite, like the official name of every porn business. I blew out a breath in exaspera-tion. That gesture left me without a lungful to lose over the following line. Mose Junior had paid PV, Inc. five thousand dollars.

"Holy—."

"Please, no cursing. Bad from girls."

"Shit!" He had already turned the ledger around and slapped it shut. "Holy shit, you paid her five thousand dollars?"

"Ten."

"Ten thousand dollars?"

"Half to begin, half after last show. From now on new policy. I pay the whole thing after. Can you believe she walked out on me?"

"You pay them all that much?"

"They're stars. You are all stars."

"Then how come you pay us nothing? How come we pay you?" In my agitation, my right breast was working its way loose from its push-up cup, not an uncommon occurrence with these wonder brassieres. Rather than supporting your breasts, these things serve them up on platters. Acci-dents are inevitable.

I hauled the flimsy burgundy satin northward while Mose Junior examined the life size poster of Ricki Rack on the wall to his right. He flicked his cigarette over the cone of butts. The column of ash skittered down the white slope and crash-landed on his desk. "Features bring in business."

We were silent for a moment. My boss was right. Plenty of pornography addicts out there were delighted to be able to see and lap-dance with their as-seen-on-TV sex partners, and happily paid the twenty dollar admission fee, day after day, for the opportunity. The features' shows were always attended by vocal throngs, eager as schoolboys to be covered with whipped cream, drink the seven-up she'd dipped her big toe in, view the bowl of stubble she'd shaved off her nether parts right there onstage. But did their patronage add up to ten grand? I wondered again exactly how much my boss was making out of this strange business.

Van Halen's "Jump" came on below us, Farrah's last song and my cue to get into whatever my show would involve taking off. "Okay. If anyone calls with news about Plushious Velvett, can you call me? I really want to send her the robe."

After a moment of searching his desk, my boss came up with a message pad. His gold pen looked too fine an instrument for his large hand. "What's your number?"

"I don't know. Whatever the phone number is to your place. The Tender Arms, remember?"

"There's no phone there. I can't have bills. You never know who these girls call, Asia, Japan, everywhere. Everywhere they got a boyfriend. Besides, they all have cell phone."

"I don't have a cell phone."

"Everyone now has cell phone."

"Are you listening? I don't."

A crescendoing guitar solo screamed up from below to the second floor office and cut me off. I didn't need to hear him to understand Mose Junior's gesture and the quick movements of his lips. What could he do? I sighed. I grabbed the message pad, wrote down my home phone number. The phone rang so often at our apartment that Geoffrey had proposed hiring a high school student to answer it evenings and weekends. Voice mail caught the overflow, but gave up after ninety-nine messages.

I got out of the club's office before I absorbed any more of the smoke stench. Customers didn't want to bring that home to their wives.

"How's the crowd?" Plantagena was re-gluing her false eyelashes in the warped backstage mirror when I'd finished my three-song set.

"Zombie-like." I got some water from the cooler. I was always sweaty and thirsty after dancing. I was also completely naked, and dribbled a little water from the dixie cup over my shoulders. It dripped down, cooling off slivers of my chest and back.

"Did you see my regular out there? You know, going bald, always wears a trenchcoat? I called him to come see me. I'm not making any money tonight." Plantagena's lashes were as long as her fingernails, and the two enhancements seemed to be getting hopelessly entangled with her efforts. "Hopefully he'll change that, if he shows."

"Didn't see him." The only people that could be seen from the stage were those who sat right next to it. Everyone else was lost in the dim lighting.

"I'm sure he's out there somewhere. He's mad at me. He and his wife are in couple's counseling over me. I don't know what the problem is. I'm not having sex with the guy. Cheryl should be happy."

"Cheryl?" I leaned over to settle my breasts into their Wonderbra.

"That's his wife. Got two kids, too. He's not about to leave her, got too much money tied up in the houses, and the kids are still too little, but the sex just isn't good."

I was once again thankful that my first and so far, only marriage had been too short to get pathetic. Conor had gone back to Ireland before his resident alien papers even came through. "He tells you all this stuff?" I arranged my thong underwear into the most comfortable position possible for a garment that has direct contact with a mucus membrane.

Plantagena shrugged. "There. It's the glue that makes these so hard to deal with." She plumped up her breasts, then pulled her sausage-casing black dress down over her soft curves just to the point where her silver panties wouldn't peek under the hem. "His wife just isn't attractive to him anymore." Viewed from behind, Plantagena had a figure like a strung bow. Her shoes were silver to match her panties, and she'd even color-coordinated her eye shadow. Her eyelids twinkled like fallout. "You can't blame him. She should do more to keep herself up." My co-worker whipped open the curtain, freeing a moldy smell, and sashayed out onto the stage.

What was the balding pervert who awaited her entrance doing to keep himself up? As I flipped my stage costumes into my locker, I sent a telepathic message to Cheryl, who was no doubt at that moment sadly stirring up some macaroni and cheese on her kitchen island in Marin, and telling the kids daddy would be late getting home from work again. Forget the properties, Cher. Run for your life.

When I saw that the man's wedding ring was accented with a pair of diamonds, glittering like red animal eyes with the club's swirling disco beams, I figured I'd found the gold mine of the evening. His blue jeans were belted, his flannel shirt bright and his Doc Marten boots beetle-shiny. But his head lacked the baseball cap with a hem of hair below it that would

44

have completed the authentic working-class look he was trying for. He told me about the ring during our third lapdance.

"Custom-made. My wife's is matching, more diamonds on hers of course. No point in not pleasing her. She works hard, too. Makes more than I do, actually."

"So she wears the pants in the family?" Normally, I dislike talkers, prefer to just grind in silence and dispense with what inevitably feels like either porn-movie dialogue or a therapy session. But after more than ten minutes of supporting my weight, my quads were screaming for a rest. When he started talking, I stopped moving.

"I wouldn't say that. I make plenty." He bared his teeth in a smile visible even in the dim lighting within our curtained-off square yard.

"What do you do?"

He laughed. "You don't have to pretend to be interested. But I'm a software engineer. Work down in Multimedia Gulch."

Multimedia Gulch was the new term for South of Market, an industrial zone across Market Street from the Tenderloin, an area of wide lanes and murky low cubes bounded by highway overpasses. South of Market's empty warehouses had been abandoned to homeless people and leather bars decades before. Now that it was Multimedia Gulch, the area was overrun with shiny-faced start-ups of both the corporate and human kind, and space in those same crumbling warehouses couldn't be had for any price.

Since I didn't have to pretend, I got back down to business. I rotated my legs outward to spare my quads. My customer was tall, but thin, and straddling him my platform shoes reached the ground. For balance, I rested my hands on his blond head. It smelled like we used the same shampoo.

When "Open Arms" was over, he declined another dance. Had to get home with dinner for the wife, was there Chinese around? His night to cook. "But you did a great job. Nothing like a good redhead."

He passed me another bill before he pulled aside the curtain.

"It's brown." With slightly reddish highlights in strong light. But there was no way he could see them in the near-blackout lighting. I tucked the bill under the pad in my black Wonderbra.

By the time I flicked on the living room light in my new temporary quarters, it was two-fifteen a.m. My sleeping bag, plumped into a worm, wiggled on top of the air mattress in the middle of the living room floor. Computer components were scattered next to it—laptop, mouse, coils of wiring.

"Turn out the light," the voice was muffled.

"Geoffrey?" He'd sworn never to set foot in my temporary neighborhood. It was simply too squalid. I wasn't to take it personally.

A triangle of my slumber-party style sleeping bag flicked downward. Vivian's short black hair stayed perfectly smooth even while she slept, thanks to fistfuls of grease. Her eyes were squinted shut.

"What are you doing here?" I asked.

"Keeping you company. Ever hear of taking out the trash? This place smells like a sewer. Put out the light, would you?"

I complied. The laptop beamed Viv's head with a cone of alien, green light. She reached to shut it off.

"No, really. What's up? Girl trouble?"

Viv flipped the bag back over her face. The city's night-defying glow combined with streetlights draping a pale streak through the open window over Viv. "Can we discuss it tomorrow?"

"Sure. What, Zan kicked you and your computer out?"

"Christ. Okay." The bag flipped down again. "The official reason I'm your uninvited houseguest is that I've got to get this thesis done. It's a semester overdue. My advisor is starting to freak. Unofficially, yes, we need space, our boundaries are blurring, whatever you want to call it. We're starting to wear each other's underwear, for chrissake. Are you satisfied?"

"How'd you get in?"

"The super. Sweet talked him." Vivian laughed. "He seemed to think I was your boss's girlfriend. I just played along."

"He thought you were Mose Junior's girlfriend?" He must have been averting his eyes. My boss went for the type who wore their leather as miniskirts instead of motorcycle jackets, who adorned themselves with fake accessories underneath the skin but only twenty-three karat and sterling where it showed. Vivian's look, though cute, was more Goodwill than Nordstrom.

Viv laughed again. "Well I obviously wasn't his porn star. Apparently your boss used to house his mistresses here. He's had this apartment for ten or fifteen years."

"Since he immigrated?"

"According to the super. Anyway, after he let me in he tried to gently inform me that I was merely a notch on the belt. I told him I was just a temporary houseguest, and he said it was good that I knew the score." Viv muffled her continuing laughter with a flip up of the sleeping bag.

"I can't believe he just let you in."

"Don't underestimate my feminine wiles. I haven't worked my charms on a man in forever."

"Congratulations. But Viv, I don't know if you should stay here."

"Why not?"

"I don't know. It's kind of a shitty place."

"If it's good enough for you, it's good enough for me. What are you trying to say, really?"

"Nothing. It just seems kind of creepy around here, that's all." Vivian was fearless, but also disdainful of violence and especially of weaponry. If she'd known I found a gun in the apartment she'd have whisked both of us out of there in an instant. I couldn't risk that. Something had happened to Plushious Velvett, I was sure of it, and more clues might turn up in The Tender Arms.

"So you can handle it here but I need protection? I'm the damsel in distress in your little butch fantasy? You're sounding more and more like some Southern cop. But I don't have to worry about being spoiled for my first husband by the neighborhood rapist, since here I am under the protection of one of the unabashed thugs of the world."

"Give it up, Vivian." I'd forgotten, in my tiredness, that it never paid to piss Vivian off. She relished all-night arguments. And she always made the most of my one-time arrest for battery.

"No, I'll be the bait for you. I'll lure the neighborhood thugs like flies with my newfound feminine vulnerability. You can attack an attacker to your heart's content."

"I've explained to you a hundred times; that guy was beating up my friend, in front of their kids. I had to hit him to get him off her."

"You had to gong him with a frying pan?"

"He lived. It's not like I killed him."

"Just hurt him."

"Just reminded him what pain feels like. Don't you get sick of hearing about women getting hurt all the time? Every day there's some new news story about a woman missing, found dead in some ditch by the highway, battered for twenty years by that nice quiet man down the block. I'm sick of it. I'm for fighting back." Vivian and I had an old argument. I patted my hot face with hands that felt, suddenly, clammy and cold.

"Of course. But not literally. Not fistfighting back. You've got to change the whole system."

"Right, the revolution. I'm not holding my breath."

"It already happened, you know. The second wave of feminism. Why do you think you have the freedom to be out as a sex worker? You'd have been completely otherized before the women's movement. You wouldn't be able to go around telling your neighbors that you're a stripper, thank you very much. Think of how far we've come."

I was skeptical that the women's movement had done much for sex workers. But to bring that up with Vivian would be to invite a sleepless night. "Want some tea?" I asked, instead. But I couldn't resist needling her a little. "Since Zan's not here to make it for you?"

"What's that supposed to mean?"

"Just that she makes you tea." I moved to the kitchen.

"Oh god, that makes her my wife, doesn't it? You think she's my wife. How horrible. Thank god I'm getting space. Thank god tomorrow I have a date."

"A what?" I dropped the kettle onto the stove with a metallic clang.

"A date."

"Not with Zan, I take it."

"Like Zan and I still go on dates. Oh god, we are married."

"Does she know about this date?"

"She will."

"Right. You'll tell her all about it, I'm sure. That's really why you're here, isn't it? To use this apartment for your tryst? Forget it. I'm not going to be involved in this."

"There's nothing to be involved in. Don't make it sound sordid."

"Don't make it sound unsordid. You're cheating on her."

"Stop being such a prude. We're non-monogamous."

"It takes two to be non-monogamous." I turned off the water that fuzzed behind me into a boil. "Make your own tea."

Zan was my gentlest roommate and though she frustrated me by being Vivian's doormat, I took her side against her overbearing girlfriend. Someone had to speak up for her, she rarely spoke up for herself.

I headed wearily for the Murphy bed. I'd been planning to use the sleeping bag Viv had appropriated, a little spooked by the bed's earlier offering. Besides, the thing didn't look too comfortable. I stretched the thick cotton of my own fitted sheet over the mattress, laid down two of Granny Leann's crazy quilts and crawled between them. After several nights on our green couch, the hard mattress felt almost luxurious. I fell right to sleep.

Chapter Six

The next morning, as promised, as soon as I got up and dressed, I tripped over the sleeping Vivian to collect the trash bag from under the sink. Morning fog made blank television screens of the windows. She was molting the sleeping bag when I came back through the living room.

"Time for your date already?"

"I take it back. It's not a date. It's coffee." Vivian reached into a pile of clothes on the floor. She shrugged her leather vest over the white t-shirt she'd slept in. The vest had once been a whole jacket. Viv had cut the sleeves off with pinking shears. She often dressed like a twelve-year-old boy. "With a woman I met in the library, at school." She pulled a crumpled wad of one dollar bills out of the pocket of a pair of jeans from her clothes pile, counted them, stuffed them back in. I left the trash bag and went to brush my teeth. When I returned I noticed a faint burnish on her lips that looked like my new shade of lipstick: Bonemeal. Viv had enhanced her hazel eyes with a swipe of black eyeliner along the inside rim of the bottom lid, the way we did it in junior high school. They had reddened and teared up as a result.

"I take it you're really into this woman."

Vivian never wore make-up, and apparently hadn't since the mid-Eighties. "Okay, stop the inquisition. I don't have to go out with just Zan. We've always been non-monogamous, you know. What's that look for? I know, the library, and coffee, godsake. Coffee's a terrible omen. You don't have to tell me that this has no future. But there might be a couple of good times before the whole things crashes and burns."

She tucked her jeans into her Doc Marten boots. Vivian was out the door before further comment.

A search in the alley behind The Tender Arms for the building's dumpster was fruitless. After a moment of poking around, I set down the trash which was beginning to leak onto my pants. Then I noticed the recess, paved in concrete, which gave light to the back basement windows, the end of the iron fire escape dangling into it like an insect's leg. There was plenty of trash in the alley, but no evidence of a trash can.

I was looking upward, mesmerized by the weave of the fire escape as it stacked toward the dissolving fog, when a window flew open on the second floor. Maybe it was the perspective, but the man's head that poked out looked unusually big.

"Hey," the young man waved at me. "Are you looking for something down there? Be careful, you might trip the alarm."

"What? Alarm?"

"Yeah, see this laser beam?" He passed his hand through the air like a swami. The movement momentarily broke the line of a red beam that shot straight down the side of the building, skimming the young man's window, the one directly above it, and mingling among the bars on the window below. A piercing wail shot around the alley. It lasted only a few seconds. "Here, I turned it off. Pretty neat, huh?"

"Yeah, great." No such line tripped across the windows on the other side, the 301 side, I noticed.

"Be careful right around the wall here. Wouldn't want you to set it off. I'm sure you're not a criminal."

"I'll be careful."

"Never know what element you're going to find in that alley. Looking for something?" He tucked a shoulder-length tendril of black hair behind his ear, smiled pleasantly around his big, white teeth.

"Can you tell me where the trash goes?"

"I can. Maybe I'll even let you do a little illegal dumping." He leaned his smile out further.

"I'm not dumping. I live here, and I'm taking out the trash."

"Oh, you live here? Great. When are we getting together for a neighborly glass of wine?"

"I prefer Coke." I leaned over to pick up my leaking trashbag.

"Coke, then. It's a date. Trash goes over there." He pointed toward my side of the building.

"Through that walkway. Right alongside the building."

"Thanks."

"When's our date?"

I pretended not to hear.

Both my shoulders almost brushed brick down the few feet of narrow passageway, currently an echo chamber for an ambient Aerosmith song. The dent that afforded us kitchen windows apparently also created space for trash collection at ground level. Gaping green trashcans overflowing with garbage bags crowded into the small paved the area. How did they ever get them out of there? Well, that was Clem's worry. I plonked my trash into one of the already full cans. The bag immediately burst, sending a mudslide of pasta-plasm down the bloated plastic belly of the bag underneath.

A cracked-open window at ground level was the source of the Aerosmith. A black rubber trashcan lid had fallen in front of it. I went to retrieve the lid. Smoke hung against the window so I couldn't see through it, but it must have been Clem's apartment—only he lived in the basement. I wondered that he could keep his window open, considering the stench outside it, but as I bent for the lid I smelled Clem's air freshener—the heavy syrup of marijuana. I pressed an ear to the window and heard a machine whine. It sounded like a drill.

I picked up the lid—tomato aspic. I would never eat it, but it had been a potluck and saladbar favorite back in Ohio. Must be a mid-westerner in the building. Some of the red-gelled concoction was was stuck to the underside, cooked to a slight shrivel around the edges under the oven of the black lid. With a section of bicycle rim I found on the ground, I gave the plump aspic a poke. It quivered for me. Specks of red slithered off. My duty as a conscientious new tenant would be to pick it up and move it to the overburdened trash cans. I picked up the lid like a tray holding the aspic, ready to dump it when something about the viscous shape struck me as somehow familiar. I no longer smelled burning marijuana but something heavier, metallic. Blood. I could taste its iron middle.

I dropped what I was holding. It seemed to take minutes as I watched my hand reach down to squeeze the thing. Around the edges, the gelatinous texture thickened into what looked like cysts.

I touched a balloon which felt dense like mercury, and remembered how Plushious Velvett had clamped my hand to her breast implant.

Someone was having sex in the living room when I got back to the apartment on Church Street. I listened from the bottom of our stairwell. The pants and moans indicated a level of activity sure to splinter the bones of our couch. Great. I announced my coming at a decibel level that I hoped would break through the abandon. My thighs reminded me of my previous long night, burning as I ascended the stairs that led directly into our living room.

I'd barely collected myself enough to retrieve a plastic bag from a drift of alley litter and scrape my suspicious discovery into it before scurrying home to my shared apartment, spooked. The twenty-minute walk in the warm blue early afternoon lent further surrealism to my recent discovery. I didn't want to think about the implications of the disembodied sac squelched in the grocery bag that dangled from my hand. Plushious Velvett hadn't made it to her next gig.

"That you, Aub?" The volume went down in mid-moan. "Come on up. We're watching Ness's work."

Geoffrey and Vanessa Sassy were settled into the couch, up to their chins in a knit afghan. Champagne and Caviar snuggled beside them in one of the sunken cushions. The dogs raised their tufted ears at me.

"Hugh home?" Plushious Velvett's breast implant, or whatever it was in the bag I held, banged against my calf, settled there, started to melt around my leg. I yanked it to the side. But I was jumping to conclusions. Hadn't I found it right outside Clem's window? And wasn't he weird? I made myself stop it.

"Sure. Relax with that package! What's in there, a dirty diaper? Come sit! Ness is giving me a fascinating narration to 'Hard Horn Morn'. Don't you want the blow-by-blow?" Geoffrey and his new best friend giggled and clinked their wine glasses. Even the hand-done blanket, knit in zigzags of clashing colors, flattered blonde and tanned Vanessa Sassy. It clung to her like a sweater.

"No, thanks."

"Hugh wouldn't watch it either. What is up with you people?" Geoffrey punched the volume button on the remote control until sucking sounds buzzed the speaker of the old television.

I found Hugh reading in his bedroom. He and Geoffrey shared the biggest room in the apartment, and the most cluttered. Geoffrey's anti-vermin crusade didn't extend to an appreciation for general tidiness. His art supplies and construction paper creations spilled out of twenty or so stolen milk crates stacked and scattered haphazardly around his single bed. The mummy bag he slept in scrunched across the bare mattress. Shallow bookshelves scaffolded Hugh's side of the room. The homemade shelves were only deep enough for cheap paperbacks, but Hugh had accumulated hundreds of these from his job at Old News Thrift Store. Hugh was their book pricer, though they only had enough work for him three days a week.

When he finished his paragraph he looked up from a water-damaged copy of *In Cold Blood*. The room smelled like mildew. Hugh looked from me to the bag I held stiffly away from my legs. "Is something wrong?"

"You won't believe what I think I just found." I offered the bag to him. He took it, looked inside. He lowered the bag to the floor, pushed his glasses up his nose, rested hands on his knees to inspect the contents some more.

"This is a…?" He lifted his head.

"I think it's a breast implant."

His eyes widened, but he bravely looked down at it again. A few pebbles and black bits of tarmac from the implant's resting place clung to it.

"Where did you get it?"

I explained my discovery of the item; described my earlier forced fondling of the very object now naked before us. Hugh held a hand to his glasses as he listened. "If this item is what you think it is, how would it come to be in the alley?" he asked.

"I don't know. I'm more concerned with how it came to be detached from Plushious Velvett. If it is what I think it is."

"At this point my concern is that you moved it. If it is what you think it is, a crime has been committed. You should have protected the evidence chain by leaving the item alone. What you have found can never be presented before a court now. But it's not too late to call the police."

"Lighten up. At this point what I found is just trash. Trash that I happen to be curious about. I was counting on you to help me figure out what it is."

"I have to refuse on grounds of contamination of the evidence chain."

"Come on Hugh. I need your mechanical mind."

"Only if you promise to turn it into the police."

"Fine. I'll turn it in. As soon as we figure out what it is."

Hugh sighed. "But I refuse to touch it." He followed me into the kitchen.

Cleaned, the jellyfish implant lolled in our battered steel colander on the Formica kitchen table. I bit my lip, thought of Plushious Velvett's complaints. The opaque orb lapped the rim of the colander, filling almost the entire bowl. Imagine hauling around two of those.

"If it's silicone, there should be some way to test it." Hugh furrowed his brows, ran a hand through his long blond bangs. "Silicon has a structure similar to carbon. It's even possible that somewhere in the universe there exists silicon-based life."

"It's called L.A." Hugh didn't laugh at my weak joke. He was hefting the colander, scientifically fascinated. I couldn't regard what I'd found with that same cool detachment. I imagined the weight of it separating my ribs. With Plushious Velvett guiding my hand I felt its impossible firmness, then mentally ran my fingers behind to the red stretch marks that had sutured it to her.

About half of the women I worked with had bought themselves surgical breast implants. They considered them an investment. They thought big tits would make them more money. And they were right.

The swinging door to the kitchen slapped open. Geoffrey came through it, carrying his wine glass at an angle bound to waste precious drops of Merlot.

"What's that?" Geoffrey exhaled wine. He didn't look too closely at the weighted colander.

"Uh, roadkill." I moved to hide the bowl from Geoffrey's view. "I was thinking of cooking up a little stew if the crock-pot's free."

"I wouldn't put it past you." Geoffrey equated Southerners with huntin' and feudin' and bad dentistry, even those of us diffused by a generation and displaced by migration. With effort, he detached the corkscrew from its magnet on the refrigerator door. "Come have some Merlot when you're done. May I add, Ness is a magnificent actress." I felt the heat from his flushed face on my own as he brushed past me back to the living room.

I made a suggestion.

"Do you think that would be appropriate?" Hugh looked nervous.

"Well, she ought to know what they look like. The surgeon probably showed her one."

"Maybe." Hugh shook his head.

"She can't think we don't know about her little secret."

Vanessa wore her baked-tan, stretched-shiny bustline with button-up shirts that quit the struggle above nipple level. On the slope of her half-bare breasts, the bumps of her augmentation were obvious. Still, I felt weird about trotting out to the living room and disturbing Vanessa Sassy from underneath afghan and wine to make such a grisly identification.

"I suppose it would be conclusive evidence."

"Vanessa Sassy?" I propped open the kitchen door with a foot, smiled into the living room. "Can we borrow you for a sec?"

Vanessa Sassy confirmed my discovery for me. I really ought to choose a smaller size, she said, that looked like an H, and she couldn't recommend more than a G, which is what she had gotten, and I should definitely see her surgeon, he was the greatest, he'd fly me down to LA for the consult at no charge, used the latest injection techniques and would anesthetize with white noise or acupuncture for an extra fee. I thanked her. So much for the FDA-banned, only-in-Switzerland myth.

Geoffrey, who had of course followed his screen idol into the kitchen, watched our conversation with his hand over his mouth, weaving as if searching for his sea legs, until Hugh ushered him back out to the couch.

Vanessa Sassy made us a snack of Wasa Bread, Brie cheese and walnuts and tucked the afghan around Geoffrey before she hurried off to her tanning bed session.

I turned off 'Hard Horn Morn', watched a close-up of Vanessa Sassy's lips and tongue spring into a dot in the center of the screen. Her muttered dirty words were replaced by a welcome moment of silence.

"You're getting implants? But why did you have to ruin that colander for me forever? I'll never drain pasta again without thinking of agar-agar and worse." Geoffrey talked to my back. I watched the TV dot slowly disappear.

"I'm not getting implants."

"Of course you're not. You look fine just the way you are. Sag is just a fact of life and anyone worthy of you accepts that."

"I found that implant in an alley. I wasn't sure if that's what it was, I needed Vanessa Sassy to confirm it for me. I didn't want to upset her by telling her it's already been used. I have a suspicion that it belonged to Plushious Velvett, who was working at Naughtyland last week."

"Well she should be awfully conspicuous walking around without it. Don't those things usually come in pairs?"

"Yes."

"Okay." Geoffrey spoke slowly, as if to a child. "What would her implant be doing in an alley?"

"I don't know."

Hugh banged out of the kitchen with a Coke, which he handed to me. The cold aluminum singed my palm.

"I'm afraid I may have destroyed the, um, it." Hugh ran a hand nervously through his bangs. His frequent hair mussing never managed to deter the blond ends from falling behind the frame of his glasses into his eyes.

"What do you mean?"

"I shook the colander to test viscosity and the outer membrane caught an edge. It ruptured. I'm sorry."

I nodded. Hugh looked contrite, but personally I wasn't sorry to see that particular item destroyed.

"The material inside is quite runny. I collected the runoff, close to a liter. Liquid and hundreds of little globules."

"So much for the evidence chain," I said. A liter. God.

Behind us on the couch, Geoffrey percolated under the afghan, giggling and hiccuping.

"What."

"I'm sorry, I can't help it. Hugh slayed the breast."

Chapter Seven

Hugh went to work, Geoffrey went to his glue and cardboard collection for an afternoon of creativity, and I went back to The Tender Arms. As I made my way around the second floor landing to the second flight of stairs, the door marked 203 whisked open. I'd been hoping that wouldn't happen. I'd been right about the perspective. His head didn't look so big at eye level. He was only slightly taller than the five-seven that my stacked-heel engineer boots lifted me to.

"Hello again." He smiled.

"Hi. Sorry about the noise." My boots were loud.

"Need some help? Third floor, huh? Here, that bag looks heavy. I'm Cassius Blakely, by the way. Don't think I got a chance to introduce myself." Cassius Blakely shook my hand, tried to relieve me of the feedbag purse that hung off my shoulder.

"I can carry it."

"They call me Cash, for short. It's kind of funny, since I'm a broker." He sprang up a few stairs, following me, his shoulder-length blunt cut bouncing behind him. Not a single split end weighed it down. "But I never got your name."

"Shouldn't they call you Stock, then, or Capital Gains? Or maybe Net Worth?"

Cash laughed, bounding up the last few steps. "I suppose that would be more appropriate." He was barefoot. The crease of his casual khakis broke against the black hair on his pale instep. "You and I are the new-comers," he said, as I went through the round of keys again at the door to 301. I wasn't saying much, so Cash had plenty of available airtime. "I just moved in a few weeks ago. Heard about the place from Sue and Todd, clients of mine. They live in 202."

"So you and your clients actually choose to live here?"

"Sure, why not? This is an up and coming neighborhood. You've heard of gentrification. It's a great thing. Brings value to these old places.

This isn't the Tenderloin anymore. The realtors renamed it Hayes Valley. Investors are missing a great chance if they're not getting into this neighborhood now. It'll be unrecognizable around here in six months, trust me. Our wine thing's still on, right? Or Coke, that's right, you like Coke. The real thing. What did you say your name was?"

I pushed the door open with a hip. "I didn't say."

Unfazed by rudeness, Cash smiled around his Chiclet teeth. "So say."

I shoved over the threshold. "Aubrey. Bye."

"Okay, Aubrey, great. Hey, I'll see you soon. Nice meeting you." He shook my hand again and sprung away down the steps. "Watch the banister," he called as he descended. "It'll give you splinters."

The late-afternoon sun had moved beyond the reach of the slot between The Tender Arms and the neighboring brick cube, but the brickwork behind the trash area had trapped enough heat to make my search sweaty. Or maybe the sheen on my forearms was goo from stirring bicep-deep into garbage. A muscle between the shoulder blades on my back gathered into a knot of protest as I ripped apart the last of the bulging white bags. Coffee grounds, shrimp shells, and orange peels sprinkled onto the ground. A sour smell wafted upward.

I tossed the bag back where I'd found it, in the trash can nearest the wall. I wasn't worried about leaving the place a mess. It looked better now, I thought, as I wiped my hands on a slightly-soiled paper towel retrieved from the asphalt, than it had ten minutes ago when I'd started ransacking the place. The trash area had been a wreck even before I'd gotten to it. Most of the bags had been slit open, their contents dumped against the wall into a bank of filth that oozed downward. With stock-owning residents in the building, its trash was a potential gold mine. A homeless person had perhaps come looking for his or her next meal, or a Lower Haight hipster for components to a found object sculpture. Trashed trash was a common sight in San Francisco. Even the public bins on Market Street were often guarded by a grubby individual eager for aluminum cans or extra French fries.

My search had revealed no more body parts. An ear to Clem's window had revealed no more suspicious drilling noises. His window was shut. A replica of the Bear Flag hung across it for a curtain.

I walked quickly, trying to leave my own growing stench behind me as I went through the alley behind the buildings, cranking open the heavy lids of corroding brown dumpsters. Several of these receptacles were parked behind neighboring buildings, more than half of them chained shut and padlocked. The three that I could open were not filled with a body or its parts, but did bulge with trash bags, cardboard boxes, cat litter and a bottom layer of mysterious sludge. I dutifully ripped open every trash bag to plow through more kitchen waste. I didn't even notice the smells any more. Not the trash's, and not my own.

Well, so much for the obvious. Geoffrey was right, of course, where there's one one-liter breast implant there's bound to be another, but I couldn't search every dumpster in the city. Besides, dusk was coming on, brushing the sky a darker shade of blue. Uneager to face my new neighbors in my current slimy state, I ascended the fire escape to the third floor. A door at the top opened with one of my keys, and I scuttled across the landing to the apartment. I had just enough time to steam-clean and disinfect myself before the night shift began.

Will, one of my regulars, was waiting for me when I emerged from Naughtyland's dressing room an hour later. My push-up bra and thong underwear always felt tight as a horse's girth at the beginning of a shift. Faces were indistinct in the club's laser lighting, but I recognized Will's silhouette from across the room. His right hip hung off his chair. Sitting, he maintained a gun-toting posture. Will was a cop.

As I approached him I noticed he was beerless. His wife, I knew, was pressuring him to quit drinking, unaware that the beer she smelled on his breath was the nonalcoholic version, the only kind with official state approval for use in strip clubs. He watched Anastasianna, a new redheaded dancer, hump the stage's metallic pole, then slide her right leg straight up the bar into a vertical split, then somehow manage to pelvic thrust the thing, using muscles few people have cultivated. I touched Will on the shoulder. He clamped his big hand over mine. Anastasianna flipped her right leg down quick as a light switch. She bent forward until her fingernails dangled like Christmas ornaments between her platform soles.

"You could acknowledge me, you know." I spoke directly into Will's ear, to be heard over "Karma Chameleon." Will and I always seemed to be wanting something from the other that he or I couldn't give.

Maybe that was another tension that drove Mose Junior's lucrative business.

"Hi, sweetheart."

"How's the wife?"

"Don't talk like that. You'll put me out of the mood."

Will turned to face my chest, the sudden torque of his heavy torso threatening to split the cheap plastic chair. He'd recently cut his springy brown hair and the gray was less noticeable in the shorter length. He pressed my hand into his shoulder, stamping my palm with the hard definitions of his deltoids.

"Come here." I leaned close enough to smell the Irish Spring. "She's making me horny," Will confided.

I pulled back. "Of course she is. That's her job."

Will turned back to the view. "You gotta way of taking all the mystery out."

What mystery? I thought, noting Anastasianna's blunt spread-eagle at the edge of the stage. Her red platforms were shot high above her head, her red baby-doll nightie a crinkle of lace accordioned high above her waist. Her bare nether parts were inches from the nearest customer, who stared at them through his mug of non-alcoholic beer.

I took a seat next to Will. It was time to make up. I had favors to ask him. "How does one go about looking for a missing person?"

"What?"

I gave him my hand to hold. This earned a flicker of his gaze and a knuckle-cracking squeeze. Will had a hard time showing the affection I knew he felt. He kept telling me I had the same problem. "Actually, I'm not sure if the person is missing. She may be dead."

That got his attention.

"Dead?" His chair wobbled, flimsy as paper under his weight.

"More likely just missing, though." I said it hastily.

Will was always telling me to get out of my profession, it was too dangerous. His precinct had booked hundreds of battered sex workers, pulled their naked, raped corpses out of the Bay, picked their body parts out of dumpsters for years before my discovery. We were society's disposables, as used up as the morning-after's condom. Sacrifices to collective shame. Not that he put it that way.

"Missing person's report. Your friend got a name?"

I picked a cuticle. Plushious Velvett wouldn't have been on her birth certificate.

"I knew it. A stripper, right? When are you getting out of this business, sweetheart?" A purple laser beam from the disco ball lit the real concern in first one, then the other of Will's brown eyes.

"When people like you stop dropping a hundred bucks a week on me."

My loyal customer shook his head. "Who's the girl?"

"Plushious Velvett, last week's feature. She didn't show up at her next job, somewhere in Texas. I found," I hesitated for a moment, "her robe.

She wouldn't leave it behind. I'm wondering if she's okay."

"Get her real name, I'll run the report."

"I can't think of any way to get it. I might have a clue, though. I found something else that I think might have belonged to her."

"What is it?"

"Just some liquid."

"Think she drank it? Poison?"

I shook my head. "I don't think she drank it."

"Easier to test it if we know what we're testing for."

"If I knew, I wouldn't need it tested. Can you help me out?"

"How do I get mixed up in this kind of thing?"

"You're the one decided to become a cop."

By the time I came back from the dressing room with Hugh's Tupperware bowl (filled with murky liquid and dozens of clots), that I'd retrieved from my locker, Will had relaxed back into his chair. I set the bowl on the table.

"I wouldn't worry too much about your friend," he said. "She probably missed her kids, took a week. Work is people's favorite place not to show up. Heck, half the time I come here looking for you, you ain't around."

"This isn't the kind of job you can do everyday." If Will didn't want to worry, whatever. I wanted some answers about Plushious Velvett's disappearance, and the naked implant's equally sudden appearance.

"How soon will you get the lab results back?"

"Couple days." Will kept his grip on my hand as we watched Anastasianna's grand finale, a series of splits and side-splits that propelled her down the stage's runway, her muscular, thin legs whirling like helicopter blades. When "Sweet Dreams" ended she somehow popped upright, collected her panties from a balding audience member, and then she was gone.

Will smiled his crinkly smile and stood, the chair springing upward underneath him. He nodded toward the nearest cubicle. "You can thank me in there," he said.

Chapter Eight

"Anybody home?" I pounded at the door marked 'Laundry Room.' I'd woken early the following day, at eleven o'clock. After my cup of Earl Grey I'd gone looking for Clem.

The Laundry Room was stubbornly resistant to my knocks, though Aerosmith from within suggested that somebody was home. The only other door along the dank, brown linoleum hallway of The Tender Arms basement floor was marked 'Janitor's Closet'. I worked it open until that door crashed into a bucket on rollers with an unholy screech of metal. "Clem? It's Aubrey, up at Mose's place. Hello?"

I pounded some more, wondered if the flimsy paneling would stand up to a kick from my stacked soles. The Aerosmith coming from the Laundry Room sounded like the same song I had heard coming from the opened window by the trash the day before. Or maybe all of their songs just sound the same. I gave up after several minutes of pounding. Clem had to be somewhere in the building. It's not like he left to go to work. Surely there was a nosy neighbor around who could enlighten me to his whereabouts, and other suspicions about the man. Maybe I'd even stumble on the super himself on one of the upper floors. Besides, when asking for Clem I could work in a few questions about the disappearance of Plushious Velvett.

Will's reassurances had failed to reassure me. Porn stars didn't just blow off ten thousand dollar gigs on some nostalgic impulse to shovel strained sweet potatoes into the maws of their slobbering children. Plushious Velvett was missing, a giant breast implant had turned up in the garbage at around the same time, and the superintendent of her temporary dwelling was inclined to let the neighborhood in. Too much of a coincidence for my liking. It was definitely time to meet the other residents of The Tender Arms.

Ten of the tenants must have either been shy or had day jobs. Only Cash was home. He opened his door so enthusiastically that the breeze lift-

61

ed the hairs that had strayed from my ponytail.

"Aubrey! Afternoon encounters with gorgeous women. Another bonus of working at home. Come on in." Cash removed a hand from the pocket of his loose green linen pants to direct me inside his apartment. His shirt was yellow and short sleeved and had obviously been pressed. His color scheme reminded me of lima beans.

"No, that's okay. I was just looking for Clem. Have you seen him?"

"As a matter of fact I've been waiting on him myself. He was supposed to take a look at my sink today. Actually, it was yesterday that he was supposed to look at it. Porcelain's cracking. Clem may need a lesson in caulk." Cash moved forward into his doorway to make up for my unconscious retreat. "Sure you won't come in?"

Here was someone eager to talk to me, someone who, being a gregarious predator type, surely had known Plushious Velvett. I dug my fingernails into my palms and agreed to meet him for drinks after work. Cokes, right? He was sure he could get some at the liquor store on the corner. He'd be on his computer until seven or so, but he couldn't wait. At least I had a few hours to brace myself for his cheery flirtations.

I had time to go home.

"Momma, it's only temporary. You can just leave messages for me here." Champagne and Caviar took turns snapping at the phone cord which stretched over them since they'd refused to give up their end slot on our green couch.

"Oh I know, sweetie-pie, but how can you live without a phone? Martha, you know, from the beauty shop, and Janie, we've got to have our daily gossip. We do a three-way call. You just act like you're going to hang up, but just hit that button real quick, then you hear beep beep beep beep, then you go ahead and dial the second number, then when she answers you hang up again real quick. Then you're all on the line. Ohio Bell charges you seventy-five cents. Eb, get this pan of brownies away from me before I sit right here and eat the whole thing. You should see the pile of corn Eb is bringing in. When's the last time you had fresh corn? Probably can't even get it there in Sin City for love or money. When are you coming home to see your old Momma?"

"I don't know." My return visits to Ross City, the suburb of Dayton where I'd grown up, had become less frequent as the years went by. There were more people there I wanted to avoid than people I wanted to see.

"Hm. Well grass is growing up real tall around that Honda. Never did run. Eb? You in the kitchen? Reach me a Pepsi, would you? Of course diet."

62

"Can't Eb help you get it running?" I had a suspicion that Eb resented the things I bought for Momma, whose job at the beauty shop didn't pay well. The used Honda I'd sent her money for had broken down on the road a hundred yards from the college student she'd bought it from. Triple A had towed it to her front yard, and there it sat. Luckily her neighbors weren't anxious upwardly-mobile types who objected to cars rusting in front yards.

It was hard to buy gifts for Momma. She couldn't figure out the fax machine. The Kenmore refrigerator was the wrong color. Something always happened like that.

"He never has time to work on cars anymore. They're keeping him right busy down at the insurance company. Then you should see his garden. I've never seen so many pole beans in all my life. Guess you can't get fat eating vegetables. That's what they used to say in Weight Watchers anyway. 'Now girls, we didn't get here by eating vegetables.' Here he is, don't you want to say a few words? She's not going to have a phone for a while, hon. No, I don't know why. Here he is, hold on."

Eb and I exchanged monosylables. He was Momma's third husband. I'd been an adult, married to my first, Conor, when the shellacked redwood sign had taken its place on the vinyl siding of the house I'd grown up in: Ebenezer and Darylynn Fosters, est. 1993. Eb and I had never really gotten to know one another. I had a number of new step-brothers and sisters that came with him. I tried in vain to remember exactly how many during our stilted interchange. I still hadn't figured out what to call the crop of step-siblings that had come and gone with Momma's second marriage. She'd met my second step-father while collecting my first step-father's life insurance. Eb had been Rodney's agent.

"I'm back. Isn't he sweet? I'll be putting up his garden tomatoes for weeks. Fifty quarts or more this year I reckon. Sigh. Your Granny Leann would put up twice that many though, had to to feed us kids. That's why her back gave out in the end. Then Rudy would turn around and be giving her preserves to the Bufords. Some had even less than we did, down in the hills." Momma launched into a long reminiscence of her eastern Kentucky childhood, one I already knew well enough to repeat along with her. I let her talk on, figuring we wouldn't be having another phone chat for a while. The Bufords had been neighbors on the old homeplace and the poorest people in the county. Mrs. Buford had pumped out children seasonally, as sure as the frogs hollered in the fall. The last one came out in pieces, a "moon baby", Momma called it, and after that Mr. Buford had been made to sleep out on the porch. Uncle Rudy, who had had a heart of gold until he was old enough to buy beer and a pick-up, and fatally crashed into a coal truck on those winding mountain roads, kept the Bufords from starving one winter by pillaging his own family's root cellar. When Granny Leann went looking for her quarts of peaches with a mind to make a cobbler and found nothing in the cellar but mouse turds, she whupped Rudy from here to Christmas. She could be heartless, Momma concluded.

Heartless, maybe, but Granny Leann had more to put up with in her life than a few thousand quarts of preserves, I thought. When she was old and I was helping her make my double-wedding-ring quilt, she'd confided that she'd spent her entire marriage to my granddad just trying not to get pregnant. Did I know about birth control because it was a blessing. She didn't know much about it herself, but if she were my age she'd make it her business to find out. Especially since I was fixing to marry an Irish Catholic. Then without another word about it she went right on piecing together interwoven rings of brown and purple calicos for my wedding gift. I'd never told Momma about this particular revelation. Granny Leann had had five children.

"You listening to your Momma? I was just telling you when the Bufords got a TV, at the Salvation Army or someplace, they couldn't afford an antenna, this was back before cable. There's no reception down in those hills. They got whatever came in through our antenna. So whatever we were watching, they'd have the same show on. When we changed the channel, theirs changed too."

"Well Momma, I should go." Momma's battery of mood-enhancing drugs kept her chattering until rudely cut off.

"Now there's cable, acourse. You have cable?"

"No."

"You're missing out! They don't have cable, hon. No. I don't know." Momma giggled. She had two laughs. The other was drawn out, two notes, like a siren. The siren was the laugh that fought off some painful subject: domestic violence, my father's disappearance then death, her moods before medication roped and tied her brain chemistry. That long, high laugh warned: drop it. Change the subject. Momma had the same philosophy about her past as Granny Leann had about her canning peaches: cut out the bad parts.

Momma's giggle, though, was the laugh that irritated me the most. The giggle was used to placate doltish husbands. "Eb says, 'No cable, what do they do out there with themselves'?" she said, when the giggle was over.

"We manage. I really have to go."

"Well it is Sin City, I reckon there's plenty else going on. When are we going to talk again? I don't like this you not having a phone."

By this point I was looking forward to it. "It won't be long. Just a few days, couple weeks at the most." Surely Mose Junior would have found an apartment suitable for his porn stars by then.

"Don't forget to call your old Momma now and then."

"I don't forget."

We exchanged goodbyes.

Phone conversation over, Hugh punched up the volume on the rerun of *I Love Lucy*. He was next to me on the couch, a thumb marking his place in a copy of *Dune* so worn that the paperback's spine was flaking off.

"Why do you like this show?" I asked him. A corseted Lucy was pouting into the camera. How did they draw all those curves into her lips?

"It's a fascinating commentary on the state of race and gender relations in the United States in the Fifties."

"Its also unbearable. Look at that phony crying." I got up, reached for my empty Coke can. Just above my left eye, the small pickaxe that dug downward whenever I drank too much caffeine took a warm-up prod. The stuff didn't keep me awake, but apparently had some other mysterious effect on my poor nervous system. Or maybe the effect was from the family phone call. I put a hand to my forehead and squeezed to combat the pain.

"Wait," Hugh looked up at me. He had on a faded red t-shirt with a glitter decal. A smiling Fonzie twinkled with the movements of Hugh's breathing.

"You want something from the kitchen?"

"No," he reached to grab my wrist, let his hand fall. "It's just that," he adjusted his black-framed glasses, "we can change the channel."

"Go ahead then. I'm getting another Coke."

"Wait, I–"

"I'll be right back. Stop acting so weird." I pulled away from the sobbing Lucy, the snapping terriers, the grasping Hugh. What was he being so clingy for? God. No more Cokes gave their cheery red glow to the interior of the refrigerator. I rubbed my forehead. It was just as well, I didn't need a major headache. Maybe that's why I'd been so snappy. I instantly felt bad for being mean to Hugh. He'd never been anything but sweet. I think that's what got to me sometimes, about him. I was probing for a mean streak. This kind of sickness on my part was exactly why I wasn't in a relationship. I pushed back through the kitchen door to explain myself.

The couch was empty.

The terriers wiggled at the top of the stairs. I heard the chatter of an entourage below. Moments later, Vanessa Sassy reached the living room. Her dogs yapped and attacked the cuffs of her velveteen pants. Geoffrey followed, his arm around a shorter, towheaded boy. The boy's straight hair was cut in careless short layers that ended unevenly above his ears, the more appealing for their tugged-at abandon. His cheekbones were made prominent by his grin at whatever Geoffrey was whispering into his ear, and when he turned, it was to look at me with gray eyes made wider by pale, almost invisible lashes. His smile cracked at one side, flirted around a sliver of exposed molars. "Hi," he nodded his head.

"Don't mind her. She's a bit slow." Geoffrey turned the boy back toward him with a tug on one of the narrow suspenders that gathered his sleeveless t-shirt to his chest. Over the shorter, blonder head, Geoffrey fluttered his eyelashes and puckered his lips at me.

I took a step toward them, close enough to shake hands. "I'm Aubrey," I said, and stuck out my right one.

The boy turned back to me. Brushed a hand across the khakis at his narrow hips. "I'm the bodyguard," he gave me his hand, small, warm from Geoffrey's escort. The handshake was firm. "Isabella."

"Sure you don't want to move back in? Maybe share the couch with Izzy? She's a slender girl, I'm sure you'd both fit." Geoffrey laughed as he poured hot water into his French press. "I offered her wine, but she likes caffeine, just like you. See, there's something you have in common. When are you going to start swinging both ways?"

"When I'm ready for a life as complicated as yours." I ground fingers into my left eyebrow. Meeting Isabella had worsened my headache, and I couldn't find Hugh. He'd left the apartment.

"Mm. You're definitely a top, but butch or femme?" Geoffrey squinted at me. "Femme, I think, but you definitely have some butch in you. You just might be a switch hitter. Lucky Iz!"

"Geoffrey."

"Femme top, I'd say. At least at first."

"Stop it."

"Oh, lighten up. If you won't have her, maybe I will. Is that too tacky, doing your houseguests? Yes, I think so," he answered himself. With both hands and a hunch of his broad shoulders, Geoffrey plunged the press' filter down through swirling coffee granules. "But she is a darling. If nothing else, this crazy scheme of your boss's has hooked us up with some interesting people, don't you think? But here I am, hogging all their time."

"It's okay. I should thank you. Thank you for taking care of them." I couldn't remove my fingers without the pulsing pain arcing behind my forehead.

"What's this, a heartfelt offering?" Geoffrey sat across from me at the kitchen table. "You look terrible. What's going on?"

"Oh, Momma called."

"How is Darylynn? Pushing husband number three toward his next heart attack in that big garden? She doesn't realize that not everyone has her amphetamine edge. I'm dying to propose that the husband take up cannabis growing, he seems to have such a talent for plants. That would pay those medical bills. May I propose it, Aubrey?"

"No you may not." Momma would talk at length to whomever happened to answer her phone calls. My roommates all knew the same details of her life that I did. I'd just heard them repeated more often.

"Kidding. Just trying to cheer you up. I'm sorry about Darylynn, I know she's difficult."

"What? She's not difficult, it's Hugh. I think I hurt his feelings just now."

"Okay," he drew out the word. "Mommy's not difficult. We'll save that one for our next session. Hate to break it to you honey, but if you hurt Hugh's feelings it's not the first time. There there, he'll bounce back." Geoffrey sprang up to find a clean dishcloth, soaked it in water from the kettle. "Hold this to your forehead." He handed the steaming cloth to me. "Why don't you take the evening off from work? I'm taking our house-guests to Trannyshack. It'll be fun."

The last thing I wanted to tell Geoffrey was that I had a date with a predatory stockbroker. He wouldn't let me leave until I'd promised to meet them that night, elevenish.

Back at The Tender Arms, I made myself an afternoon cup of Earl Grey and a fried baloney sandwich, my first meal of the day. It was five o'clock. My new neighbors should be getting home. I'd found Vivian in front of her laptop on the floor of the living room, blank blue screen and glazed television-lit eyes staring each other down. At least she was alone. I didn't ask her about her date. I elicited gagging sounds from her with offers of half my sandwich, then left her to her nail-biting. With her free hand, she wrung out one of the succulent leaves of the snake plant, as if to squeeze inspiration from its sap.

"I'm going to meet some of my new neighbors. If I'm not back in three hours, come looking for me."

67

"Yeah, yeah," she said. "Maybe I'll have the subtitle done by then."

"The subtitle? How long you been working on that thing?" I took the final bite of sandwich, the dry, mealy corner. Baloney should come in squares.

"Couple weeks." She wasn't looking at me, but at the glowing screen of her laptop. The screen did seem sparsely populated. In fact, the copy that flickered there couldn't have been more than a sentence long. "I had to come up with a title."

"It took you two weeks to come up with a title?"

"Yep. My advisor insisted it better be good, and it is."

"What is it?" I'd lived with Vivian throughout most of her two-year graduate program, but had only the vaguest idea of what a Master's in Women's Studies would entail, except spending afternoons scribbling onto coffee-stained papers and being generally surly around exam time.

"'The Male Gaze: A Penetration into the Construction of the Discourse of Entitlement.'"

"A penetration?"

"I know. I'm subverting the concept. Don't you think it should include something about Access?"

It sounded like the kind of paper Early Lyle, my ex-father, would have ripped into fourths and stacked in the outhouse, next to the hole. Pointy-headed academics were about as worthwhile as the pissants that crawled latrines, in his opinion. Not that he'd had first-hand experience with academia. Until he was drafted at age eighteen, he'd worked as a plumber.

Viv didn't seem to notice that I didn't answer her. Someone was rustling in the hallway outside, and I decided that a casual meeting would be advantageous in my quest for information about 301's previous tenant.

I was too late to question the person who turned out to be my immediate neighbor. I just caught a glimpse of a black flare of polyester hem over navy hose and flat pumps, the shoes of the kind made of giving material and spongy soles, before the door marked 302 closed behind them. Those weren't real pumps. Real pumps are made for women with mettle, for those willing to recast their feet into the shape of a canoe for fashion's sake as my Momma's were. I knocked on 302 long enough for Vivian to come out and tell me to shut up, she needed to concentrate, but Comfortable Pumps never answered.

304 wasn't home or wasn't answering either, but at 303 I got a taste of things to come. The door's opener was tall and thin, with short gelled hair, small-rimmed glasses that barely managed to circumscribe her mascara, pelvic bones that rigged out the denim lap of her jeans. Her white silk

shirt draped backwards in accordance with her no-weight-problems-here posture. Her boots, suede with a brushed-up nap, were cowboy boots. She tapped one as she looked down at me.

I explained I was her new neighbor, and she asked me what I wanted. I asked her if she'd met Plushious Velvett, describing her when the name got no response. The description got this response: "Seen a million like her coming in and out of there." I explained that Plushious was missing, and asked if she had any information. Her information was this: "We're tired of your type in and out of that place and it's not going to go on much longer." She raised the bottle of microbrew that she held. I stepped back. She didn't smash the bottleneck against the doorframe and wave resulting fangs of brown glass at my throat. She only sipped her beer, then closed the door.

Well.

The hall was silent. My conversation with Cowboy Boots had been as quiet and as charged as two schoolgirls whispering gossip in the back of algebra class. I headed down the stairs. I'd start again as far away as possible from Cowboy Boots.

"Tea or coffee, honey? I'm a Southern gentleman, and my Momma would swat me if we got to talking without a little something first to wet your throat."

There was no getting out of Southern hospitality. "Do you have Earl Grey?"

"Let's see here." My host, who had introduced himself as DeeDee, rustled through his kitchen cabinets while I tried to rearrange my backside into a comfortable position on a small wrought-iron seat, part of the bistro set in his living room. This apartment, directly beneath mine on the first floor, had the exact same layout but was more run down than Mose Junior's weary place. Water stains threatened most of the square yardage of DeeDee's ceiling, its surface painted in a dispiriting puce color perhaps chosen to match them. A pair of homemade curtains, thin as cheesecloth, scraggled over the window. They filtered the waning sunlight into the yellow color of old toenails. The window sill held a shallow pot of blooming narcissus, the source of the acrid smell. The built-in bookcase was missing its shelves. Nevertheless, the hollowed-out space was filled with reading material, slippery stacks of women's magazines with faded paperbacks mortared in between. Plenty of overgrown foliage plants contributed to the Italian garden atmosphere, as did the wicker living room furniture mere inches away from the bistro table. Every personal effect in the room seemed to have been recently removed from a trunk in the attic. The place was a firetrap.

"There was Tetley or Lipton, so I went with the Lipton. It's really a toss up, don't you think? Momma always swore by Tetley. Sugar?" DeeDee balanced carefully on the matching iron chair opposite me. He passed me a sweating glass of iced tea. A beginning pot belly strained against his navy muscle-T, sagging bare beneath the shirt's hem for a couple of white inches. The sleeveless shirt did show off defined deltoids and biceps, though the solid muscle rooted sagging flesh. Belted seersucker shorts matched the blue of his shirt. "Oh, let's clink," he raised his glass. "Now tell me what you're up to."

We touched glasses. I was glad there was someone underemployed in the building. DeeDee explained that he was a hairdresser for little old ladies during early afternoon, post-luncheon hours. He was always home by four. The other residents of the first floor hadn't been.

"I'm living upstairs—"

"301, right," DeeDee cut me off with a wave.

"Uh, right. Anyway, the previous resident didn't show up at her next job. After she left here, she disappeared."

"That lovely girl with not much hair? Whoever did that dye job should be shot, or at least sued. Poor thing looked a bit plucked." DeeDee stirred his tea, the sugar making a white swirl in the brown liquid.

"You knew her, then. Ever talk to her?"

DeeDee leaned back and sighed. "I try to have all you 301 girls down here, for a little homegrown hospitality. It's a cruel living. I should know; I was a dancer myself in the seventies. We've got to stick together. Sometimes I don't get a chance to meet every single one of you. Last week's, though, came down to tea."

"Really?"

"Don't make that expression, sugar. You'll give yourself wrinkles. They start right here," DeeDee touched his forehead, above his nose. "She mostly smoked." DeeDee's voice fell into a conspiratorial stage whisper and he leaned forward. "It's for guests like her that I have an ashtray with a little built-in fan. The Smoke-Sucker, it's called, only nine-ninety-five at the dollar store over on Polk. You've got to get one, they're great. No smells. No one will suspect, whatever your habits. No smoking building, you know, new regulation." His voice returned to normal. Laugh lines cut across his wide forehead and carved the beginnings of jowls into either side of his mouth. "But you won't tell on me, sugar?"

"No, of course not. Did she mention anything that might explain why she's gone missing?"

DeeDee tapped his glass onto the metal table in a slow rhythm, and with a finger idly traced the outline of one of the cabbage roses that tessellated across his faded wallpaper. "We talked about the business, mostly. And The Seventies. You can't imagine how much fun it was back then. The worst you had to worry about was herpes; there was always plenty of cocaine, everyone was single and hated Nixon; we'd just party all the time. And the clothes! Those tight hips. It was a sad day when they went out of fashion. Anyway, I still use the name I gave myself back then. I was christened Dwight David, can you imagine? We really did it in cages. But you wouldn't remember those days." DeeDee looked at me with an expression of sympathy. "She did." He reached backward and through the doorway to his kitchen counter, offered me a plastic tray form-fitted to two neat rows of cookies. The cookies had come under a blow-gun of granulated sugar. "Windmill cookie?" he asked.

"No, thanks. Did she say where she was from?" I shook my head clear of the image of a coked-up DeeDee, thinner and polyestered, go-go dancing in a dangling cage.

"She'd just moved to L.A., she said. From somewhere else, Illinois, Colorado, someplace like that. Is she really missing? How dreadful."

"Would you voluntarily pass up a ten thousand dollar gig?"

"My goodness, is that how much they're paying now? I've got to find out if Nob Hill Cinema might be hiring. I suppose it's hopeless, with this fetish for youth." DeeDee made fluffing motions against his blue rinse, to little effect. His hair was crenelated into immobile waves. "I'm afraid I'm not much help."

"You didn't hear anything suspicious, say, last weekend?"

"Last weekend, last weekend. They all kind of blur together, don't they? Let's see, I had a party here Friday night. That's right, she was there! I invite all the lower class residents of the building to my parties and make them be as loud as they can. It drives the yuppie bloc crazy. Mr. Tate always shows up, god love him, comes creaking across the hall behind his walker. We'd keep him up anyway, he says, so he might as well enjoy himself. He still loves his vodka."

"Plushious Velvett was there?"

"Oh, just for a moment. I found her in the lobby and did she look like she needed a drink. Clem put a stop to our festivities before she could get half of it into her, unfortunately."

"Clem stopped the party?"

DeeDee refilled his iced tea glass, a tall one made for the purpose and decorated with flowers painted in an inexplicable olive green. "He never lets us go beyond two. He's at the beck and call of the yuppie bloc, you see."

"Who're they?" I guessed that I'd already met two of them. I shook my head to an offer of the ice tea pitcher. It was aluminum, lurid green, the size of a chemical toilet. Cubes of ice, mint green from reflection, floated counterclockwise in the brown liquid.

"The newcomers to the building. The ones who aren't living in the Tenderloin, because they're in the North of Market. They ran out of fashionable neighborhoods to invade and they just love these charming built-ins." DeeDee gestured toward his shelfless bookcase. "They turn the places into lofts the second they move in. It's like a compulsion with them, kick out a wall and slap up a platform bed. God knows how they have sex on those things." He downed his tea like a post-game beer. "Maybe that's not an issue. I think Sue, that little prude, organized a raid on the whorehouse down the block last night. Did you hear the sirens?"

"No." I hadn't, but years of living in the city had inured me to nightly howls of the siren family. I could easily have slept through a police raid down the block.

"Yuppies are lining up to take over these apartments, so little rules come up, like we can't have pets anymore, or hanging plants. We're not supposed to hang towels out the windows, and the curtains that face the street are supposed to be white. And no smoking inside!" DeeDee waggled his finger in imitation of a schoolmarm. "No wine drinking, then, I said. Did that turn some heads. If you don't conform, and honey, I'm an individualist, with these little violations of your human rights, Clem can see to it that your days are numbered."

"What do you mean, your days are numbered?" My mind began to race. Hadn't Clem told me that Mose Junior's place was a bargain? That someone would "kill" for that rent-controlled apartment? Had that been Plushious Velvett's fate? If her disappearance was the result of slum clearance taken to a new level, I, making the neighborhood a bad one with my mere presence, was next in line for the program. But it didn't make sense. Mose Junior paid the rent on 301, not any of his porn stars.

"The forehead, the forehead!" DeeDee was saying. "Watch those wrinkles! You really should think about drinking aloe vera juice. Look at my skin, and I never put anything on it. They're looking for excuses to evict what remains of us lower-class types. I've been in this place for twenty years. The building used to be full of hustlers and whores, and drugs, all of which I fully approved. When the Vietnamese moved in we had such fun acculturating each other. Things did get a little crazy with crack." He whispered the last word. "I lived in this apartment through it all. An old-timer, that makes my rent low. The landlord could be getting a lot more for it. He knows it too. The old coot tried to evict Mr. Tate next door, and the poor man is lame."

"How long has Mose Junior been renting 301?"

"Five, six years. Between you and me, he kept his girlfriends there until he started using it to house his weekly features. The girlfriends stuck around a little bit longer than a week. He got in long before the boom. Us real old-timers pay three hundred a month, and you'll just want to ask Sue and Todd and them how much he's taking them for rent."

"How much?"

"You wouldn't believe it if I told you."

"How does the landlord get away with it?"

"Market value in this neighborhood was low even a year ago. But now this old place is just as valuable as anywhere else in the city. This isn't a last resort neighborhood anymore. They've gone and gentrified the entire city of San Francisco."

That did seem incredible. The Tenderloin has the worst image of any neighborhood in the city, long known as a fine old refuge for crime and drugs and homelessness as well as for the sex trade. The neighborhood never made the papers without the descriptives "notorious" or "crime-rid-den" or the alliterative "troubled" buttoned to its name. I was skeptical of these adjectives, aware that Drinking In Public was the bulk of the "crime" in the neighborhood where I'd worked for almost two years, and Solicit-ing no doubt a close second. I didn't feel particularly threatened by either criminal activity.

The Tenderloin is as geographically challenged as it is newsworthy. It's a hollow between San Francisco's famous hills, viewless and stagnant. It's in the middle of the peninsula, far from the ocean and the bay. No breezes cleanse it. Even the fog that churns over the Tenderloin on sum-mer afternoons seems merely to seal in the gamy exhale of the Asian restaurants, laundromats, saloons, and sex shops rather than retreat with these impurities back to the Pacific.

"There's no last resort neighborhood left in San Francisco, then," I said.

"It's called Oakland, honey. These people would love to see us cross the bay. Over my dead body. Have you ever been there? It's a cultural dearth."

"Never been."

"It's on BART. But there's absolutely no reason you should ever go."

"So, Plushious Velvett came to your party and that was the last you saw of her?"

"That was it. I had to send her home half-sober. Let me know what you find out, would you? I'd hate for us to lose another one." DeeDee swung his teaspoon like a pendulum inside his glass. It made cheery clinks. "We've such a dangerous profession."

Chapter Nine

DeeDee agreed to meet me later that evening, when the lower class neighbors, as he called them, would be home. He'd introduce me, and I could ask away about our co-professional. With the reception I'd been getting, I agreed that double-teaming with DeeDee might be more productive in my search for clues about Plushious Velvett's disappearance.

I climbed back up to 301 to change for my date. I'd be dressing down.

"Hey, Aubrey. Hey, great, come on in!" Cash scraped a hand along his center part and smiled. His hair fell back exactly in place, the even ends sweeping his shoulders. He'd changed into a pair of loose denim painter's pants with an undershirt of the type Geoffrey favored, sleeveless and ribbed, bunching out over the waistband. Clearly neither shirt nor trousers had ever been used for painting. The pant legs were wide enough to completely conceal Cash's bare feet. He waved me inside.

"Sorry I'm late." I glanced around his place. The fading sunlight fell through several windows, creating faint columns that highlighted galaxies of dust. The place seemed to be under construction.

"No, hey, that's great. Gave me time to change. You, too, I guess, right?" Cash looked me over. I'd let my hair keep its aggressive clumping tendency, which could have been softened into auburn waves with attention from a brush. I'd put on the baggiest clothes I owned: a used pair of Levi's laddered with rips and a black t-shirt with stains around the collar. This was my hair-dyeing outfit, salvaged from Hugh's thrift store. Vivian had assured me that I looked great, so I knew I'd reached a fashion depth. Though Viv offered to loan me a pair of threadbare Converse, I'd opted for my new black leather lace-up boots. They went over my calves and were visible through the bottom rungs of my jeans.

"Look, take a seat, okay? Here," Cash stooped to shove a pastel cushion back down into a low Scandinavian-style couch. "Make yourself at home. Please."

"Thanks. Working on the place?" It smelled of new paint.

"Not anymore. Well, painted the place last week. Like I say, I'm new here. The previous owners did some work on it, I think. Here, let me get you something. I think I know just the thing. A spoonful of sugar, right? Just a sec." Cash grinned and padded across a rust-colored runner to his kitchen. The runner itself stretched over paint-splattered dropcloths. The mustard yellow and watery olive green smeared over the walls were not the only colors represented on the white sheets. Brown and blue had once been dribbled over it, a few blotches of brick red provided contrast. Perhaps Cash had had his floor coverings professionally splattered. From the kitchen, I heard the spine crack on a tray of ice.

Next to the sofa was a glass-topped desk with spindly metal legs. On the desk, and reflecting into its greenish, beveled surface, was a humming laptop computer. A halogen light matched the desk chair in its jointed, barebones design. All the furniture—the desk and the couch were all there appeared to be—was clustered under a broad plywood canopy jacked to within a foot of the ceiling. A futon slumped on top of the plywood, creating a loft.

Not only was Cash's hardwood floor completely covered with speckled tarps, but his dividing wall was gone. What in Mose's place and DeeDee's had provided a bedroom, however small, had been knocked out in this apartment. The Murphy bed closet was closed. It was painted with the yellow, to match a foot-tall stripe that ran around the entire apartment at just about head height. Below the yellow was the thinned olive green.

"Like the paint job?" Cash, a glass of Coke in each hand, stopped on his runner to gesture around. "Took my decorator hours to come up with the colors. That's Green Tea all over, Dijon accent. He said it would unify the space. I don't know," he shook his head as he resumed walking toward me. "Does an apartment that's all one room need unifying? Here you go." He ducked under the loft to set the glass on the tarp at my feet.

"Thanks." I sipped the Coke.

"You like Al Green? You know, you have to promise me another date. Sue and Todd are about to come by for wine tasting. I had to invite them after I ran into them down at Beverages & More. I couldn't get out of it. You shop South of Market?" My host clipped a CD into a boombox that sat among folds of the dropcloth in the room's far corner. "Let's Stay Together" came on. Cash joined me on the encounter couch, positioning himself so that the sun sparked up his blue eyes. I shifted before he could casually slide over an arm.

"So, you just moved in?"

"Couple weeks ago. Sue and Todd got me the place. I love it. Up and coming neighborhood. They're clients of mine. We try to get together, do the neighborly thing. Sometimes we've had Gloria, from 303. She's your neighbor. But...," he took a big swallow of Coke, raised his eyebrows against the inevitable throat pain. Cash didn't seem to be well acquainted with carbonated beverages. "...Let's just say Gloria is a gnarly chick. You know? Have you met her?"

"Wears cowboy boots?" Neutral answer. I wasn't sure if being a gnarly chick was good or bad.

Cash looked down at his bare feet and frowned. "Could be. I didn't really notice her shoes. So," he settled sideways against the stiff cushions, threw an arm across the seat back and tucked his hair behind his ears. It was the 'attracted, interested' posture from the body language dictionary. "Where are you from?"

"Ohio."

"Oh, Ohio."

"You know it?"

"Oh absolutely. I fly over it all the time, whenever I go back home. Patchwork fields. Corn, right?"

"That's Oklahoma. The other O state. I know it's confusing. Ohio has more factories than corn. Flying over it you might notice the smog."

"Sounds like Hackensack, New Jersey. I'm from the east coast too."

"It's the midwest. Ohio."

"All back east from here." Cash gestured his Coke in the direction of east. He wasn't making much progress on the drink.

"Hackensack sounds like a lovely town."

"It's a shithole, but what can you do? Go west, right? I came out here for college. Just graduated last year. Business degree. I'm in stocks, like I said. What do you do?"

"I'm a stripper."

"You got stock?"

"No."

"You should have some. It's a perfect investment for you. I assume your earnings are high, and at this time of your life, no kids, right?"

"No."

"No kids, no mortgage, you're saving anyway. You should be putting that money where it can earn more for you than one percent in your savings account."

Savings account? I hadn't had one of those since grammar school. "I'm not much of a gambler," I said to Cash. I saved less than he probably

77

thought. I helped out Momma and my old college roommate, Melissa, who had two young kids and a husband in jail, with a good percentage of my earnings.

He grinned. "Leave it with me, it won't be a gamble. You can ask Sue and Todd how much I made for them last year."

"I'll think it over. Listen, speaking of my job, did you happen to meet the woman who was living in my place? Last week? She was there until Friday. She left sometime after that." I wanted to get to the point of this date before the stockowning couple arrived. I planned to leave as soon as they showed up. Somehow I didn't think we'd have much in common, and conversation would be strained.

Cash wiggled. It was his first sign of lost cool and it was over quickly. "You mean Sophie?"

Sophie? "I didn't get her name. Bleached blonde, well-built?"

"That would describe her." Cash began a repetitive motion of smoothing an imaginary moustache.

"Do you know when she left town?"

"Haven't heard from her since the middle of last week, but she said she'd be here until Sunday."

"Did she happen to give you a forwarding address? She left a few things behind." I watched Cash closely. He'd dropped the flirtatious posture, seemed a bit embarrassed, but not in a state of guilty panic. Something had obviously happened between himself and "Sophie," but I didn't think dismemberment was it.

"Forwarding address? No." He smiled weakly at his drinking glass.

"Did you get her last name? Maybe I could track her down."

"Last name, last name. I'm sorry, I just keep repeating everything you say. Okay." He thought for a moment. "Wow. This is bad, but I don't think her last name ever came up. She was from Denver, though."

Sophie from Denver. "Can I use your phone?"

"Sure." He pulled a cell phone from a pocket of his painter's pants and handed it wordlessly to me.

I walked it into the kitchen, punching the number for information, got the area code for Denver, called information there.

"PV Incorporated, please."

"Checking," said the female voice. A male voice had followed me into the kitchen.

"Is it long distance? Cause it's okay if it is. I mean," Cash grabbed my forearm and quickly let go.

"Sorry. Hey, I don't want you to think it was just about sex. We

78

talked, you know."

"Hold for the number."

"While you were talking, did she happen to mention being in mortal fear for her life? You got a pen?"

"Hah! No. Joke, right? Pen. Pen. Here. Shit, that's the door. Look, as soon as she told me she had a boyfriend I told her we had to break it off. I'd better get that."

I dialled the number the electronic voice gave me. PV Inc.'s phone started to ring.

Cash's kitchen was a recognizable Tender Arms original, unlike the rest of his apartment. I leaned against the cracked porcelain sink. The cabinetry had been sponge-painted, obviously with cosmetic applicators, for the familiar small wedge shape was a repeated theme. The paint job looked like the result of a toddler play-date.

After about ten rings, "Hello, this is Plushious Velvett" came on. I couldn't remember what she sounded like. The one time I'd talked to her, she'd been in a cussing mood, and the cooey recording was done in her best breathy-porn-star style. "Thank you for calling the star of all your favorite movies, including…" she inhaled. "*Dildo Gravy, Ankles Away, Ho the Line*…" Cash had answered the door. Damn. I'd wanted to make my exit before the arrival of Sue and Todd.

"…*Row Row Row Your Bone*…"

I peeked through the kitchen doorway while Plushious Velvett continued on with her extensive credits. Cash was exchanging air kisses with a thin young woman under her spiky hairstyle. The woman held her green wine bottle like a baby, tapping its pastel-brushstroke label with her French manicure. Her finger movements allowed the diamonds in her wedding band to seize the weak sunlight and beam it back around the room. She had apparently arrived without her matching man.

"…and also covergirl of all your favorite magazines. *Big Honkin' Tits*…"

This could go on forever. I watched Sue brush a hand up Cash's bare arm, lightly, to his shoulder. She massaged his deltoid. Then he whispered something in her ear and she turned to look at me. Her frosted brown smile fell.

"…*Anal Aggressive*. You can mail-order any of these…"

"Let's Stay Together" ended. Who buys CD singles? In the sudden quiet, Sue's words became a shout. "….Didn't know you had company."

"…or just say hello. I'm looking forward to hearing from you! Take it sleazy." And the machine beeped.

"Hi." Shit. I never thought these things through beforehand. "Hi. Um, my name's Aubrey and my stage name is Aisling, I worked with you at Naughtyland last week." Sue and Cash turned their gazes from each other to me, their conversation stopped, the wine bottle dangling at Cash's side, forgotten. Shit. "I worked with you last week at um, there and I have something of yours. So please call me if you get this message." I gave work and home numbers. "Okay? Give me a call. Thanks." I examined the phone.

There didn't seem to be any way to hang it up. I walked across the room and handed his cell phone to Cash.

He began to babble. "Wow, a Napa Valley Sirah. And you have a whole case? But where's Todd? He's totally invited. In fact, he wouldn't want to miss this. I'll give him a call right now." He used a thumb to dial his phone. "Sue, this is Aubrey. Another newcomer to the building. She's a stripper, don't you think she should be investing? All that cash just sitting there depreciating. It's like she's never heard of inflation. I can't think about it. Convince her to be my next client, would you? Aubrey, this is Sue."

"Cash," said Sue. Her cheeks had flushed.

"Hey, just advertising. Mutual funds, Aubrey. They're no gamble. But not much is, really, in today's market. Tell her, Sue."

"But how long can that last? And mutual funds grow relatively slowly. I'm still convinced that the best returns are on real estate." Sue smiled at Cash, who smiled back. Did this kind of talk pass for flirting in their circle?

Cash held up a hand and turned toward the kitchen, phone to his ear. "Todd, dude!" he began.

Sue politely recovered a memory of her smile as I shook her small hand. "Hello." Sue's eyeglasses were small as bifocals, the frame the same deep brown as her hair dye.

"I was just leaving," I answered.

"What a shame. For good?"

Cash flipped the phone shut. "No way. You're not leaving without trying this Sirah. Or should we wait for Todd before we crack it? He's on his way."

"Yes, he'll be along. No, we don't have to wait." Sue was a bit distracted, since she was checking out my person with the same scrutiny I'd given hers a moment before. Happily, I'd been able to do my assessment from a more discreet distance. Her gaze lingered almost as long as a customer's on my chest.

Sue's appraisal of my breasts had a scientific quality. She was measuring, calculating, comparing.

Customers, on the other hand, eyed my breasts like a desert wanderer would an oasis, or sunk into them as they would a hot bath at the end of a day.

"They're real. Not all strippers have implants," I reassured Sue.

She affixed a smile. "So how long have you lived in Hayes Valley?"

"You mean here, in the Tenderloin? About two days. You?"

"We moved to Hayes almost a year ago. We've seen the neighborhood improve a lot since then. I'm active with several neighborhood associations. Between you and me, Hayes Valley won't be the sex capital of San Francisco for much longer." Sue traced my figure with her stare again, settling her gaze on my shit-kicker boots. "But why did you choose to live here?" she asked me.

Sue didn't blink much behind her bifocals. I thought of a few smart comments—great shopping, I crave the smell of urine, I'm never far from my drug supply. What a question. Of course the reason anyone "chose" to live in the Tenderloin was money; they didn't have any. It was still the cheapest neighborhood in San Francisco. Immigrants, sex workers, blacks, and Mose Junior could afford it. Cheap rent was why the sex palaces opened there, cheap liquor encouraged their patronage, cheap tenements housed whatever groups currently worked for the cheapest wages. Simple. But rich people, strangely, never seem to understand that what motivates poor people as much as it motivates themselves is money. Immigrants, sex workers, blacks, or whatever group's representatives riot the evening news across their television screens have no puzzling genetic defects or outstanding moral failings—they're not aliens, they're just poor.

I finally answered Sue: "It's close to work. You?"

"It's up and coming."

"No condos left in Twin Peaks?"

"This city has a one percent vacancy rate. Heaven for landlords, hell for tenants. You're in 301, aren't you?"

"That's right."

"Then you won't be with us for long. Things are about to change around this place. Like I said, this neighborhood is improving."

"Yes," I matched Sue's appraising stare. "I can see that. Thanks for the Coke, Cash." I'd left my glass on the floor in front of the couch, and like the well-trained recipient of Southern hospitality that I was, I picked it up and took it to the kitchen sink.

Sue didn't know, I thought, whom she was up against with her neighborhood "improvement" fantasy. Some powerful and motivated people had made the seamiest part of the city into the gloryhole it was today. Johnny the local pimp came to mind. I rinsed the glass. Before I wiped it dry on my shirt I noticed a dishtowel nailed to the doorframe and moved to use it.

Al Green's voice softened into a warble. I couldn't be seen from the furniture cluster. I dried my glass and overheard Sue.

"...thought what she got last week would have gotten rid of them for good..."

Somehow I managed to hang onto the dishtowel. The glass bounced off my boot before smacking crisply onto the floor. Shit. Cash was on me in an instant. Don't worry about it, sale at the Crate and Barrel, there's seven more where that came from, and get one for yourself, you must at least just try the Sirah. He didn't seem to have a broom. He'd take care of it later. He grabbed my hands when I offered to pick up the shards, and playfully kissed each of them.

"Don't worry about the glass. And don't sweat her. Jealous, you know?" he murmured, then said .louder, "Shall we have a drink?" His smile broadened the cheekbone stratum of his angular face. I could tell the effect was often charming. Before I could answer him or ask Sue what she'd been talking about, Cash's rudest client was answering a loud knock at the apartment door.

His flannel shirt was a different tartan, but the clean belted jeans and the beetle-shiny Doc Martens could have been the same pairs that he'd worn the other evening. He reached out to shake Cash's hand, and over our host's shoulder he caught my shocked expression. He smiled at me, confidently, stalked across the room to make his greeting. As he bent to air kiss my cheek, he whispered in my ear.

"See, I was right, you are a redhead."

Chapter Ten

Meeting a customer off the premises was my worst nightmare. It was to avoid such encounters that we strippers went through elaborate security procedures, from choosing anonymous stage names, making up alternative life stories to tell the customers who inevitably think they had the right to know all about us, never scheduling shifts in advance. Threats posed by stalkers were all too real. We'd all heard stories of dancers who'd been followed or found, then assaulted, even killed. We were publicly naked like women shouldn't be and the property of no one man like women should be, and we knew, on some level, that every customer who walked into Naughtyland hated us for it. That hate put us all in danger.

"I'm leaving." I twisted out of Todd's grip.

"So soon?" he said.

"But we're just about to have wine. I know you prefer Coke, but once you've had this—"

"Todd, why don't you walk her back upstairs."

It felt like I'd been trapped in this pseudo-loft for an eternity. "No, I don't need to be walked home."

"Take her up, Todd," Sue repeated.

Cash took my hand as I left. "Well, it's just great you stopped by. I'm sure I'll see you soon. We have a deal right? I'd really like to be alone with you."

God. I didn't answer. Todd proved he was good at following orders by seeing me out the door. Perhaps I could sprint ahead of him up the stairs. Why were they making a big deal about escorting me across a few feet of faded carpet? Maybe Todd was Plushious Velvett's killer, doing Sue's dirty work to rid the building of certain elements. Was that what her comment "what she got last week" meant?

Plushious Velvett was last seen then. I quickened my pace and was halfway up the stairs by the time Todd shut Cash's door softly behind him.

"Wait."

"Forget it."

Todd loped up a couple of steps. He was younger than the gentleman farmer look he cultivated might imply. Probably around my age, mid-twenties. But damned if he was catching up with me. I swept around the hairpin turn in the staircase, leaving him where I could look down on the off-center part in his light brown hair.

"What's your wife up to, anyway? Killing off the neighbors? She seems to really hate us strippers."

"Of course not, what are you talking about?"

"I don't know, she seems the not-in-my-backyard type. Too bad she moved into the backyard herself, and right over the septic tank." Todd hadn't moved, but I ascended a few more steps anyway.

"You're right, she's not thrilled about the procession through 301. But that's not what I wanted to talk to you about. Stop. Listen, it's for your own good."

"Don't presume to know what's good for me." I didn't pause.

Todd followed me, pounding the stairsteps out of rhythm with his words. "Sue knows, or suspects that I have, let's say, extracurricular activities going on. Of course I can't stop you from telling her anything. But if she finds out that we've, well, met before, she'll have you out of the building. Quickly, too. Just a warning."

"Thanks. That works out very nicely for you, doesn't it?"

Todd rubbed his five-o'clock shadow. "I suppose it does. Bye."

I didn't bother to answer. How would Sue have me out? On a stretcher? In pieces? Is that what her comment about what went on last week had meant? Ignoring Vivian, who was in the same position I'd left her in an hour before, I fell into the Murphy bed to think.

At nine that evening, an hour we'd agreed upon as comfortably beyond dinner but well before bed, DeeDee and I began my introduction to the lower class. Mr. Tate had met her, yes, the blonde, yes, the one with the ripe melons, at DeeDee's party. Our conversation began and ended through his closed door.

"Haven't seen hide nor hair of her since then, but I wouldn't mind it." He turned up the volume on "America's Most Wanted." We considered ourselves dismissed. Young Vietnamese families complete with several bouncy pajama-clad kids were crammed into the other two ground floor apartments, but though both harassed fathers were friendly with DeeDee, brief conversations yielded no information from either. They'd attended the party between dinner and story time, left well before Plushious Velvett's arrival, and hadn't heard anything suspicious since.

Only one apartment on the second floor merited a knock from DeeDee. I was nervous that Cash would poke his head into the hallway any second, but it never appeared. Cash's immediate neighbor was a black woman, thin, middle-aged, and flustered. She cracked open her door after DeeDee assured her that it was him. DeeDee called her Shirley, and how had her mother liked her hair-do? She'd liked it fine, except for the curls were too tight around the ears. Shirley had no clue about Plushious Velvett. Anyway, she had to go.

That was a long shot, DeeDee explained on our way to the third floor. Shirley keeps to herself, since she's technically an illegal resident. She took over 204 from a previous tenant who had died, and paid the artificially low rent with checks forged with his signature. He'd been some kind of relation to her, lived there fifteen years.

He knocked on Comfortable Shoes' door. My neighbor was apparently lower class. I found myself strangely relieved. She didn't answer.

"Bay's another strange one. Keeps to herself, as well. Hasn't come to any of my parties. But I don't judge. That's as far as I can go, sugar." He pointed to the door that Cowboy Boots had rebuffed me from, earlier. "Gloria," he mouthed, and pinched his nose. He continued in a whisper from behind a cupped hand. "And Nico in the other corner. Pretentious artist type. And no politics. Heinous! Ask him what's he wearing all that black for, and he doesn't even know! At least in the old days, people like that had politics." DeeDee patted my arm. "Shall we try Clem?"

"Sure."

He led me to the elevator. "Weak knees," he explained. "Going down is harder than going up. Honey, I am getting old. I never thought I'd be saying that."

The elevator settled into the basement with the slowness of arthritic joints. I followed DeeDee to the Laundry Room door. He covered his ears, the movement recreating that troublesome gap between shirt and waistband. "The music," he stage-whispered. "Heavy-metal." He made a face. I knocked. I knocked again.

No response.

"Where is that little so-and-so? Probably grouting the tile up in 203, or giving Sue and Todd new kitchen cabinets or something. It's not like he can leave. House arrest, you know." DeeDee's dramatic stage whisper returned. "He wears one of those electronic collars. Around his ankle. It's like prison, only in your very own home. Leave a certain radius, and eeeeeeee!" He shrieked in imitation.

"House arrest. What'd he do?"

DeeDee shrugged. "Must have got caught for the pot at some point. He's my supplier and by the way, I can really recommend his stuff. It'll take you there. Anyway, he doesn't seem to have the gumption for a more stimulating crime, does he? Can you picture him mugging someone? Too slow."

"How far can he go before his alarm goes off?"

"No more than fifty feet or so from the building. I guess the cops give allowance for having a yard. Poor boy can't even shop for groceries."

He couldn't drag a body too far, either, I thought.

"Bet you he can't hear us over this roar," DeeDee said. "He's half-deaf from heavy metal. Let's go in. I've got the key."

"You've got the key?"

"We all do, honey. This is the laundry room." DeeDee gestured to the sign. Grimacing, he removed a hand from his ear and dipped into his pocket. He handed me a keyring and replaced his hand.

"I thought it was Clem's apartment."

"What?" DeeDee tapped his sandaled foot impatiently while I struggled to unlock the door.

Once I'd swung it open, the Aerosmith volume rose to a level requiring hand signals. We passed into the narrow laundry room. Its linoleum floor was a seamless extension of the basement hall's. An avocado green washer and dryer set hummed under a scaffold of industrial shelving. A bleach odor and the stale breath of dryer exhaust stung the close air. A laundry basket on top of the dryer brimmed with floral blouses and stretched-out full-cup underwire bras, someone's whites, or dingy grays. Didn't whoever it was know better than to put bras in the dryer?

"He didn't tell me there was a laundry room," I said.

DeeDee was already pushing open a flimsy door cut into the right-hand wall. "I've got to turn that music down before I do another thing. We'll leave him a note if he's not in," DeeDee said and disappeared inside, calling for Clem.

A bright country smell emanated from the cracked-open door—fresh-cut wood. I followed the scent into a dining room that, except for the cement floor, wouldn't have been out of place in a New England farmhouse. A round wooden table and four solid oak chairs took shape in the sodium light glow. A dark-stained buffet with curved edges and a standing candelabra stuck with half a dozen white taper candles flanked the heavy dining set. Clem must have inherited. The glow came from the transom window, the same window I'd spotted along the ground by the trash cans the day before. I'd noted it had been unbarred; now the long, narrow pane was broken. Fangs of glass dangled from the upper casing.

Clem must have been trying to get a breath of air into the place. The recycled air from the clothes dryer seemed to suck the oxygen from the neighboring rooms. Even with the window gone, the air was eerily still. The nighttime fog didn't seem to fold into the batter of the Tenderloin's air, but rather, to catch the lowland smog immobile beneath it.

The music was still at top volume and the guitar solo was getting uncomfortably near. What was keeping DeeDee?

Clem's kitchen was tucked behind the common laundry room. Fanning my face, I stuck my head in. Yellow cabinets, bright and still oozy with resin, were guilty of the dominant smell. Saws, files, and various other serrated, scored, and pointy metal tools scattered over the countertop among yellow curls of wood. A square pan of brownies was also on the counter, missing a quadrant of the treat. The thick door of the old refrigerator was flung open. Its interior light had burnt out above the snarl of celery stalks, opened Tupperware, broken jars and accompanying cascade of jam, ketchup, mayonnaise, and leftovers. The mess dripped through wire shelves and into the crisper that jutted halfway out at the bottom, cracked and askew. The blaring boombox sat on top of the refrigerator. I pulled its plug.

This was more than bad housekeeping. I shouted for DeeDee, too loudly in the new silence. I turned from my examination of the kitchen and moved slowly underneath the broken window to an archway that separated the kitchen-dining area, bracing myself for whatever the rest of Clem's apartment had to offer.

After what I'd seen, it couldn't be good.

At the far side of the archway, I stumbled into DeeDee's feet and almost fell over his body. DeeDee sprawled at a twisted diagonal over Clem, who was lying prone. The former dancer covered most of the super. Clem's face was visible above the intersection of their chests, eyes bugged and following me, the beard stubble on his cheeks dark as ink spackled onto eggshell. A silver smile was pasted across his mouth from chin to nostrils. The duct tape had been taken from his boots, leaving their soles to flap away from the leather insteps. A row of toes the color of marble poked up from the split black leather. When I looked at Clem's face again, it was turning the same cold color.

Chapter Eleven

"DeeDee, get off!" I wrenched one of his arms behind his back. DeeDee's torso was weightier than its hollow look implied. I kicked him in a place that I thought might deflate a lung, hard.

I clawed at one edge of the duct tape that sealed Clem's mouth, not caring that four small skidmarks of blood welled across his jaw in the path of my nails. The rest of my body was busy punching and kicking DeeDee about the head and shoulders. The super's eyes opened even wider when I ripped the tape off. I tried to make it fast. Tears came to his eyes anyway. Clem struggled for a breath, flailing enough to elicit groans from the dead-weight on top of him. Or maybe the groans were Clem's. DeeDee had clearly knocked the breath out of him with his fainting spell, and held it out of him still. I planted my feet and grabbed hold of the muscle T and prepared to haul.

At that moment DeeDee jumped to his feet and started to scream.

Clem heaved in a breath.

"Are you okay?" I knelt down to ask. Clem nodded, still bug-eyed. I waited a moment until a red undertone awakened his face before I went to the kitchen to retrieve one of the sharp implements from the counter. Clem's wrists and ankles had been bound with wrappings of duct tape, though I hadn't noticed with DeeDee on top of him and he hadn't mentioned it. A hacksaw did the trick.

Once freed, Clem's limbs flopped. I stood up, the hacksaw dangling at my side. The super didn't seem prepared to explain his situation. I left him to puddle into his concrete floor. DeeDee needed checking on. He'd moved his screams into the dining room but had since fallen eerily silent.

I found him sitting calmly in one of the solid oak chairs. His hands were folded in the lap of his seersucker shorts.

"Is he okay?" DeeDee spoke in a whisper, albeit an urgent one.

"He's trying to breathe. Color's coming back. Are you okay? What happened?"

"I know. Sorry. Little fit of the vapors. Memories of Nam." He breathed deeply and rationed it back out, yoga style. "I'm okay now. Screaming helps. 'Don't bluff it don't stuff it.' I'm in a group."

"I'm sorry." Early Lyle had been in Nam, too, and my father had familiarized his small family with the battle that never got won in your head. He'd done so, unfortunately, nonverbally.

"Don't be, sugar. We've all got to be working on something, right? I'm pushing away my victim stance." He inhaled, drew his hands up his chest as though tracing his lungs, punched them forward with a karate yelp. "There it goes. Let's go see how he is." DeeDee stood, shrugged his shoulders back and walked a few steps toward the scene. He paused before the doorway to reach backward for my hand.

Clem was just across the threshold, struggling to sit up. I helped him prop himself against the wall, away from the pile of broken glass under the window that, with the lighting so dim, I hadn't noticed before.

DeeDee busied himself by fetching washcloths, a cool one for the forehead, a damp one for the beads of blood from my fingernail scratches, rough ones to rub the circulation back into Clem's hands and feet. The nearest light fixture hung from the ceiling over a picnic bench next to Clem. Pot plants grew on the bench. The florescent tube was shaded in plastic, the kind that hang so low over the table that they get tangled up in the pool game. I switched it on, shielding my eyes against the sudden red and white shine of a Budweiser logo. A groan came from the direction of Clem.

"Naw, man," he said.

"What. Is the light disturbing the growth cycle?" I asked him. But Clem was looking behind me, at the wreckage of his room. The room seemed to double as bedroom as well as nursery, but it was hard to tell under the heaps of strewn clothing if the object in the far corner was a bed. Finely varnished dresser drawers scattered across the floor amid their contents: tube socks, gym shorts with white piping, flannel shirts, dark blue jeans flipped out of their accordion folds. The pile was tufted with tools, books, plastic cassette tapes emptied from their boxes.

"Aw shit," Clem said.

"Who did this?" I asked him.

"Whoever it was got you good right here." DeeDee was dabbing at the bloody scratches next to his mouth. "Aubrey, did you see these claw marks?" I didn't answer.

"I don't know." Clem winced. "It stings."

"You don't know? What, you weren't in the room?" I asked.

"I was, I think. I don't know. Can't remember."

"Why would anyone ransack your place?"

"Listen up," DeeDee stepped back from his work. The bleeding had been slight, and had stopped. "Sometimes it's better to forget these traumas and just hope they don't come back to you in the middle of the night so you wake up to your own screaming." DeeDee layered the washcloths over his forearm. "All better? I hate to be negative to my fellows in drug abuse, but everyone you deal to knows you keep cash in here. One of your customers must have tried to rob you."

"Rob me. Shit. I've got to look for something." Clem tried to get up. His feet scrabbled beneath him.

"What is it? I'll look." I said.

"Under the sink in the kitchen. Fanny pack. You know, one of those you put around your waist."

"What's it look like?" I moved toward the mess in the kitchen.

"Gold colored."

"What's in it?"

"Cash money. Man, five bills at least."

I found the bag among overturned cans of Raid and industrial strength cleaners. Fortunately, none of these had leaked. It was metallic gold. A string of velveteen looped to read "Graceland" across its front.

The bag was zipped open, and empty.

I brought it back to the two men. "I think it might be a good idea if you did try to remember what happened." I felt DeeDee's glare.

"Money there?"

"Gone."

Clem sighed. He furrowed his brow. "Fuck. Don't know, man. I was lit." He shook his head. "The last thing I remember I was taking out the trash. What's today?"

"Thursday night," DeeDee answered.

"You don't remember anything? I assume your apartment doesn't always look like this. Whoever was looking for your money must have made quite a ruckus in the process."

"It's prime herb, all I can say."

DeeDee nodded.

We were all quiet for a moment.

"I think I remember someone coming through the window. I was pretty out of it." Clem looked at the shards of glass scattered on the floor to his right. The window they'd come from was no more than eight inches tall.

"That's impossible. Look how narrow it is."

"That's right. It was a woman." Clem said. "Or maybe I was dreaming it. She crammed a brownie in my mouth. Or maybe I was dreaming that, too."

I went back into the kitchen, dug into the brownie pan. My fingernails came back flecked with green. Eating pot was reportedly a more psychedelic experience than smoking it. I remembered a college friend who had eaten a poppy-seed and marijuana muffin while preparing her final art project, and ended up ruining her work by pouring buckets of exterior house paint down the canvas. She couldn't be talked out of it at the time. The next day she hadn't remembered a thing. The "landscape" got an F.

"When did you come to?" DeeDee had helped Clem to one of his dining room chairs.

"Right about when you fell on me."

"The woman wasn't anyone you know?" I asked him.

Clem shook his head.

"Remember anything about her?"

He cleared his throat, skittered his eyes downward. "Well,"

"Well what. You remember something."

"Why are you encouraging him? Would you think of the post-traumatic stress?"

"If someone's breaking into the building, it could have a connection with our missing friend. Why aren't you encouraging him? What about not stuffing it?"

DeeDee and I turned to look at Clem. Clem was staring at my chest.

"Why are you staring at my tits?"

"This chick, man, she had enormous breasts."

"That's what you remember?"

"That was your psychedelic trip? Oh Clem, you're so very ordinary." DeeDee patted a fake yawn.

"No man, it wasn't. She came at me, they came at me like fists."

"Well that's a little more interesting," DeeDee said.

"Man, I've got to take a leak."

"We're on a need to know basis, Clem. That would be our cue." DeeDee motioned me toward the door. "I take it you won't be filing a police report?"

Clem laughed, an odd chunk of sound. "You kidding? I'm still on probation. Besides, they'd take the rest of my plants."

Chapter Twelve

"…ruined forever."

I hoped the cup of tea I was making for him would lower the volume of DeeDee's wailing. As much as I'd wanted to, I hadn't been able to go straight upstairs and collapse—gently, to avoid breaking the rusty springs—into the Murphy bed. DeeDee had begun to experience more vapors on the stairwell up to the first floor from the basement. Though he had assured me he was only "having a moment," he had accepted my offer to make him a cup of tea. I stirred several teaspoons of sugar into the bitter Tetley. The mug I'd found in the sink had a leopard-skin pattern rolled onto the ceramic.

Though his apartment had become, with the windows opened to the summer night, damp and cool, DeeDee fanned himself on the wicker love seat in his living room. The fan was one of the free kind distributed at Southern funerals. A rococo Jesus on a cardboard cut-out stapled to a paint stirrer. The Jesus pumped in front of DeeDee's sweat-beaded face.

"Thank you, sugar." He set it on the floor next to his feet. "I'll let it cool."

"Did you want ice in it?"

"Oh, that would be perfect. You're a dear."

I returned to the kitchen. Iced tea didn't seem nearly as comforting, but to each his own.

"You'll be okay?" A moment later, I handed him a cold glass.

DeeDee looked up at me. The only part of him that wasn't sagging just a little bit was his crisp hair.

"I will be," he said. "Might switch to a laundromat for a while." He took a long drink. "Here I am keeping you up till all hours without even the excuse of a party."

"It's okay."

"No, you be getting on up to bed. I think I'll do the same." He clunked the empty glass onto the floor. "Shall we?"

I saw DeeDee to the doorway of his bedroom. After goodnights he headed for his Murphy bed. His was dressed in a pink chenille spread with a matching bedskirt that ruffled like a prom gown until it skimmed an olive shag rug. A pair of praying hands hung on a shiny plaque above the headboard. Carved through the shellac below the hands was a cursive message: Have You Tried Prayer?

The next morning I found Vivian in the small kitchen. She had the kettle boiling and was searching the cabinets, pawing aside several rusting cans of Chunky soup, sliding a bag of C&H Sugar through its leaked grit.

"Not even instant."

"Have tea."

"I should. Coffee would just remind me of Greta." Vivian poked her tongue at her lip. "Yum."

"Listen, Viv, the guy who let you in the other night got held up yesterday. Someone stole five grand."

"That guy had five grand?" She smacked the cabinet door shut.

"Yeah."

"Don't you want to hear about my date?"

"No. Just be on the lookout, okay? There seems to be a rash of crime around this place."

"I've got nothing to steal."

I got the Earl Grey out of the cabinet. The water was beginning to boil.

"Greta's this beautiful young actress. Black hair. She shaves it all off; it's just growing back."

"You having tea?"

"Baby butch. Is it too soon to call her?"

"I don't know."

Vivian leaned toward me, her coconut smell settling after her. "Is it too soon? I don't want her to think I'm desperate. Or pushy or obsessive. Come on, help me out." She had a habit of running her hands through her hair. They came away visibly greasy. She wiped them onto her jeans.

"I can't help you." I sniffed the milk. It felt warm.

"Stop being such a prude. I told you Zan and I are non-monogamous. Or are you jealous? When's the last time you had a date?"

"You know why I don't date."

"Right, the nobody wants to date a stripper litany. Or if they do want to date a stripper, it's for the wrong reasons. So lie."

"What?"

"Don't tell them what you do. Don't be in a relationship, you're terrible at those anyway. I'm talking about one night stands. Don't sacrifice your sex life because people can't get over your profession."

"I don't think I'm cut out for the one night stand thing." I always seemed to get deeply involved with people, creating a level of intensity after, say, the first date. Another reason I wasn't currently dating.

"Just the cure for your tendency for over-involvement."

"Right. So I should lie, like you're doing to Zan? How's that going? Well enough to recommend it?"

"I'm not lying to Zan."

"So you've told her about this Greta person."

"No. I haven't." Viv straightened and clapped her hands together like an efficient schoolmarm. "But let's take care of that right now. There's nothing to eat here anyway."

We didn't say anything to each other as we walked the twenty or so city blocks back to our old home.

Our shared lunch was pasta with greens and roasted garlic. The wine was a Chilean red, leftovers from the dinner Vanessa Sassy had made the night before. She and Isabella had left with the dogs for the terriers' grooming appointment, and Vivian and I had missed them.

"Oh, that was good. Even better the second day. Isn't she multitalented? And I've always wondered what to do with arugula. Who knew?" Geoffrey levered himself from the floor to the couch.

Our kitchen wasn't large enough for big dinner parties, or even small ones. We had eaten sitting on the livingroom floor.

"Arugula. We've taken our first step toward yuppiedom."

"God forbid."

In a rare show of domesticity, Vivian gathered all the plates. She motioned for Zan to help her in the kitchen. I watched the greasy stack of dishware disappear through the swinging door, wondered if they would soon be flying through the air at one or the other of the non-monogamous couple.

Geoffrey had unfolded a copy of *People* magazine over his face. The pages fluttered upward with his slow breaths.

This left Hugh and me alone.

We were silent. I was working myself up to an apology. Not my strong point. Hugh picked at the sole of his Nike sneakers. They were vintage 1983.

"Sorry about the other day."

"It's okay." Hugh's eyes met mine. They were the color of Coca-Cola behind pale lashes. He'd been avoiding me since I'd arrived, seating himself between Geoffrey and Zan while we ate, taking refuge from the mealtime conversation by paying undue attention to Hodge. The cat had been trying to stay asleep in a curl on the couch.

But why were you being so weird? I wanted to add, but remembered that wasn't polite. Hugh obviously required a more delicate touch than my usual. Silence squatted over us once again.

"How's Hodge doing?"

"Do you want a detailed account?" Hugh was serious.

"Why not?" I smiled at him, but the ice wasn't broken.

"He eats about half a cup of the dry in the morning, sleeps until midafternoon, takes some exercise by running or stalking, and after that can usually be found on top of the refrigerator. He's getting along remarkably well with the terriers. They learned to respect his distance after he batted at their faces a few times." Hugh continued to pick at his shoes, which over the years had softened into the formless shape and nameless color of an old laundry bag.

"Any blood drawn?"

"No." Hugh pushed up his glasses. He always used his middle finger for this job, poked against the thick bridge of the black frames. The shoe-picking stopped. "How's your new place going?"

I told Hugh about finding Clem. My story was interrupted at times by snores from Geoffrey strong enough to riffle the magazine on his nose. Hugh listened to my account of finding the trussed super with increasing attention. By the time I got to Clem's sparse accounting of events, Hugh was transfixed, our earlier awkwardness forgotten.

"A woman broke into his apartment, forced him to eat a pot brownie, bound him with duct tape, and proceeded to ransack the three rooms?"

"So it seems."

"That's a lot to go through for some cash."

"Well, it was a lot of cash."

"Five thousand you said?"

"Yes."

"Well whoever took it must have been pretty desperate."

Geoffrey interrupted by snuffling in the *People* with a hydraulic snore, waking himself with the noise. "I can't believe you two let me fall asleep like that. Haven't you ever heard of sleep apnea? I could have suffocated."

"Sorry, the warning label just said supervise those aged three and under. Haven't you ever heard of a bed?"

"For sleeping? No." He fanned himself for a moment, cracking Tammy Wynette's glossy headshot on the downstrokes. His raised eyebrow expression went to one, then the other of us. After a moment, Geoffrey got up and went into the kitchen. We clearly weren't in the mood.

"Look, I've been snappy lately. Lack of sleep or something. Are we friends again?"

Hugh nodded. "I just—"

Geoffrey banged out of the kitchen holding a refill on his glass of wine. "What's wrong with all of you people? Everyone's so touchy today. I don't recommend going in there. I should be working anyway—did I tell you that a curator is interested in my Receding Hairline pieces for an upcoming show of urban youth expressions in mixed media?" He toasted himself. Hugh and I congratulated him.

"And thank you for being the most patient, understanding roommate." With a gush of enthusiasm, Geoffrey pounced on Hugh and kissed his blond-stubbled cheeks. "All those nights I kept you awake with the overhead projector may not have been for nothing."

Hugh blushed but after a moment hugged Geoffrey back.

"You," Geoffrey used a finger that would have better served to support his slopping wineglass to point at me. "Check your messages." He scrambled off Hugh's lanky figure, smoothed his baby blue undershirt over the wavelets created by years of Abs & Buns classes. "Your dear biblical boss keeps calling."

"Mose Junior?"

"Is there more than one? How hard that must be to keep track of." Geoffrey drained his wine. I had the phone in my hand and began punching in the numbers for the voicemail. "I've got to get to work," he said. "I got so excited by my bright future that I went and bought quite a few new materials. I'm afraid you might have to sleep out here while I work with them, pumpkin." Geoffrey swiped at Hugh's blond hair. "Sorry, meant to rumple it affectionately. Am I too drunk to work? Well it's just plate glass." After answering himself, Geoffrey headed for the bedroom he shared with Hugh.

"Plate glass?"

"Stacked on my bed," Hugh said. I was skipping scores of messages from Geoffrey's would-be or current lovers, listening for Mose Junior's voice. Finally I heard his unplaceable accent, the familiar tenor filed with a slight whine. He'd called the day before, five p.m.

"Phone call came," was all he said.

I hadn't planned on working that evening, but that message changed my mind. It was four-forty, which left me two hours to prepare for a night at Naughtyland.

I got to work at six-fifty. The night shift started at seven o'clock. Since Mose Junior had bought the business and imposed a hundred-dollar fine on dancers who arrived one minute after seven, I was no longer late for work. Ever. Dallas opened the door for me. He was stationed in the lobby. A wad of cash from the entrance fees he'd been collecting made a pad in the chest pocket of his gray t-shirt. His worn jeans were accented with a red bandanna tied around the thigh. He waved me in with the proper aversion of his eyes.

Kevin, our other bouncer, stood immobile behind the bar. Mose Junior hadn't provided him a chair. Nevertheless, Kevin's position serving up non-alcoholic beers and making correct change was considered a promotion from doorman. Spotlights animated by the disco ball flitted red and blue over his shiny hair, dyed deep black. He was clothed entirely in black, as well, and his body seemed to disappear into the dark interior of the club's one room. When he saw me, he lifted a glass and a stainless steel hose and sprayed me a Coke.

"Hey, Aisling," he mouthed. He spoke too softly to be heard over the Scorpion's song that Moana danced to onstage.

"Hey, thanks." I accepted the glass, leaned on the bar to drink it. The glass was slender and stuffed with ice. It held about two teaspoons of liquid.

"No problem. Slow day." Kevin scratched what was left of one of his eyebrows. He'd shaven both of them to the point where they had almost disappeared, in order to make room for more makeup to bloom up his forehead. Today his few remaining eyebrow hairs were worked in to the black lines of a spiderweb. All the sockets of his face, cheeks, eyes, were blackened, while the highlights were powdered stark-white. A thick paste of eyeliner rimmed his blue eyes.

"Real cadaver-like with the eye stuff. Good job."

"Thanks." He smiled shyly. Kevin was a Goth.

"Growing in is the itchy part."

"Tell me about it."

"Mose upstairs?"

"Should be. Counting his money."

"Don't let them get too rowdy tonight." I handed him back the empty glass.

"Right." Kevin ducked his head shyly, bent to wash the glass. Mose

Junior had hired him for his intimidating looks, figuring that anyone who dressed in black clothes held together by safety pins and painted their face like Dracula must be a violent anti-social type, perfect bouncer material. Kevin had disappointed him by being a shy pacifist. Luckily, most of Naughtyland's customers thought along the same lines as Mose, and Kevin was seldom challenged.

Our boss was sitting behind his desk, mercifully unaccompanied by offspring. Bony elbows propped him into an alert posture, as if there were more on today's agenda than fiddling with his pinky ring, though this was how he was occupying himself. The gold ring flattened between his knuckles into a diamond-encrusted M big enough to cover most of the joint. He stopped twirling it when he noticed me.

"New ring?" I asked.

"Present from my wife." If I hadn't needed information from Mose Junior just then, I would have asked him, which wife?

"Nice. You called me yesterday. I assume there's some news about Plushious Velvett?"

"Yes I called you. I'm nice guy, no?"

"Sure, I guess. Thanks."

My boss shrugged his shoulders inside his gray suit. Like all his suits, this one was large enough for him to turn around in. Perhaps the sizings his tailor was given were too narrow and tall to be believed. "I am not sure the call is about her. A woman called. I can't understand her. Some foreign language. Prank calls, I thought."

"What language was it?"

"I think maybe Spanish."

"What makes you think she has something to do with Plushious Velvett?"

"She says her name. Maybe. Hard to tell with the accent."

"Did she say who she was?"

My boss shrugged again. Asking him where she was calling from brought the same response.

"And they come every day? Why didn't you tell me before?"

"I just hung up on her. Yesterday, she called, she was crying. Woman crying all sound the same. I thought it was my wife. I stay listening. Then I heard her say the name of the star, Plushious. I thought it must be about her, then I called you."

"Why didn't you get Mamacita or Carmela to talk to her? Or one of the other girls who speak Spanish?" Enough Latinas worked at Naughtyland to fill the dressing room with rapid-fire Spanish on almost every shift.

"I thought it was some crazy woman."

"Will she call again?"

Shrug.

Though I felt like strangling him, I politely asked my boss to give the crazy Spanish-speaker my number if she called again. I'd have Hugh talk to her. He'd studied Spanish in school. With his photographic memory, he had surely retained enough of the language to have a conversation with a hysterical woman about the possibly grisly fate of our mutual acquaintance.

Backstage, Amarantha was wiggling into a black vinyl shorts and halter-top set. Once on, it looked like her torso and crotch had been dipped in ink. She slammed her locker shut, stepped away from the gray row so I could get into mine.

"Should be a good night," she said.

"Why?" I asked as I threw my leather jacket onto the pile of underclothes in my locker. Talk like this always went on at the beginning of a shift, a mantra against uncertainty, a prayer that money wouldn't be owed when the lights went on at two a.m.

"It's Vanessa Sassy's next-to-last show, no major sports events are being televised, we're still near enough to the beginning of the month that welfare checks haven't run out, it's not tax time and there hasn't been a holiday since the Fourth."

"Sounds like a winning formula."

"Just you wait; I've got a good feeling about tonight. That looks good on you."

"It's the same old bra I always wear."

"You tried the Wonderbra? It lifts them."

"This is a Wonderbra."

"Well, it looks good."

"Thanks." Compliments were rare between us dancers. We were, after all, each other's competition. "That outfit looks good on you, too."

Amarantha said thank you and left, black-lacquered hips torquing under the swayback spine that high heels give, to work the floor. I stepped into a pair of red thong underwear and my acrylic-sculpture shoes. I decided against another layer of make-up. It was dark out there.

"You got a boyfriend?"

I wasn't having a good night. I'd worked the floor for the first hour, asking the loosened ties and dusty workboots of the afterwork crowd for lapdances without success. I'd reluctantly followed Amarantha's advice and changed outfits. Soon after, I was in one of the curtained-off cubicles, grinding the bottoms of a purple sequined bikini into the lap of a young white man whose lunch break, from the breath that wafted from my cleavage past the brim of his baseball hat and up to my nose, had clearly included Fritos.

"Yeah," I lied. I didn't want this guy announcing his candidacy.

"He lets you do this?" He nosed his Raiders cap into my sternum.

I didn't bother to answer the familiar refrain. It was certainly true that a lot of my coworkers' boyfriends weren't supportive of their partner's profession, even when it supported them, and did so in grand style. Some of Naughtyland's strippers did manage to keep their occupation a secret, prioritizing paying the bills and avoiding flak over the California dogma of 'honesty' This system worked well until, inevitably, in walked your cousin on some Friday night, or your mother's coworker with a big mouth was part of the lunch rush, or the very object of your affection himself paid the place a "never been here before I swear" visit. On one recent occasion, Naughtyland's plate glass window had been shattered with a jealous patron's gunshot.

Yet more reasons I remained celibate.

"Sweet Child O'Mine" by Guns-N-Roses was coming to an end, finally. Nothing like a lengthy heavy-metal ballad for inducing leg cramps. I cranked myself upward and off my customer, wincing as my knees straightened. I felt like a Model-T that needed some oil, wondered again how long my body could keep up the dancing. What would I do for money once this gig was played out?

"Your boyfriend is a very lucky man." The Frito fan slapped me on the butt.

"I'll tell him you said so."

He smoothed his dented brown hair and replaced his cap. I went looking for another twenty bucks.

Among the solitary figures at the plastic tables was a familiar one.

My night was about to get worse. The figure was Todd.

I stayed backstage for a while, but Todd had the advantage. He didn't have to make money at Naughtyland. He could show up anytime he had the twenty dollar entrance fee and a few hours free of the wife. With his income and Sue's obvious if inexplicable interest in Cash, the two events could conflate often. Hiding would only be counterproductive. I adjusted my bra to high-heft and walked back out, dipping to talk to a few other customers before I reached Todd's table. He'd chosen one in the back.

"Can't find anyone suitable? What'll it be tonight, a good blonde, perhaps? We have an array of them, be sure to pick a breast size."

"Nice to see you again. I was thinking about a blonde, actually. That one over there, perhaps. I'm mad for her French accent. But I wanted to talk to you first."

"Hate to tell you, but Madeline's not really French. She's from the Central Valley, Modesto I think. She thinks the accent makes her more money. She's right. I don't like to chase away business, but I'd appreciate it if you didn't come in here."

"I can come in here whenever I like."

That was, unfortunately, true.

"Don't leave," He said to my back.

"I almost feel sorry for Sue." I turned back, saw the hundred dollar bill that Todd pushed across the table.

"For two minutes of conversation," he said.

"Fuck you."

"I've arranged for your stage fee to be waived tonight. I paid it to the young gentleman there." He indicated Kevin, at his post behind the bar. Kevin looked away from us quickly, his spiderweb rippled by furrowing brows.

"What do you want?"

"To explain myself. Then I promise not to visit here again. I know you think I'm an asshole. But you want people to pay for your services, and I'm one of the people willing to do it. Glad to do it. Generously, too, I think." We both ignored the bill on the table. Todd leaned back in his chair, stuffed fists into the pockets of his cuffed jeans.

When it became clear that I wouldn't be joining him by taking the offered seat he continued. "I'm a straightforward guy, you see. Sue's a busy person. To be frank, she doesn't have time to take care of all my needs. And I'm fine with that. She's a modern woman, own career; works sixty hours a week sometimes. I'm proud of her. I'm a man of the nineties, I can take care of myself. In places like this I'm happy to pay for any services; it works out well all around. Everybody's happy. It's like buying take-out instead of cooking. More exciting. No dishes afterward. Tastier. Well," he was smiling, "you get what I mean."

Oddly, I saw his point. Todd's did seem the kind of case best handled by professionals. It's not like he was taking money away from his children, since he didn't have any. And Sue got a break from the guy. I wondered if Todd knew about his wife's interest in their other new neighbor. He didn't seem the type to appreciate subtle cues.

"Well, thanks for the update. I hope we meet less often in the future."

I turned to go.

"Besides, sometimes, I don't want a woman. I want a stripper…" Mercifully, I was soon out of earshot. The rock music that washed away Todd's voice for once felt soothing. I turned back when I reached the entrance to the dressing room. Todd was gone, and Madeline was holding up his abandoned hundred-dollar bill to various colored spotlights. I could see her grin from across the club as she tucked it into her bra.

Champagne and Caviar preceded their owner backstage at a quarter to midnight. The terriers jogged through the piles of costumes and spike heels that dotted the dressing room floor as the night shift melted down, licking toes bared by the going shoe style, jouncing leashes behind them. They caused an exodus of tired women back to the floor. No one wanted to smell like dog. Before I could join it, Vanessa Sassy caught me in a lung-targeting hug, and squeezed me like a bellows. Over her shoulder, I watched Champagne and Caviar play tug-of-war with someone's thong panties.

"We missed you last night. We wanted to go and check on you, but dear Geoffrey warned us that your neighborhood isn't safe at night. Geoffrey so wanted you and Isabella to get to know each other better. But she's coming with some of my things, and now you can."

I was let go. One by one, my lungs popped back to life. It took me a minute to remember what Vanessa Sassy was talking about. I'd promised Geoffrey to go out with them last night and I'd completely forgotten about it. Isabella, dressed in denim faded to the grey of her eyes and steel-toed black boots, pushed into the room. She carried a large duffel bag.

"Missed you last night." She gave me the smile that darted around her back teeth.

"Thanks. Yeah, I got a bit sidetracked."

"Don't worry about it."

"Is my corset in that bag? If it is, we better start getting me into it." Feature stars had their own dressing room, a converted broom closet at the end of the row of lockers. Vanessa Sassy stood in the doorway of it, naked. She was a startling sight. Her hips were narrow, her legs strung with muscles, her calves pinched short by the thrust of a pair of stiletto mules. Her arms were slender. Her tan was even. Freckles dotted her small nose. She had the body of a tomboy, albeit one who sunbathed nude, and the breasts attached to it looked all the more out of place.

"I brought the black one. Well," Isabella turned back to me, "time to bodyguard."

There was no point in trying to hustle up a lapdance before Vanessa

Sassy's much-anticipated show. The customers would be frozen in place until it was over. I moved to the mirror, pushed aside a few smoking curling irons, began to retouch my make up. It looked like someone had pulled the plug on my face.

Everyone behaved themselves nicely at Vanessa Sassy's next-to-last show, and Isabella's duties were light. She hurried the series of cast-off costumes backstage: the sequined cop uniform with breakaway snaps down the inseam; its shined, billed hat; a lattice-laced black corset; a geodesic dome rhinestoned bra.

The thong panties were gone. Vanessa Sassy had snapped them into the air like a rubber band and they'd landed somewhere amid the enthusiastic crowd, scrabbled after like the game ball. Isabella placed the faux-bearskin rug over the runway for Vanessa Sassy's floorwork, folded it neatly and collected the hillocks of dollar bills from the stage when the show was over. Then her work was done. I immediately got a lapdance from one of the frenzied customers. When I retreated backstage to rest my legs, Isabella invited me out for a drink.

"My shift's not over till two."

"Come on. You look like you've had a bad day." She was frisking the cop uniform smooth over a hanger. The sparkly navy top came only to the midriff and was built like a box.

I touched my face. What did that mean? "My sets are over for the night. I guess I could go. But I don't drink."

"Hey, I'm in recovery too. We'll have coffee, or Cokes, or something. Shoot some pool. Ness, you in?"

Vanessa Sassy appeared in the doorway of her dressing room, tugging a v-necked t-shirt around her torso. "Sure. Where can we go?"

Somehow the thought of us being a threesome put me more at ease. "Hollywood Billiards is right down the street," I offered.

"Can we walk there at this time of night?" Vanessa Sassy asked.

I eyed the porn star's chest. Her shirt reminded me of a child's butterfly net around two basketballs. It just wasn't engineered for the task it was put to. "Well, we do have a bodyguard."

"How soon can you be ready?" Isabella asked.

I opened my locker. My leather jacket slumped out onto my feet. "Five minutes. Just let me get dressed."

Fifteen minutes later we snuggled up to the horseshoe-shaped bar of Hollywood Billiards, Vanessa Sassy between us. Isabella and I ordered

Cokes. The porn star ordered a Harvey Wallbanger.

"How do you stand that level of sexual harassment all the time?" I asked her. We'd been treated to pelvic thrusts and catcalls that stretched to the length of descriptive sentences as well as the familiar "Hey-baby"s and whistles during the short walk to the pool hall.

"I know, it gets old, but I say to myself, that's just the city talking back." Vanessa Sassy shrugged off her jacket, a quilted powder-blue number with a fake fur collar. The jacket didn't meet over her chest, and the extra layer had done nothing to ease the enthusiasm of oglers. "You keep a positive attitude."

I'd almost slugged the pelvic thruster, and even Isabella had countered one of the spicier catcalls with a muttered, "Suck my dick."

"Nothing else for it. I knew when I got these implants that they were coming with a price. But they're what customers want. In movies you can't compete without them these days. I call them my girls, Cash and Flo." Vanessa Sassy took a long sip of her drink. She held the martini glass next to her face while she swallowed, then downed the rest of her drink in one shot. "You ever met a guy who didn't like big tits?" Vanessa Sassy set down the empty martini glass. Pink lipgloss kissed its rim. The bartender moved immediately to get her another.

I thought about it, hard. "I guess I haven't surveyed all straight men, but I see your point."

"I can always get them removed when it's time to move on. At least deflated a bit. Till then, they're a tax write-off. Business expense." The porn star patted off the remains of her frosty pink lipstick with a cocktail napkin. She'd deglazed herself of layers of makeup before we'd left Naughtyland, leaving only a smudge of black liner to enlarge her blue eyes, and a sprinkle of powder blush over her freckles. She didn't need the makeup to hide flaws, I thought, or to hide age. She wore it to hide her innocent, tomboy beauty. The wrong kind of beauty, in our business.

"Who wants a game?" she asked.

The bartender and several men who'd been staring from the opposite side of the bar volunteered, but Vanessa Sassy only smiled at them, and picked Isabella to play against. They were evenly matched, trading wins, occasionally letting a lucky male patron play the winner, then inevitably beating him, whether through skill or distraction I wasn't sure. Both were good players though, Isabella better on the angles, Vanessa Sassy on the long shots. It was obvious they'd played together often. Harvey Wallbangers and Cokes kept coming, until I was enough in my caffeinated cups to try a game myself. I overshot everything.

104

I'm not the best pool player. Isabella took the cue from me, won the next game, and confirmed my suspicions by getting a bright kiss from her opponent for her skill. Isabella followed up on the kiss with a flicker of her tongue across Vanessa Sassy's upper lip, collecting precious, forbidden drops of Harvey Wallbanger.

I didn't have to worry about Isabella, I realized, with a slight sadness that surprised me. She was already taken.

"You sure we can't walk you home?" It was three in the morning and the side door of Hollywood Billiards swung to behind us, heavy and final. The deadbolt scraped behind it. We'd been the last customers and the previously flirtatious bartender had asked us to leave in the middle of a game.

"It's out of your way. I'll be fine."

Isabella's cheeks were as red as Vanessa Sassy's, but in the bodyguard's case, the flush must have been due to the cold. I scrunched into my leather jacket. Fog had dithered downward, fuzzing the purple light that gave the city a perpetual glow. The stained sidewalk we'd been evicted onto smelled like a latrine.

The porn star sagged against her girlfriend. She'd taken off her high heels, complaining about a bunion. Barefoot, she was short. Her head came to Isabella's shoulder, and lolled there. Vanessa Sassy held onto her stiletto heels by their straps.

"Less go home," she said.

"We're on our way, honey. We're just going to see Aubrey home first."

"Cold here. Not like L.A." Vanessa Sassy's knees buckled, and no wonder, with her center of gravity artificially high.

"It's cold at night there, too. Just not so clammy." Isabella thrust a hip out to balance Vanessa Sassy's slow collapse.

"Really, I'm fine," I said, as her bodyguard caught the porn star by the armpits. Giving up on hauling her upright, Isabella gently settled her charge onto the concrete. "I'm just a few blocks."

Isabella frowned at me. "If you're sure."

Of course I was sure. I never took too well to being babied, even when I was a baby, Momma said. Always an independent little cuss. Isabella and I hauled our companion to the bus stop, a few feet away on Market. Before I'd walked out of sight, the two were climbing onto the F line. Isabella turned and blew me a kiss.

The four blocks toward my temporary home were deserted. I walked quickly, trying to warm up. The flared pants I was wearing hadn't even been adequate against the afternoon and the air had chilled considerably since then. Without daytime's lively ground-level stratum of humanity to distract me, I noticed the fine architecture of many of the neighborhood's buildings. Those four or more stories high were often elegant cubes of brick with pilasters softening their corners. Gargoyles yawned out from some of the cornices. Large windows with frames painted in a contrast trim created precise patterns across the brick faces. Iron fire escapes slashed down the sides.

Only at litter-level was grime apparent. Cigarette butts, McDonald's wrappers, crushed soft drink cups and newspaper inserts rolled around the streets, tufts of day-glo colors, proof that consumers were simple as bees looking for the brightest flower. Higher up, the brick was red or painted white and dissolved softly into the night.

I was walking through one of San Francisco's oldest neighborhoods. Neglect had mercifully spared its blocks from the invasion of post-1930s architecture. In San Francisco's trendier areas, lurid structures that resembled moon-landing vehicles rubbed shoulders with Victorian rowhouses. I imagined the strait-laced Victorians averting their bay-window eyes.

The restaurant on the corner of Taylor and O'Farrell was closed but still bright with flattering yellow lighting. It was a glassed wedge around a sparkly counter and new metal tables and chairs. Hayes Valley Eats, said the sign. I squinted through the floor-to-ceiling plate glass at the menu. A three-foot-high blackboard listed only coffee drinks. A shorter blackboard listed bagels, flavors, fillings, cheaper by the dozen. The place had been a Chinese food and Donut restaurant a few weeks before—one of the florescent-lit, linoleum-floored eateries, ventilated by a grill's hood last degreased during the Depression—that had fed the Tenderloin's residents for generations. Spacepod dwellings couldn't be far behind, I thought, turning toward home. There goes the neighborhood.

I was half a block from The Tender Arms when the neighborhood talked back.

Chapter Thirteen

The arm around my neck was thin and strong as piano wire. It had come from behind, quick and silent. Long fingernails dug into my neck. My upper vertebrae crunched against my captor's collar bone. My head was wrenched sideways. A cold metal mouth pressed into the small of my back.

The voice was muffled by proximity to my ear. "I want the bag."

Fear started in my gut. It felt like someone was striking matches on my stomach. I searched around for the pocket of my leather jacket. The hundred or so dollars I'd earned on my bad night was in there.

"Where is it?" my captor said, more loudly this time. She pulled me tighter, skewered the gun toward a kidney. My fingers stumbled over the rough grain of the leather for a long moment until they found my pocket. In family payday tradition, I'd spent a proportion of my earnings at the bar, and what was left was a thick packet of ones, fives, maybe two twenties, and some coins. In my nervousness, I spilled the money over the sidewalk. The change hit loud as hail.

"Shit, you're clumsy. I'm talking about the bag. You know what I'm talking about."

"No, I don't, I don't carry a purse. That's all I got. Please just take it." My protest was loud and, no doubt, Southern-accented.

Unexpectedly, she loosened the clamp of her arm. She yanked me around by the shoulder. "Where the fuck did you put the bag? I know you were there." I was close enough to note speckles of flame lipstick on her teeth and smell orange soda pop on her breath.

We were in the middle of the block, in the pocket of dark where outstretched arms of corner street lights fail to meet, but I could see that my assailant was the teenaged Asian prostitute who had solicited Hugh. She was wearing the same outfit she had on when she'd been knocking on our cab. Her strapless red mini was fashioned from the square yardage of an Ace bandage. She stood inches higher than me, jacked up by four inch heels. She was slender enough that her kneecaps stood out with almost the same ferocity as her artificial breasts. Her pistol glinted like jewelry in her small hand.

Getting mugged by an acquaintance is somehow a less frightening, if more surreal, experience. The gun was currently aimed at my heart.

"I'm Buddhist; I don't like to kill," she told me.

"Great, I don't like to die. I'm just going to collect the money now and give it to you, okay?" I bent over and concentrated on breathing and collected the money as quickly as I could and handed it to her.

I watched her count the bills. She kept the gun to my chest while the long nails of her free hand flickered through the short stack of green. She stuffed the money into her Hello Kitty plastic purse.

"Where's the rest? You work all night, only come home with seventy?"

"Sorry."

"I thought white girl whores made good money."

"Sometimes it's okay."

"You're too old, maybe."

"Don't you ever have a bad night?"

"No."

"I'm still having one."

A sudden scream from my assailant caused my hands to clap over my ears almost of their own accord. Her vocal cords were on a level with my eardrums and less than a foot away. I froze. She was looking at a spot over my right shoulder. Her eyes had opened wide, the whites luminous as her gun.

"Vampire," she shouted, and turned and ran, wobbling on her high heels.

What luck that my mugger had hallucinations. I rubbed my strained neck, held a hand to my chest for a moment to steady my breathing. I watched her clatter up to the door of the Lotus Leaf, pausing instantaneously in the shallow indent that led to the unmarked door. She was evidently more facile with keys than I. Or maybe someone had been waiting for her arrival.

"Halt." The voice broke midway through the syllable. I turned around and met my mugger's vampire.

"We have a neighborhood watch here…" The young man took a wavering breath. "…and, like, we don't tolerate crime." After his assertion, he anxiously tucked a flop of Clairol Blue-Black hair behind an ear. He was a Goth, in whiteface with black lips and black doodles around his eyes, tall and thin so that his trenchcoat fell around him like a cornhusk.

"That's wonderful. Since the crime seems to have already been tolerated, I'm afraid I'm missing your point."

"My point is that the police have, like, been notified of your suspicious activity."

"Great." My legs accepted commands once again. I started toward The Tender Arms.

He followed me. "We have neighborhood watch. The police have been notified of your suspicious activity."

"You mean me getting mugged? You're right, that was careless of me. I'll think twice about doing that again, now that I know there's a neighborhood watch." It wouldn't have occurred to me to report the mugging myself. Tenderloin cops took little more than a mocking interest in the constant petty thievery that plagued the marginal residents of the neighborhood. As far as they were concerned, one sex worker robbing another was just as pathetic and inevitable as a schoolyard fight between two of the class's friendless losers. A precarious grip on our ill-gotten gains was considered part of the price we paid for being part of the criminal underclass.

"If you were getting mugged, why did that woman run away screaming?" His voice had that "gotcha" tone that I remembered from elementary school.

"Why is this block full of teenagers tonight? She was running from you, okay. She mugged me. Now stop following me." I wearily climbed the steps to the front doorway of the apartment building.

"From me? No way. Hey, you live here?"

"Didn't I ask you to stop following me?" The key seemed to have swollen since the last time I used it. I mashed it into the lock, flipped it, mashed it in again.

"Let me get that. I'm Mikey. New doorperson. Security, you know. So how'd I do?" I was too tired to register much except the movement of his black lipstick around the words.

"We have security?"

"You do now. Don't you feel safer? I'm new."

"Who hired you?"

"Sue somebody. You okay? Like, I'm just learning. It's like my first night. You got mugged, huh? Must have happened fast. By the way, that stuff about the police being notified, don't worry, cause that was bullshit. Sue told me to say that." He laughed. "And that other stuff about neighborhood watch and tolerating crime. She made me memorize it, like say it back a few times to get confident. Did it sound, like, rehearsed? I didn't think I'd get to try it out so soon. Hey, you look tired."

He held the door open for me. I answered his "Like, good night," and climbed wearily home.

I woke up in the late morning of the next day, Friday, out of a dream in which I'd opened Mose Junior's room-sized fridge, put in a baby, and took out a beer. I'd shut the refrigerator door and was listening to the suck of its hermetic seal when I woke up.

Though exhausted, I hadn't slept well. After I'd fallen into bed I'd lain awake, feeling the pattern of Murphy-bedsprings brand my back, strangely attuned to the fragments of arguments, the keening of car alarms, the crackles of far-off collisions that made up the normal restlessness of the urban night.

Knocks rapped against the apartment door. They must have been what had awakened me. I heard Vivian open it, say, "It's about time she got up." A moment later DeeDee was rumpling up my quilts with his seersuckered bottom.

"Wake up, honey."

"Why?" My mouth was as dry as if I had a real hangover, not just the aftershock of gallons of Coke.

"We've got to talk about this rash of attacks. Didn't you say your dear predecessor is still unaccounted for? It's a class war, they're picking off the lower classes one by one."

"Who is?" I rolled groggily, but wasn't able to pull the quilt after me to dislodge my guest. Polyester doubleknit, as well as having a long half-life, is heavy.

"You know very well who. The yuppie bloc, that's who. They can't wait to get this building all to themselves. They have meetings you know, from which the lower class is conspicuously absent. Yesterday they hired a doorman. You should see him; he looks like he's been rolled in flour and his hair-do is just like Halloween—a fright wig. They're trying to take over."

"That may be, but they're not about to kill anybody. They don't want to raise the crime rate in their zip code. They don't want "convicted murderer" on their curriculum vitae. How do you know it was them who hired Mikey?" The new doorman had told me as much, but it didn't seem like DeeDee had actually talked to him before jumping to conclusions.

"You've met him then? What do you make of that hair? They hired him, all right. And who are they to be hiring security? They're not the landlord. Let's just say I have my sources. Look at the pattern. First your friend, who just happened to be a stripper, then Clem, who just happened to be a maintenance man and an ex-con. Or presently a con, since he's still

110

in that ankle bracelet. Then you, last night."

"How do you know about that?"

"I have my sources, like I said. Who's next? Mr. Tate, or I am. They're starting at the bottom, working their way up." DeeDee's voice had raised in pitch. It sounded like he really believed this stuff.

"What do you mean, the bottom? Plushious Velvett was living on the third floor." I didn't want to delve into my mugging story. It certainly hadn't been the yuppie bloc that had victimized me.

"Don't you get smart with me."

"Well, I don't see a pattern, is all. Plushious Velvett and Clem have nothing in common. With her income, I wouldn't even call her lower class."

"You know it has nothing to do with income."

"At any rate, I've got a theory about who attacked Clem." DeeDee's talk of patterns had made it clear to me.

"Who? Tell."

"A woman who works at the Lotus Leaf." My attacker had been bold, fearless, and clearly desperate for money. Just as, Hugh had pointed out, whomever had hogtied Clem and ransacked his place would be. She wore shoes capable of breaking windows. Clem's window was on the side of the building nearest the Lotus Leaf, was at ground level, and unbarred. And her breasts, artificially firm, matched Clem's description.

There was silence for a minute. I was in danger of drifting back off to sleep.

"How do you figure?" DeeDee grabbed my shoulder and shook me. "Look at me."

"Ow! It's just a hunch."

"What are you going to do about it?"

"Look for evidence."

"Oh, so scientific."

"Well, what's your method? Paranoid Marxism?"

"We'll see how paranoid I am. Just you wait, they'll be coming after you again, missy."

"I'll be on the lookout. I'll let you know how things develop. You can keep me informed about your theory."

"You just aren't prepared for the class war."

"Guess I need more sleep first." I pulled the quilt up over my head, dislodging planted seersucker in the process. DeeDee took his cue and left.

After a shower and careful avoidance of Vivian, who asked about my late night and if I'd gotten lucky, I paid a visit to the laundry room. The door that led to Clem's was locked. This wouldn't have been possible a few days before. He must have gone out and bought himself a padlock. I knocked.

In a moment Clem's bristly hair and stubble framed the door's bright new anchoring security chain. Below them, a stripe of shirt seemed to hold his features aloft on a tartan flannel stick. We exchanged hi's. The door was not swinging open to let me in.

"New security measure, I see. But didn't she come in through the window?"

"Replaced it."

"Good thinking. You know, I have an idea of who might have robbed you the other night."

Clem's face drained of color. It hadn't much to begin with. "You turning me in?"

"What? No. What are you talking about?"

Clem scratched his brown beard stubble. His bloodshot eyes were the other color contrast on his face. "You saw my plants."

"I'm not turning you in. I'm just trying to jog your memory. Was your attacker a young Asian woman by any chance?"

"I was attacked?"

"Yes, you were attacked. The other night. You spent hours hogtied with duct tape. You came to when a two hundred pound man fainted onto your lungs. I found you, that's why I saw your plants. You don't remember?"

Clem looked dazed.

"Nothing?"

He shook his head. I wouldn't be getting any clues from the perpetually stoned Clem.

I decided I deserved a long bath and a burger at Massimo's before going to see if Hugh was home and waiting with him for a phone call that might never come. During the bath another wedge of the ceiling rained down through the steam, silting the water and narrowly missing my arm. I ate my Avocado Burger next to Massimo's rear booth, its table still covered with empty Juice Squeeze bottles, a ketchup-smeared plate and napkins sodden with salad oil and smeared with plum lipsticks.

The Converse-wearing waiter bounced over to bus it, pocketed a twenty dollar bill he'd found among the mess. "Great tippers." He smiled at me. He clattered the dishes into a plastic tub. I wondered if that was one of the twenties I'd been forced to donate the night before. Good old Johnny.

I found Hugh watching a rerun of *All in the Family*, patting Geoffrey awkwardly on the arm. Geoffrey's face was tear-streaked, though unbloated.

"What's happened?" I sat next to him on the couch. Crying didn't swell Geoffrey's features into hives as it does to most of us. Tears magnified his blue eyes, slurpy snuffles pouted his lips attractively.

He shook his head dramatically.

"The curator rejected his pieces," said Hugh.

"Oh no. The hairline ones? I thought he'd already committed to taking them."

"Turns out he just wanted to sleep with me, the bastard."

"I'm so sorry. There'll be another chance. You work on your art all the time, someone will take notice. Don't give up."

Geoffrey shook his head, lifted his ribbed sleeveless t-shirt to blot at his eyes. The tears made fuchsia dabs out of the pink that he'd dyed it. "That was it. I'm through. I'm going to take up computers or something."

"That's crazy," I said, and Hugh added,

"I don't think you'd find that field to your liking." Hugh was a Luddite. He mistrusted machinery.

"Well I've got to do something. I spent my rent money on those new supplies."

"The glass?"

Geoffrey nodded. "It was expensive. I thought I was about to be a real artist."

We reassured him as best we could.

"Well what am I supposed to do for money?" Fresh tears welled up.

"What do you mean? Call daddy and ask for more funds," I said. Geoffrey had never confronted the money problem before. He was supported by his father, a Hollywood actor whose B-movie career had peaked in the '70s but who still occasionally landed a bit part. Dear old Dad had been sued by more than one mistress for child support, and presumably didn't keep close enough track of his litter-trail of offspring to realize that Geoffrey was years past eighteen.

"Daddy dear is at his beach house in Maui. He only gives that number to his legitimate children. What am I going to do?"

"You can always borrow money from one of us." Mose Junior had paid my rent, after all, so I had a little extra. How much extra, I had no idea. I kept my net worth an intriguing mystery by seldom balancing my checkbook.

Hugh nodded in agreement.

"No. I won't. You two work too hard for it." Geoffrey snuffled deeply and composed his face into a determined expression. "Well at least Aubrey does. I refuse to impose on my friends. I'll find a way."

The phone rang during *Star Trek*. Hugh watched with a critical eye, but for me television was just a mind-enema. After the events of the last couple days, I needed the mental blankness that television viewing provided. After three rings, a memory sloshed out of my slack-jawed neurons. I was waiting for a phone call. I grabbed up the receiver.

"Hello? Hola?"

Hugh looked at me. He was chewing his lip. I'd briefed him about the Señora Loca, as we'd begun to call her, and he'd reluctantly agreed to interpret between us if she should call. He tried to get out of it by telling me his Spanish wasn't all that good. I was sure he was just being modest.

"Aisling?" The voice was quick and gruff.

Only one man with my home phone number called me by my stage name. He couldn't get used to Aubrey.

"Will?"

Hugh's chest sunk in further with his sigh.

"Call me back from a pay phone." He gave me a number. Will lived in Daly City, south of San Francisco.

"Why? What's happened?"

"Call me in ten." He hung up.

Will was paranoid about losing his job with the Force if anyone found out that he was a regular customer at Naughtyland. He was also, more logically considering the vast number of cops that were regular customers, paranoid about losing his wife. He was thirty years married and a grandfather too. We didn't normally communicate outside of my office hours. Whatever he had called me for, it had to be big.

Plushious Velvett must have been found. That's all I could think of.

"You all right? You seem shaken. What did Will want?"

Hugh knew about my relationship with the cop. He thought it quite practical to have a good friend in the Force. So far, it hadn't kept me out of trouble.

"He didn't say. I'm supposed to call him back from a pay phone."

"There's one in front of Safeway."

I spidered my fingers nervously. "I'll tell him I ran." I punched in the phone number. Paranoia is something I've never been good at, along with patience.

Will's wife answered, a strong voice that seemed to be pumping fresh air, as though she'd just come in from out-doors. I knew she was a gardener. I knew that tea tree bushes, jasmine vines, agapanthus, and lemon trees wove her tract house yard, and I heard about it when the California climate teased open a summer carpet of her flowers, flashy as tinsel. I knew she knew nothing about me.

Hubby was on the phone within seconds.

"Aisling?"

"It's me."

"Where did you say you found the liquid you gave me two days ago?"

The liquid? I was expecting to be talking about a body. It took me a moment to think of the right answer. I'd almost forgotten the tupperware bowl filled with implant innards. "I didn't," I finally answered.

"This is serious. A serious federal offense."

"What are you talking about? An aesthetic offense, maybe. Did you find silicone?" Hugh watched me from his propped up position on the living room carpet. It was the way he always watched television. No wonder his elbows were red, rough skin.

"Do you have any more of the substance in your possession?"

"Why don't you tell me what the substance is and I'll let you know."

"Heroin."

I must have repeated the word. Hugh's expression of horror caught the shockwave of my own.

Chapter Fourteen

"If you've got more of it, you'll need to turn it in to me." Will's voice was gruff, a tone I seldom heard him use.

"Of course I don't have any more of it."

"I don't know what you're up to, but half a kilo isn't messing around. Do you know what kind of jail time we're talking about? Distribution is a major crime."

"Since when are you such a good cop?" Will's visits to Naughtyland often coincided with his swing shifts. Since I'd known him, he'd demonstrated only a lackluster interest in policing.

"When I see you get mixed up in this stuff I start to take an interest."

"Are you trying to say I'm a drug dealer?"

He laughed. "No, sweetheart. No one but the gangs deals in heroin. I'm saying my little girl has maybe got mixed up with an organization that offered her a lot of money to help them out in some way. A bad organization. Where did you get the substance?"

"You're crazy, Will, as well as condescending. I'm not connected to any organization. Just because I'm a stripper doesn't mean I'm involved in all the underworld dealings in town. I found it in the trash."

"That's not something someone would just throw away."

"Well that's where I found it. Would I have given the stuff to you if I'd known it was heroin? Don't you think my connections would be displeased with me for putting their supply straight into the hands of a cop?"

"It's hardly a supply. Half a kilo is piddly stuff."

"Half a kilo sounds like a lot." I thought about the weight dangling off my chest.

"Just over a pound. A pound of number four, ultra-pure. Golden Triangle extraction, no one else makes it like that. Worth quite a bit of money, little girl. Profit margin on that stuff is astronomical."

"Really?"

"You gave me pure powder, kiddo. Just off the boat. Worth a hundred, hundred-twenty-five thousand once it's cut for the street. That's just the

116

profit. That little bit you handed over they might pay twenty grand for, but it gets cut a few times with baking powder and such. It's a multi-tiered operation usually, every tier cutting the junk and swiping some profit. Huge operation. I know you're really a good girl. You don't belong in that lifestyle you're in. I can keep it quiet where the substance came from. Just promise me you'll end your involvement right now. However much the gang's cutting you honey, it's not a good business deal. You need extra money, you ask me."

"I belong fine in my life. And I don't need extra money." If I did, a regular customer would be the last person I'd ask for it. It didn't pay, in the long run, to be in a customer's debt. I was beginning to get it. That's what this phone call was really about. Will wanted to wrangle me into owing him something. He wanted the upper hand in our relationship. Will didn't really believe I was a drug gang's dupe, or care if I was, beyond some genuine glimmer of concern for my safety. In the crime hierarchy of San Francisco, a smidgen of heroin didn't even rate. This whole scenario was just feeding his daddy/whore fantasy. "You're loving this, aren't you?" I said. "Getting to be my protector?"

"You did hand over a chunk of smack to a police officer. I'd say that puts you in a compromising position."

"My blackmailer, then. Are you threatening me with jail unless I behave? You'd miss me too much if I went to jail. And oh, let's see, where are you going to tell your superiors you acquired this substance? From your favorite stripper, the one you often pop in on while still on the clock? They'll laugh, or fire you. I don't think you exactly have me where you want me, Will. As much as you'd love to get the upper hand in our relationship, you can't go anywhere with this."

"Time to break. Don't contact me. I'll come see you soon."

Will hung up. I'd said "blackmail," a word that would dilate the pupils of whatever government geek with earphones Will believed monitored his phone line. I dangled the receiver slowly into its cradle, letting the rubber coil pull apart my fingers.

Hugh was hugging his knees. A look of concentration wrinkled his forehead and his glasses needed pushing up.

"Remember that evidence you insisted I hand over? I gave a cop a pound of heroin. Luckily it was a sleazy cop, since he'd love to use it against me," I told him.

"No. You gave a cop the innards of a breast implant."

"Half a kilo of heroin. Over one hundred thousand dollars worth. Well, eventually worth that much, once it's diluted for sale."

"It's the perfect smuggling scenario."

"What are you talking about?" The thought of being in possession, however unwittingly of so much heroin had shaken me. My experience with drugs was limited to the pharmacopoeia that had spilled out of the medicine chest over Momma's pink-tiled bathroom sink. Since an array of cute pastel pills had whisked Momma away quite effectively, and served up something leftover and lukewarm as her replacement, I wasn't inclined to experiment with chemicals. I'd never, to my knowledge, seen heroin, or any other hard drug. Even the roster of losers that I'd dated hadn't included, by some miracle, any junkies. Of course I was familiar with marijuana. Geoffrey and Zan sometimes smoked a bowl after dinner if there was no chocolate for dessert.

Hugh continued his thought. "Smuggling heroin into the country in breast implants,"

"What?"

"It's ideal. The women could just walk through customs, carrying heroin inside her breasts. If half a kilogram's worth a hundred thousand or more, that's almost a quarter of a million dollars' worth divided between two breasts."

"But is it worth it? Think of the surgery. Twice. In and out."

"It must be worth it, for whoever's profiting from it. People go to all kind of extremes to smuggle heroin. Swallowing bags of it to recover from excrement for example. And that carries the risk of the bags bursting and killing the carrier. With breast implants that risk is eliminated. And drug-sniffing dogs wouldn't detect it. Women are seldom detained at customs in any case and due to social proprieties, when they are their breasts are certainly not examined. It's a foolproof smuggling scheme, and that's worth a lot to someone."

I thought about it for a moment. It did seem like a foolproof smuggling scheme. But how many times did the poor smugglers have to go under the knife? Though I'd heard from many of my coworkers that breast implant surgery was quick and easy, this foolproof scheme had to be a man's idea. And the profit gleaned from a pair certainly didn't go to the heroin's carrier.

"But I didn't see any heroin in that stuff. Will said it was powder."

"I think I've figured out the method. Remember the cysts?"

"Yeah." I'd felt the thick lumps when they were still inside Plushious Velvett. We'd seen milky pebbles drifting around the bottom of the fluid. Some had been as big as skipping stones.

"The drug must have been encased in small sacs. We thought they were congealants of the fluid."

I thought about that for a moment. What an effort to go through, to cling-wrap anthills of heroin, seal these into silicon pillows, and surgically implant them into perhaps unwilling young women. But for that many American dollars, I suppose it was worth it, for somebody.

"Will said it was super pure. From the Golden Triangle."

"The great majority of the world's heroin comes from Myanmar, formerly Burma. From there we get China White. China White is pure, and expensive. It's grown in what's known as the Golden Triangle, a highland area in Southeast Asia, where Thailand, Laos, and Myanmar join. The area also borders Vietnam and China, hence the drug's nickname. The packets we saw looked milky. I'm betting your discovery was China White."

Despite what his parents back in Connecticut feared, Hugh's work as a book pricer at a thrift store wasn't at all a waste of time. He read everything that passed through the store's dented shelves. "Had your friend travelled to Southeast Asia?"

"It's possible, I guess. She was a travelling porn star."

"She might have found a way to make her career even more profitable."

"But why would she throw her profit into the alley?"

"It could have been a drop-off point. A place to deliver the drugs to whatever connection would actually be selling them."

"I can't see her hawking heroin on some street corner."

"Clearly not. You don't see lay people selling drugs down at Sixteenth and Mission." Everyone in San Francisco knew where the drug market was. The boisterous homeless and hooker crowd that animated the sidewalks of the Mission district intersection was backgrounded with a quieter group, men in their twenties and thirties, dressed neat and muted, without a smell, innocuous as white noise. Ghosts among the mortals, they floated out of sight but drifted up to you if you wanted them. They knew who you were, and what you wanted. "Most of the drug trade is controlled by organized crime," Hugh continued.

"The Mafia?"

"In the case of heroin, more likely the Chinese Triads. Obviously, an operation like smuggling involves a lot of people, a lot of money, and therefore a lot of power, for someone. No one's smuggling freelance."

"So that heroin—"

"It's part of some drug ring." Hugh suddenly paled, and stilled his rocking. He looked at me, eyes lasered tight. "Did anyone see you take the implant, or know you had it?"

"Heroin? I didn't even know I had it." The trace of protectiveness in his voice annoyed me. I began swinging my foot in my cocky way.

119

"Sarcasm won't help you if a Chinese Triad member comes for his boss's contraband. They don't play. And if you did find it at a drop-off point, someone was watching it. A lookout."

"Well no one's come after me so far. It's been three days."

Hugh dropped eye contact. He braced himself, as if the roller coaster was inching over the crest. "I should have said this before. I think for your own safety, you should move back in."

So I had my second fight with Hugh that week. I could take patronizing from Will, in small doses, since there was money in it. From friends who should know better I wouldn't. I was all grown up and could take excellent care of myself, and of whoever else was tagging along. Hugh wasn't trying to be patronizing, he said. He was worried some heroin drug lord would hear tell of my theft of his property and render me into another grease spot on the rancid streets of the Tenderloin, he said. He was sorry he brought it up, but he didn't want anything to happen to me, he said. Nothing was going to happen to me, I said.

The phone rang again half an hour later. Hugh was in the kitchen, making spaghetti from a can. Vanessa Sassy and Isabella were out enjoying their second-to-last day in town, and had gone for Italian in North Beach, leaving us without a gourmet dinner. Geoffrey was out with a group of his young boy fans reassuring himself that despite his career's setback he was still desirable, and Zan was sulking in her bedroom. She'd taken up cigarettes again. She thought she was keeping her habit secret by smoking in her room with the door closed. I could smell secondhand smoke from the living room couch, faint acrid cinders.

As soon as I lifted the receiver, I regretted it.

"Aubrey, it's your little old Momma. Haven't heard from you in ages."

"Hi, Momma. I told you I didn't have a phone."

"Well that doesn't seem to be true. I'm just sitting here watching *Soul Train*, too lazy to get up and change the channel, thinking about my little girl out there in Sin City. You're my only daughter, you know. What are you doing?"

"Just sitting here watching *Star Trek*."

"You like that show? I never did get the hang of that show. How do they memorize those funny words? That Dr. Spock, he reminded me of your father. Now, we are harvesting the biggest beefsteak tomatoes you ever seen in your life this year. Don't you wish you were here to eat a slice of one? You never tasted anything so good in your life as a slice of one of Eb's beefsteak tomatoes with salt on top. Don't suppose you can get homegrown where you're at. When are you going to come see your old Momma?"

"I don't know, Momma. I'm pretty busy."

"I don't like this you being so far away all the time. You're my only daughter. Well Eb isn't doing so well lately with his veins acting up on him. It gets so bad in the evening he just has to set up here with his feet elevated. On the hassock, you know? We just sit and watch the programs."

"That doesn't seem so bad. You got that nice couch set." It filled up the rec room in their suburban ranch, a modular sofa connected with plush curves, with pop-out footrests at both ends. I'd bought it for her the summer before.

"Oh, that set's too hot in the summer. That velour just doesn't let you sweat. We got the TV set up out here on the deck and we watch from the lawn chairs. Don't we hon? Here's Eb and you should see the state of his legs. Thank you hon. Yes, that's plenty of ice. Will you just set and stop fussing over me? You know Retha's husband Hank did such a great job on this deck. I tell you he built it for us from scratch? He loves his old Daddy, doesn't he Eb? He calls Eb daddy, even though he's really daddy in-law."

"Okay, I got the deck is-better-than-sofa set thing. Am I supposed to start calling Eb daddy? Is that what you're trying to say? I was twenty-two when you two got married. I barely know the guy." I should have just gone along. That would have been the adult thing to do. But for some reason I was unwilling to explore I often felt compelled to crash-land Momma back into reality.

"Oh sweetie-pie, I don't know what you're talking about." She laughed her siren laugh. "Eb just whipped up some strawberry daiquiris. Could you reach me one of them packages of Sweet-n-Low, hon? Thank you. You know the doctor told me to lay off the Tab. He says it's bad for my kidneys. Well, not much else going on here. It's state fair time coming on. Sure do miss making those place settings with you, sweetie pie. My eyesight's going or I'd whip something up on the sewing machine to enter in."

"Stop talking like you're old. You're only forty-five."

"Well you know people in this family die young." Momma launched into a full rendition of Death Roster. This was a popular sequel to the Hospital Talk she'd been indulging in before. In sum, brothers, uncles and fathers had died young and drunk. The coal mines had taken the older generations, the grandfathers and great-uncles. The females all the way back endured decades longer than their spouses. They survived childbirths, snakebites, and the inevitable palette of diseases, detailed in Hospital Talk, that strike the poor in Kentucky until their hearts gave out, as described in Death Roster, from a lifetime of hard work and putting up with their male relatives' infuriating shenanigans.

"You be careful with your kidneys, Momma."

"I'm not drinking Tab."

"Daiquiris probably weren't the substitution Dr. Hillman had in mind."

"But it's so hot. They don't have many calories, with Sweet-n-Low in. My size eights are getting tight so I've got to watch it. Have you gained weight? Is that why you're home on a Friday night?"

"No." I should have just told her I was in hiding from a drug lord's thugs, and that was why I was home on a Friday night. That might have ended this conversation.

"You've got to work at it if you want to meet yourself a man. Why don't you go down to the Adult Children meeting? That's a good place to meet people. Of course you're not supposed to date. You're not supposed to say last names. But it happens all the time."

"You realize this is insane advice, don't you?"

"Well, I'll let you go." Momma changed to a whisper, made coarse by her mildly drunk condition. "I got in trouble for running up too high a phone bill last month."

I hung up. I was trying to choose between feeling anger or guilt when Hugh stuck a plate of spaghetti onto my lap.

"I'm turning this off," he said, and walked over to hit the knob on the TV. "I think you've been watching too long. Your eyes are glazed over." He sat next to me and gave me concerned looks between cramming in bites of spaghetti. "Who was on the phone?"

"Darylynn." I stuck the fork through the red sauce to the noodles, began twirling it.

Hugh nodded in sympathy. "She still on the stimulants?"

"She'll be on meds for the rest of her life. The way she mixes them up with alcohol and Sweet-n-Low that might not be much longer."

"She's suffered a lot, you know. They give her a break." Hugh could be so diplomatic.

"I know; I was there. I lived through a lot of what made her suffer too, you know. Watching someone get beat up is almost as bad as getting it yourself. Personally, I'd rather just take the blows. It's simpler."

"Of course you would, darling." Geoffrey's voice boomed up the stairwell, followed by the heavy sound of our apartment's security door coupling back into its iron latches. "You've never been subtle. It's that crude hillbilly blood. Come on," he hopped toward us, smudging a citrus scent of cologne into the living room. He wore his glitzy red leather jacket, and struck his arms out like a jazz singer. "I've figured out the way to make rent! We're going gambling."

Hugh had successfully begged off this foray, suddenly becoming tethered to an age-flaked copy of a Brother Cadfael mystery. I'd been necessary to the gambling expedition, though, as Geoffrey's 'gun moll.' I agreed to go along. I felt too hideous to work. To Geoffrey, my agreement was a formality. He dressed me in some slinky silver number dug from one of Vanessa Sassy's matching bags, the bodice of which fluttered in rolls like belly fat down my relatively inadequate chest. Geoffrey propped my unruly auburn waves into a scraggle on top of my head and pinched them into place with a banana clip. I was allowed to accessorize myself in my leather jacket and a pair of chunky black heels, though by the time I returned from the bathroom, kissing off most of the 'Bloodshot' lipstick he'd applied for me, Geoffrey had taken the shoes outside and spray painted them silver. "I'll buy you a new pair with the profits. Let's go."

We were halfway across the Bay Bridge and the night wind was hunkering me into my jacket and down the seat of the red Renault convertible Geoffrey had somehow gotten hold of when it occurred to me to ask where, exactly, were we going.

"Oakland, of course."

"What, is there an Indian reservation there?" I'd never heard of gambling being allowed anyplace else, except in Nevada.

"No, silly. This wind is doing disastrous things to your hair."

"You could put the top up."

"But it's a red convertible, you see." Geoffrey adjusted his sunglasses, another pointless and perhaps, at this time of night, dangerous fashion statement. "I'll fix it once we get there."

The East Bay night was warmer and darker than San Francisco's. Once we exited the freeway and left behind the hot coughs of car exhaust, the air was drier. Geoffrey nosed the Renault through a flickering neighborhood quilted with freeway overpasses. Dark buildings shouldered by, the low bland architecture of banks and fast food joints, an astonishing amount of speechless empty space between them, now and again a block of battered Victorian-era storefronts, plate glass fractured and repaired with duct tape. The stores inside sold wigs, vacuum cleaners, paint. There were pawnbrokers and bars.

"Parking lots and everything. It's like suburbia."

"This was life before gentrification. Don't you miss it?" Geoffrey had stopped for a light, and shouted over the windshield at a man crossing in front of us. "Can you tell me where Bloke's is?"

The pedestrian stopped. He was holding a bag labeled Church's Fried Chicken. "Bloke's is right around the corner there," he swung the bag of chicken to point the way. "Up on the left." As he crossed in front of me, he gave me a familiar appraisal. I braced myself for a catcall, but none came. I must look worse than I'd feared. Or maybe the silence was because I had a male escort.

The male escort was repinning my hair-do. Wind had plucked it apart and garbled it. Then Geoffrey was gunning through the intersection, swiping into a parking place, ignoring the meter, and ripping me out of the car.

"You look great."

"Aren't you going to put the top up?"

"No need. I'm feeling lucky tonight. Your part is to distract potential bouncers with your beauty. Gregor taught me a foolproof method for winning." Geoffrey whispered in my ear as he propelled me down the block. "It's called counting cards. Remember when your math teacher said you'd never use it in real life? He was so wrong. In fact, card-counting is a great life skill. Why didn't we learn it instead of all those empty sets and algebras?"

"A life skill. Like typing?" Everybody, from guidance counselors to Darylynn's second husband, had urged me to take typing class in high school to guarantee a future as an underpaid secretary. I had refused.

"Exactly. And one I plan to base a career on."

We turned the corner onto what had been a main thoroughfare in some other era. Now the signs were muffled, the buildings shed paint. Bloke's, a thin building with a facade of fake boulders tacked up to the second story windows, had no sign, just a red awning and a palace guard of bouncers to announce itself.

We showed ID. They asked us if we were cops. We said no. Then, miraculously, the suited phalanx let us through.

Bloke's glowed with red carpet and upholstery and a cherrywood bar. It steamed with beery exhales from a close-packed crowd. The place smelled like decades of spills. We ordered beers. For different reasons, neither of us was planning to drink. To further keep up the facade that we were simple folk rather than potential swindlers, we each took a freshly microwaved hot dog. The hot dogs were free, a promotion. I decorated mine with a string of mustard.

Geoffrey fought a gag as we made our way to a noisy back room, palming cold bottles and the papery skin of cheap hot dog buns. He acted like he knew where he was going, and I followed along, aware we were parting waves of stares. We were the only white people in the place. We were also horrendously overdressed. Or perhaps, I thought as I watched

Geoffrey's jacket shimmer in the lower light level of the back room, and the stripe on his tuxedo pants spank back the green glow, we were simply horrendously dressed.

The back room contained two pool tables. No one played pool. At the end of each table a card game was being dealt—blackjack.

"Eat this," Geoffrey crammed the hot dog into my already occupied hand. "You know I'm a vegetarian."

"How long do I have to stick around here being your accessory?" In more ways than one, I was tempted to add.

"Don't pout. Well, pout a little, it's not a bad effect. As long as it takes to win rent. What is my rent?"

"Three hundred-fifty."

"For our tenement? You're joking. The place is a hellhole."

"I'm not. We all pay three-fifty."

"For a roach-ridden, closetless, prison-gray, prewar-applianced—" My escort pulled a hundred dollar bill out of the pocket of his tuxedo pants. He snapped it crisp. "Well it's home. My last hun," he said. "Come be my lucky charm?"

He smiled, ducked his head, fluttered his impossibly big blue eyes at me. This strategy of his seldom failed. Receding hairline or no, Geoffrey, with facial bones that looked like they'd been attended to by a team of sculptors, enormous Mediterranean blue eyes, and straight hair that kept getting blonder, was one of the prettiest people most of those he encountered had ever met. "Come on. I'll take you to Denny's after with the winnings." He put a hand to my face. "I know how much you like Denny's."

Despite his bravado, his palm was damp with nervousness. I found a little desperation hidden in the pucker of his shapely eyebrows.

"All right, then." I said.

We passed over to a game on the back half of the left hand table. A new round was being dealt.

"Hi, guys," Geoffrey said. "Deal me in."

An hour and a half later, I was holding my queasy stomach and Geoffrey was holding one thousand and fifty dollars.

Chapter Fifteen

I couldn't manage more than coffee at Denny's. It mixed warily with the hot dogs in my stomach. Geoffrey ate a plate of scrambled eggs and rye toast, talking all the while about how easy it was to make money and how he wished he'd tried it before. The sense of independence from earning your own way was just thrilling. When grovelling to daddy got tiresome, as long as you knew when to double down, rent would always be within your reach.

I listened glumly. Geoffrey could gamble all his life, make money at any age. What would I do when I got too old to be a stripper? Already I was watching younger girls, nineteen, twenty-one, hatchlings with moist skin and radiant hair and unarthritic knees, take much of Naughtyland's business. I was almost twenty-six. Almost washed-up. I'd put myself through college on the usual array of service sector jobs: waitress, cashier, fast food. I'd been bad at all of them. Even after I married Conor for financial aid, after tuition I never had enough money to live on. Dinners throughout my four years of study had consisted of two cigarettes. Stripping had relieved me of poverty in a way that my history degree, I knew, wouldn't. I might have a year or two left, but still was only one injury away from unemployment. With the amount of time I spent in high heels, injury was inevitable. What would I do instead?

Geoffrey had put one of his slender hands over the thick porcelain rim of my coffee cup. The cup was an inch from my lips. "Stop it. You've had enough, my dear. She's warmed it up six or seven times." As he spoke, the silent young woman in nurse's shoes who was the one graveyard shift server plodded up to us. She absently tipped her coffee pot to top off both of our mugs with half-inches of thin brew. She was gone in an instant to coffee the rest of the patrons, her beat from table to booth to table worn into the carpet like a mule path. I could almost see varicose veins worming up her calves. I imagined her turning into myself, my thin ankles treading the mule path until they swelled, my body swelling the polyester uni-

126

form as time went by, then shriveling and stooping within it, my attitude consistently too bad to earn good tips. "Let's pay before she comes back around again. They seem determined to make you leave with a full cup of coffee on the table. Here you are in your beautiful ball gown biting your nails like a traumatized child. It's so Monroe. What's wrong with you?"

I told him as we walked out to the car.

He told me to stop being such a victim, and offered to teach me to count cards.

Geoffrey refused to drive me to The Tender Arms, not at any time of day, but certainly not in the middle of the night, certainly not in Gregor's Renault. I could take a cab or spend the night at home.

A night on the anorexic green couch suddenly appealed to me. At least I wouldn't run into my teenaged mugger on the sidewalk or the overly cheerful Cash in the morning.

I hauled myself up the stairs, behind Geoffrey's bounds. He'd heard voices in the living room and couldn't wait to tell whoever was waiting up for us about his success at Bloke's. When I reached the top of the stairs he was kissing cheeks and waving his cash roll from Vivian to Zan to Vanessa Sassy to Isabella and even to Champagne and Caviar. All were occupants of the couch that I had planned to fall asleep on within the next minute.

Though exhausted, I could tell something was wrong. It wasn't just that Zan was frozen against the embracing slouch of Vivian draped over her, and smoking furiously. Or that Vivian was there, clinging uncharacteristically to her girlfriend when she should have been at The Tender Arms writing her thesis or shoring up her boundaries. Or Isabella's long, compassionate glance at me. It wasn't just Vanessa Sassy's compliment, though her words cemented my fears.

"You look great in my dress, honey, what a pretty outfit," was the compliment.

"What happened? They found her?" My stomach coiled into a corkscrew.

"Found who? No, now don't you worry, we're going to straighten this out with Mose Junior just as soon as it's light tomorrow. As soon as he gets to the office, anyway." Vanessa Sassy pushed one of the terriers off the couch as it hopped over the lap of her pajamas. "Go give Aubrey a kiss."

My ankles were soon swabbed with dog tongues.

"Straighten what out."

"Check this out." Vivian reached into the back pocket of her black overdyed jeans. She withdrew a folded envelope and handed it to me.

I pulled out a three day notice of eviction from 301, 1432 Taylor Street. Dated Friday, August 14. Yesterday—now that we were in the wee hours of Saturday. Across the bottom was scrawled: Second Notice.

"I pay rent, I pay rent." Mose Junior was flipping through his check-book, damaging the thin tissues of carbon paper with his haste and over-sized hands. "Look, first of month." He spun the checkbook around.

Vanessa Sassy and I leaned over to see. The check was for four hundred dollars, dated August first, made out to Realty Conglomerates.

"Realty Conglomerates?" I asked.

My boss shrugged. "Owner over there change all the time."

"If you paid the rent, why are they evicting you?" Vanessa Sassy asked. I had a good idea of why, but settled back in my chair to hear his explanation. Mose Junior had quickly provided a seat for his special-guest porn star when we'd arrived an hour before Naughtyland's noon opening time to speak to him. He'd then had to provide one for me. I'd never actually sat in his cramped office before. A lower viewpoint gave a whole new perspective to his girly posters. "Thank you." Vanessa Sassy accepted the Marlboro he'd tapped halfway out of the pack.

"No idea. But don't worry. You leaving tomorrow, right?"

"Tonight, actually." She leaned to aim her cigarette toward Mose Junior's lighter. I noticed her unconscious hunching movement to keep her breasts from poking the desktop. "Izzy and I got a red eye back to Chicago. We're leaving right after the midnight show."

"You need a limo to the airport?" He moved his lapel aside to slip the lighter into his shirt pocket. Over the negative space of his chest, the lighter stood out like bagged kill.

"Sure, why not. You've been so nice."

"What about me," I said. "Sorry to break up the party, but I'm the one living in the place. What am I supposed to do when the new feature shows up? That would be tomorrow, right, or Monday? My apartment didn't grow by one bedroom in the last week."

My boss sucked on his Marlboro. He and the porn star exhaled in unison. I tasted ash.

"Who's coming for next week?" Vanessa Sassy asked.

"Shy Anne and Shy Honey," he said.

"There's two of them?" I said.

"Oh, I know them. The Boobsy Twins. We did a movie together, some locker room thing, I forget the name. They're the cutest things. You should see their hula hoop act. You'll like them."

"I'm sure I will. That's not the point. They'll bring a bodyguard, that's three people. Where are we going to put them all?"

"Her place really isn't all that big, Mose," said Vanessa Sassy.

"Okay okay. I start looking for new place."

"You haven't been looking for a new place? This whole setup was supposed to be temporary. And you can fight this eviction, you know. You don't have to just take it. Renters have rights. It's illegal," I said.

"It is?"

"Sure. This says second notice." I tapped the notice on his desk. "Did you ever get a first?"

My boss shrugged.

"And you've been paying rent. There's no grounds to evict you. They just don't want sex workers in their building." I was sure Sue was behind this. Aided and abetted by Cowboy Boots and the rest of the Yuppie Bloc, as DeeDee called them, no doubt.

"It's okay. They don't want us, we go. Who knows but we get sued or something. I don't want trouble."

"You'll never find another place that cheap."

"It's okay. I heard of new place, apartments going cheap."

"Where's that?"

"Oakland." He blew me a final taste of Marlboro. Diamond rings winked as he ground out his cigarette.

Dispirited, I walked the three blocks over to The Tender Arms. The day seemed to share my wilt. The summer sky was a blue-gray monochrome, pale, as though an eraser had been rubbed over it. Litter lay flat as the lighting. Billboards, dull in the lack of sun, hadn't the energy left to scream. Homeless people and drug sellers were still and quiet, waiting for the lunch rush to pass by and make an outdoor market out of cravings and spare change. A black man in a wheelchair paused at the curb to drain his urine bag into the gutter. He splattered his bare, propped feet, and the stench of the concentrated waste filled the block.

I paused in front of the Lotus Leaf. The facade was nondescript, the sign a scrawl on the lid of a shoebox stuck in the corner of a curtained window. A small video camera aimed at me from above the door. I waved to it. No doorbell. They checked you out, then buzzed you in.

Mikey of the neighborhood watch apparently didn't work days. I let myself in, trudged up the stairs. I'd made the final turn onto the third floor landing when I heard Cash chirp.

"Hey, Aubrey."

I was keying the lock on 301 when he caught up with me.

"Hello." I said it to the doorknob.

"Hey. Let me help you with that. These old doors get a little tricky. Listen," the door opened easily under his coaxing, "can I come in for a minute? I've got something for you."

"I bet you do." I pushed past him, inside. I went to the kitchen looking for one of Hugh's Cokes. I hadn't eaten. Vanessa Sassy and I had gone to see Mose Junior as soon as I'd rolled off the couch and rubbed the bedsores it had made overnight. They were at precise intervals down my body, corresponding to the ribs of the couch's frame.

He laughed, a bit sheepishly. "It's not like that. May I?"

When I didn't answer he continued from his spot in the doorway, kicking to one side in a casual lean. "See you've got your Coke."

The living room was a mess. It smelled like Chinese food. A ragpile of Vivian's torn flannel shirts and distressed jeans carpeted the hardwood. I kicked through her wardrobe to her computer. A glowing green light indicated that the laptop was still on. The screen was dark, but ghosted into it, centered top to bottom and left to right, was an afterburn of her thesis' title: *The Male Gaze: A Penetration into the Discourse of Entitlement.*

Cash had crossed his arms and looped the shiny black hemispheres of his hair behind his ears. "Well, I'd rather no one heard about this, but—" He looked behind him, out into the hall. He ripped open the velcro pocket of his cargo pants and extracted a pad of bills. "The coast is clear. This is for you." He held out the money.

"What for?"

"I took the liberty of investing some money for you. Earmarked five hundred dollars so whatever I made with it I'd give to you—to shake your lack of faith in the market. I do a bit of day trading, and I had a good one yesterday. So here you go." He once again offered me the pad. It was doubled over but still thick and I could see that the outer bill was a twenty.

"Is this compensation for evicting me? Or evicting Mose Junior?"

"No it's not."

"So you knew about that."

"I'm really sorry. Look, I know you'll find another place. I can help you. Several of my clients are landlords."

"I'm sure they are, but I don't need your help, I've got another place."

"Well I hope this doesn't mean we won't be seeing each other anymore." He once again tried to hand me the money wadded in his hand.

"No, thanks. Why don't you keep it. I'd just waste it by spending, but you'd reinvest. Capitalism is counting on you."

"No. I made it for you. It's not much, but if, you know, momma needs a new pair of shoe—"

"She'll be in her Kmart flip-flops till the first frost."

"Okay, okay." Cash laughed, but he placed the money on the hardwood floor and slowly backed away, like a samaritan feeding a rabid dog. "Enjoy it."

I shut the door behind him and made my way to the small kitchen. A few pairs of chopsticks, the light wooden kind that restaurants give for take-out, fermented in the sink. I threw them away, ran some water into the kettle. The apartment had come with basic pots and pans as well as the small amount of furniture. Surely I wasn't expected to pack this stuff up, I thought. The landlord would throw it out on the street for free. The kettle was getting heavy. I turned off the water.

I looked up and through the window over the sink just in time to see the venetian blinds in 302's corresponding window snap horizontal.

I leaned over the sink to stick my face closer to the window. This apartment lacked curtains. How long had Comfortable Shoes been spying? I looked down the triptych wall. 202's window was buttoned up with a treatment done in a happy yellow and red tomato pattern. The first floor windows were black-barred, the frontline of urban defense. The bloated-belly bags of the trash pile beneath them lolled over the tops of the green trash cans like escaping slugs.

I smashed my forehead against the pane. Craning one's neck, one could see most of the street-level trash area from the third floor. One could see the very spot where I'd found the most valuable item ever mistaken for tomato aspic. Back across at 302, the venetian blinds still swayed a bit. I could almost hear the aluminum slats click-click-clicking, like teeth on a spoon, against the glass.

I thought about the Smith & Wesson, which I'd hidden, in the old-time tradition, between the mattress and the rusty springs of the Murphy bed.

And I'd thought paranoia wasn't my weakness. Rubbing my forehead, I set the kettle on the stove. The only thing in the cabinet was the yellow box of Earl Grey. I settled a bag into a mug. Hugh had me spooked with all his talk of drug lords, drop-off points, and lookouts.

Still, when the knock on the door came, I jumped. And this was pre-caffeine.

DeeDee had brought up a copy of Sheila's eviction notice and a joint.

He lit one and flapped the other as he went in agitation over to the couch. "Can you believe this? These people are outrageous. I knew they were up to something, but eviction! The cheek of it. Poor Sheila. You know what GA pays her to live for a month? In the most expensive city on Planet Earth?"

I was relieved to see DeeDee instead of a heroin dealer with an assault rifle.

"What? By the way, they evicted me, too. Or I should say they evicted Mose Junior."

The noise that followed was either the boiling kettle or DeeDee's screech.

"Come on! They won't get away with this." He seized my upper arm and steered me out the apartment's door and swept me down the staircase. Without a word to the startled Sheila, who answered her door as warily as I had, he collected her by the sleeve of her blue polka-dotted blouse and wheeled the two of us in front of the door to her neighbors'.

Sheila tried to bolt.

"Oh no you don't." DeeDee kept his grip on both of us. "No more hiding. Aubrey, you knock."

"Okay." I did. Though my upper arm was painfully wrung by DeeDee's grip and would have an unattractive bruise tomorrow, for some reason I felt like giggling.

Sue answered, her eyebrows surprised high as her hair.

"You're responsible for this," DeeDee's voice was squeezed and thick. "Look at these poor people." He shook us. "Look into the faces of the human beings you're throwing out onto the street! Even welfare queens and whores need places to live."

"I'm not exactly a–" I said.

"I'm not a welfare queen," said Sheila. "I have a job."

I think I was the only one who heard her. DeeDee had raised the volume of his rant. I watched Sue's expression go from wide to narrow. She slipped her hands into the pockets of her casual weekend khakis. Her leather flats were braced. Todd puttered up behind her.

"I know you're behind this and I'm going to fight it! I know about your meetings, your little committee. What you're doing is illegal."

"Are you finished?" Sue asked.

"Certainly not."

"Well then let me interrupt. You say what we're doing is illegal. I'll have you know that what they're doing is illegal. This one," Sue pointed to Sheila, "illegally took over a lease. She," Sue indicated myself, "is last of a long line of subletters. Subletting is illegal. This isn't an SRO hotel, rented by the week."

"It was a better place to live when it was! I'm taking this to court. Just because you pay more rent doesn't mean you dictate who lives in the building. You can't go tattling on everybody to the landlord." DeeDee let go of Sheila to dramatize his 'you' by stabbing the air in front of Sue's chest. Released, his former captive fled through her door and slammed it.

"We don't have to. We formed a co-op and bought the building. You see, we are the landlord."

My arm felt tossed up by the sudden release of the vise grip. A moment later, I was propping DeeDee against the hallway wall along the stretch that separated Sheila's door from Sue and Todd's. He hadn't exactly fainted, but the vapors seemed to be after him again.

"You okay?" I asked him.

He could only nod and claw at the fuzzy yellow fleurs-de-lys that patterned the wallpaper.

"It's okay, we'll be repapering soon. Isn't that Victorian stuff hideous?" Sue said. She and Todd had stacked their heads around their doorframe. They smirked at DeeDee who was hyperventilating. I fanned him with my hand. His face reddened under his gray crash helmet of hair.

"Hey Todd honey," I said. "Haven't seen you down at Naughtyland lately. All the girls miss you. It's that charming little grin you get when your face is an inch from their crotch. When can I tell them you'll be coming back?"

Todd flushed furiously and his soft brown coiffure barely escaped being caught in the door slam.

He pulled back just in time.

Chapter Sixteen

"So that's what they were all about, the meetings. The Yuppies were onto this co-op scheme. I should have known they were on about something to do with profits, and investments, and screwing the lower class. Property is theft."

"You did know." I answered, in my most soothing tone. It came out sounding sarcastic. I'm not the nurse type. DeeDee was stretched out on his bed with a cool washcloth over his eyes. I'd helped him home after the encounter and he'd gone straight to bed.

"But I should have seen this coming. They bought the building. I can't believe it."

"More tea?"

He sat up, still balancing the washcloth across his nose. I stuck the tall flowered glass in his hand, and he took a prim swallow.

"I'm going to have to move. After all these years."

"You weren't evicted."

"It's a matter of time, honey." He lifted a corner of the cloth to reveal one gray-blue eye. It was a child's washcloth, decorated with a teddy bear. "They'll find some excuse to get rid of this old queen. They can get four times what I pay for this place. Don't be naive."

"I try not to be."

"I'm going to have to move."

He let the cloth fall back over his eyes and reclined onto the pink chenille spread. His breaths were deep and slow to take advantage of the aromatherapy candle he'd lit, pine-scented for relaxation. The artificial scent of Christmas cloyed the room. DeeDee's t-shirt and shorts were as rumpled as the bedspread. Both garments were jarred toward the headboard, as though someone had grabbed his sneakered feet and yanked.

After a moment I asked, "Who is the woman in the apartment next to mine? Do you know anything about her?"

"She's legit. Pays full rent and is on the lease."

"Okay. But what's her deal?"

"Definitely lower class. She'll be on her way out too, now that the capitalist running dogs have taken over."

A moment passed again. DeeDee was pressing the washcloth directly into his eyeballs with finger and thumb.

"Yes, but who is she? What does she do?"

"She's a Vietnamese immigrant and she works at the dry cleaner's over there on Golden Gate. Just the kind of person the capitalist lackeys like to screw the most. Charming woman. Impossible to tell her age, she's that kind of person. Lived through the war though, we talk about it sometimes. She doesn't bear a grudge. Barely speaks English. She comes to my parties and she always participates in the dance contest. Now she'll be out on the street with the rest of us." DeeDee rolled over.

"What's her name?"

"Bay. Means 'six.' That tells you she was the sixth child in her family."

"You know Vietnamese?"

DeeDee nodded into his pillow. "My interest in the culture didn't begin and end with the girls. Before Nam I'd never been too far from a dirt farm. Once there, I studied Vietnamese. Most GI Joes didn't get beyond 'suckee fuckee.' Who knew we'd all meet up again in some American ghetto?"

Who knew.

"Now go on home, cookie. I'll be all right. I need to think."

I climbed up to 301, pausing on the landings to give my left knee a break. Pain shot across it with every lift on the ascent. Saturday night was a good night at work and I had to go. That gave me a few hours to soothe the knee. I'd ice it, if ice could be found in the dorm-sized refrigerator at Mose Junior's. Maybe my favorite Vibram-soled platform clogs were too heavy a footwear for those of us whose joints had been clobbered by high heels, lap-grinding and pole tricks.

I hadn't told DeeDee, but despite Hugh's concern I'd decided I'd better move back to the old homeplace immediately rather than stay the two further days granted to Mose Junior's lease. Sue had kicked Mose Junior out, but if Todd saw me again there was no telling what he'd feel justified in doing or saying to me since I'd tattled on him to his wife. He seemed the petty revenge-taker type. I tried to think of any possible way he could get me fired, but couldn't. I'd gotten suspended for hassling customers off Naughtyland's premises before, but that time there'd been eager witnesses.

The second floor was quiet. Sheila was no doubt laying even lower than usual. Perhaps Sue and Todd had taken her neighbor and secret crush, Cash, for a Saturday afternoon wine tasting cruise through Napa Valley. Was Cash in on the co-op deal? He'd made a lot of expensive alterations to his 'loft' for a renter. I hesitated to call them improvements. He'd known about my eviction. But he also seemed the too-carefree-to-settle-down type. I wasn't interested enough in the answer to try and find out.

I ratcheted my leg up the final flight of stairs, using both hands to lift my thigh onto the step above.

It was interesting, I thought, that Comfortable Shoes was Vietnamese. Hadn't Hugh said that most of the heroin trade came from that area of the world? Could she be a lookout for the local gangs, and could our trash area be a drop-off point? When I thought of gangbangers, I thought of young men with extra testosterone and ridiculously baggy pants. Perhaps I was being unfair and gangs were more equal opportunity than I had supposed. If women were bringing in their heroin, perhaps they were guarding it, too. But I was being ridiculous. Fifty thousand Vietnamese immigrants lived in the Tenderloin, most of them families. They weren't all members of some drug gang. The Chinese Triads, Hugh had said. There you had it. Different group altogether. I was getting anxious about nothing.

When another knock on the door came an hour later, I removed the plastic bag of ice from my propped knee and answered it with confidence.

"Time's up."

The Hello Kitty purse, the size and transparency of an oversized ice cube, travelled toward my gut. The handgun was clearly visible inside it. She'd redone her nails in pink.

I backed away. She shut the door behind her, softly.

My relentless pursuer wasn't looking good. Her hair, formerly a pour of black ink, was rough and greasy. Mascara smeared black sickles underneath her eyes. She was dressed in her usual evening wear and spike heels. One of her knees was skinned. She waggled the purse at me.

"Time's running out," she said. "I know you have the bag. I'll kill you. Hand it over."

"How did you find me?" I had backed up against the raggedy love seat and sunk involuntarily onto it. "I don't know what you're talking about."

"I know you have it." Emerald sequins on her minidress sparked as she hobbled toward me. The dress tweezed her legs knock-kneed. I wasn't sure how she was going to fire the gun, since it was enclosed in her purse and her grip on it was mediated by the thin plastic. Her expression left no doubt that she would find a way.

"You're going to have to tell me what bag you're talking about. Can you describe it or something?"

"You know what I'm talking about. Quit stalling." She kept the gun trained on me and knelt to fling through Vivian's clothes. She'd somehow managed not to trip over the pile. She was better at heels than I.

"In here somewhere?" She shook a pair of stained jeans. "Under the couch?" She lunged toward me, skittering over the floor. I recoiled, but she only stuck her free hand under the loveseat. It came out gray with dust. She put her tongue to a finger to lift a stripe of gray from her pale brown skin.

That action pounded an idea into my head. I'd seen crack addicts lick the floor when desperate for their fix.

"Heroin. The bag you're talking about is the implant full of heroin?" I felt as triumphant as I could with a gun trained on my navel.

She was unimpressed with my powers of deduction. "Now you remember you have it all of a sudden. You've got ten seconds. I'm waiting right here. Ten."

Panic slapped my stomach. She was a junkie without her fix. No wonder she looked so bad. When she found out I didn't have her junk, she'd certainly kill me. I wasn't human to her, just an obstacle in the way of her high. I had to get the gun away from her before I broke the bad news.

"Five."

What to say? I tried to breathe life into my wits. She was lithe and little but strong as a farmer. I remembered the piano wire bandiness of her arm around my neck.

"Two." She was unsnapping her plastic purse. "One."

"What's your name?" I blurted. I squeezed my eyes shut. "I promise to help you."

"Marilyn."

For some reason, she hadn't shot me. Why not? I kept my eyes closed. "I can help you get a fix." I didn't have a regular supplier or anything, but I'd happily join the drifters at Sixteenth and Mission to score my life back. Why didn't I feel a bullet searing my internal organs? Maybe it was the Buddhism thing.

"I'm not a junkie. Smack's for losers."

"Dealer?"

"Give me my bag."

"I would if I had it. I'd really love for you to have it."

My two-time assailant kicked spastically at Vivian's mess, not caring when her open-toed shoes collided with the furniture. "You live like a pig. Where are you hiding it?"

"Look I'm not hiding it. I had the bag for a short time. I don't any more. I gave it to the cops. It's gone. Sorry."

"It's gone?"

I opened my eyes. Marilyn's face had softened into utter shock. Her plum-colored lower lip wobbled. There was an innocence to her terrible expression, as though she were a child first comprehending that the world was really rather indifferent to her fate.

"It's gone. I'm sorry. I didn't know what it was, or that it was yours."

Marilyn collapsed as thoroughly as an abandoned neurotic. She curled up into Vivian's dirty clothes and sobbed into the soft flannel of one of my roommate's cut-up shirts.

A few moments later I had recovered enough to pull the spaghetti purse strap from Marilyn's shoulder. It stuck to her skin a little bit, perhaps from sweat. She didn't seem to notice as I unwound the strap from her arm. Her arm was a deadweight, and nearly as thin and limp as the strand of plastic. After extricating the purse, I replaced the arm at her side, onto the scratchy sequins that collected her underfleshed parts.

I took the encased gun and pressed it under the Murphy bed mattress next to Plushious Velvett's Smith & Wesson. If she got to it again, at least we'd be even.

Marilyn's crying was just as ferocious after I boiled tea water, filled two mugs, steeped for five minutes, let cool and began to sip. I set a mug of tea on the windowsill for her. Still the crying continued. I went to lean over her. Her face was bloated and wet with tears, snot, drool. A rash of pimples stippled her forehead. She was, I thought again, just a kid.

"Wipe your face," I handed her another shirt of Vivian's, a cotton T that was part of the pile. She hurled it back, aiming for my eyes, and sucked a breath for another round of sobs. I couldn't help but admire her spirit.

I'd often been grateful that I hadn't had to earn my living as a sex worker until the relatively mature age of twenty-four. It was a career that didn't mix well with the traumas of adolescence. I'd had a marriage and several affairs notched in my bedpost before I'd been introduced to the charms of paying customers. Watching Marilyn quaking on my floor reminded me of the most terrible denominator of youth: ineffectualness. As a teen I'd had, as Marilyn seemed to have, no idea of how to go about making good things happen. She'd mugged me, arguably twice, but watching her dampen the laundry with tears, my anger at her drained. Marilyn wasn't a good mugger. Too scared of vampires. Somehow I couldn't hate her for trying. She seemed to throw herself at problems with blunt ferociousness that no one had managed to beat out of her yet, and, though she'd thrown her fury at me, I admired her ferocity.

She also had stamina. While her crying jag carried on I finished my Earl Grey standing at the kitchen sink and watching Bay's Venetian blinds. They made a smooth white surface to the world as I watched them. No cracks.

By the time I finished my tea, Marilyn had quieted a bit. I reentered the living room. When she saw me, she heaved herself onto all fours and crawled toward the front door.

"Oh no you don't." I ran to block her path. "I want you to tell me some things first."

"Fuck you."

"How did you find out where I live?"

"Get the fuck out of my way." She charged my knees. The right one held but it didn't matter. The strobe of pain from the left one floored me. I grabbed it as I fell. Marilyn clambered upright.

"Do you want your gun back?" Her hand was on the doorknob. She turned to me, wiped a streak of snot off with her hand. She passed the snotty hand down her sequined front.

"Where is it?" I didn't answer. I rubbed the throb that was my knee. "Okay. What do you want?" she asked.

"How did you find out where I live?"

"Saw you come in."

"How'd you get in?"

"Rang bells." I nodded. That was my technique too.

"And how did you know which apartment?"

"Man in the hall said."

"How'd you know who to ask for?"

"I just asked for whore's apartment." Her tone was matter-of-fact.

"What makes you think I'm a-"

"You said. I saw you with that guy in the cab. I saw you at Massimo's. He was your customer. Now you give me my gun. You can't keep it. It's mine."

"Why do you need a gun?"

Marilyn's customary look of fury came back to give a steel frame to her face. "Because I stole heroin and now I have no money to get away. You gave it to police. I wanted to buy out with it. He's coming around tomorrow night for pick-up. I have no more time." After these cryptic comments, she called me a few names. I was beginning to feel like I deserved all of them. She seemed to be finished crying and stared at me coldly. She grabbed her tits to reposition them under her dress and tugged the cloth to compensate. The dress, uninterrupted by hip curves, fell into a straight green cylinder beneath the one-two punch of her breasts. "Your fault I'm going to die," she finished.

Even for someone without a predilection for guilt, that was a tough accusation.

"Marilyn," I said. "If you want me to help you, you better explain."

Because I refused to give her back her gun, I got an explanation. I made her sit on the couch. I brought her one of Vivian's t-shirts dipped in warm water for her to wipe her face with but she refused it, so I tossed the wet crewneck on top of the clothes pile and took a seat next to her. The love seat crowded us close enough together for me to smell the candy scent of her body spray. Viv would love the new odor that had been wallowed into her clothes.

"My name's Aubrey Lyle. I'm a stripper over at Naughtyland."

"Good for you." I'd been hoping she would reintroduce herself. Marilyn, obviously, was going by a stage name. Diva and movie star names were ever-popular choices. She'd chosen, or someone had chosen for her, an improbable pseudonym designed to conjure the mystique of Monroe from a skinny child. I obeyed sex worker etiquette and did not ask her real one. Her torso strained away from me. The armrest must have been breaking her back.

For a moment I wished I had some of Cash's easy charm. I tried a compliment.

"You speak English really well," I said, immediately hating myself for coming up with no better opener than the cliché. Naughtyland customers often addressed our Asian dancers with insulting "me so hawny" phrases, genuinely surprised to get fluent English in response. And why not? People learn the language they make money in quickly. Marilyn did speak English well, with an accent and with fewer struggles for syntax than the average second-language speaker. I attributed her fluency to her youth.

"Watch TV all day and learn. What do you want?"

"Okay. I found your bag in our trash pile—"

"That's because that's where I hid it."

"Right. Well I thought it might belong to a friend of mine who was missing. The previous occupant of this apartment, actually."

"She a whore too?"

"A stripper. And a porn star. Plushious Velvett. Ever heard of her?"

"Porn is for perverts."

"Anyway, she was missing and had implants, and since she'd last been seen here, I thought that what I'd found might have been hers. You know, with women getting attacked around here all the time." I looked pointedly at my attacker.

Marilyn looked sullen. She picked at one of her larger pimples with a fingernail.

"It was mine," she finally said.

"It didn't come from Plushious Velvett, then."

Marilyn shook her head. We were silent for a while. Marilyn inspected a strand of her hair.

"Do you mean it came from you?"

She shook her head again. "I'm old girl. New Thai girls came last week."

"I see. And they travelled with breast implants filled with heroin."

She just looked at me.

"So you come over from Thailand with breast implants filled with heroin. Then they're surgically removed, replaced with normal implants and it's time to start working for Johnny?"

"Taiwan."

"Taiwan?"

"Implant surgery in Taiwan."

"Why Taiwan?"

She shrugged. "Lots of implant surgery there. How much money do you got? You owe me for the bag."

"I don't know. I don't really keep track."

"You're too old. Can't make much money. Any cash left from last night's tricks?"

"How much do you need?" Although I made quite a bit of money at Naughtyland, I seemed to spend it just as quickly as it came in. And why? What's the money for?"

"Ten thousand to pay Johnny off."

"You owe him money? I thought you were working for them. Do they make you pay a fee every night you work?" That's how it worked at Naughtyland.

"They bring us here, we must pay them back. Forty thousand dollars."

I didn't say anything for a minute because I was stunned. I had to block the thought of how hard Marilyn had worked to earn the twenty-five thousand she had already paid her pimp. I assumed she'd given him the five grand she'd taken from Clem's Elvis bag.

"I'm not from here. I'm Thai." Her tone was somewhere between contemptuous and mocking. "From Thailand. They send me over here, I work for them and pay them fare."

"Johnny brought you over here?"

"I can't apply for a green card. He arranges green card."

"So Johnny gets the heroin and a prostitution ring. Efficient gangster."

"He just gets girls for Lotus Leaf. Smack is payment to another gang to leave him and Lotus Leaf alone."

"Wow. A bigger fish. They get the heroin, and Johnny pimps in peace."

"Not fish. Gang."

"Johnny's doing okay then. A plane ticket from Thailand doesn't cost forty thousand dollars."

"It costs fifteen hundred. Change in Los Angeles."

"Why don't you just buy yourself a ticket and go home? Use that five grand you stole from Clem."

Her arms crossed like guards' swords under her breasts.

"Because. Spies all over this neighborhood. We're locked up most of the time. We can only go out with Johnny."

"You left to come rob me. Twice."

"I pay someone, she says she never see me. Pay another one, she says she did. Two hundred dollars. I get one hour. Then room check."

"But if you buy yourself from Johnny—"

"I go."

"But what was all this about me being responsible for your death? If you don't pay Johnny now he won't kill you. He benefits more by you paying him back over time. That way you stay longer as part of his team of professional virgins."

She glared at me for a while, arms still folded, exuding her candy scent. Her sticky face had attracted filaments of hair but she didn't lift a hand to unstick them. I fought the urge to reach across to her and do it myself.

"Gang man comes for heroin tomorrow night. I stole from him." She'd spoken slowly, as if I were a thick-headed child.

"I see."

"My plan was to pay Johnny and go before he comes. Before they will see some smack is missing. I had almost a week before you stole my bag. Now one day, and no smack."

"I see."

Marilyn stood up. "I decided. You made this problem. You solve it for me. I need ten thousand dollars by tomorrow. Your problem. If you don't have the money, I'll send the gang man your way." I watched her kick towards the door. She overturned a flannel shirt, revealed the money Cash had left earlier. I'd forgotten all about it. Marilyn fanned the bills expertly and riffled the stack of twenties to count them. She folded the bills in half, then in half again, and plugged the roll between her breasts. She found her purse and shouldered it. "Ten thousand not so much for a pretty white girl whore. Nine thousand seven hundred and fifty now. Your neighbor I paid not to see me. Had to. She works for Johnny. She sees everything. If you don't pay me, she'll know where you go."

As if on cue, when I looked out the window across to my closest neighbor, the venetian blinds at her window were swinging like a bell.

"And I know where you work too," Marilyn said. "Keep the gun. You need it now. See you tomorrow."

The door clicked shut behind her, a quiet punctuation.

Chapter Seventeen

I put on low-heeled, sensible and comfortable shoes for my walk to the bank. I found the old workboots in Vivian's pile. Sensibly, calmly, I measured my steps down Jones Street, breathing evenly through the four blocks to Market, the left turn and the long choked blocks to the nearest Bank of America, a whole BART stop away. The Tenderloin had only check-cashing places on its urine-watered streetcorners. Real banks clustered northward on Market, lapping up on the Financial District's skyscrapers. The silver razors of downtown's tall buildings reflected the sky, still the color of a worn dime. I walked into a late-afternoon breeze that tossed my hair and would have made me cold if I'd been in a different state of mind. For grounding, I pinched the bank card in my pocket.

The line at the bank machine was tourists caught between the Ferry Building and the cable car turnaround at Powell Street. I waited behind them and their tethered children, our short line adding to the turbulence of sidewalk traffic flow.

There couldn't be more than a thousand in my account. I never checked my balance. Perhaps, by some miracle, there was two thousand. Even so, that would be only a fifth of what I needed. No one I knew had eight grand to spare. Vivian lived on student loans. Zan did too, and on what she earned as a guinea pig in medical experiments. She'd sold some of her eggs to pay for her last semester. Hugh had the lifestyle and budget of a monk. Geoffrey's dad was unreachable.

Geoffrey, I thought as I moved up to the head of the line to replace a matching couple in tennies and two warm-up suits shiny as their respective pate and cornsilk hair. My newly-employed friend. I'd give him what I had, and he'd just have to gamble it up.

A moment later I withdrew seven hundred twenty dollars. I left a balance of fourteen cents.

I worked that night in even more of a frenzy than usual. I wanted to

144

set Geoffrey up with the biggest ante possible. By ten o'clock, three hours into the shift, I'd increased my net worth by another three hundred dollars. The night wasn't even that busy, and the number of my coworkers who had showed up to work the lucrative Saturday shift was legion. I wasn't sure how I was doing so well. Normally, sheer desperation didn't sell. I must have moved beyond it into some more marketable state.

I thumbed through the bills in front of my locker. Mose Junior strode by, making a rare appearance in the dressing room. His lanky gait was led by his wrists.

The flutter of greenery made him stop. "You have my money?" He looked toward the back wall, but he was clearly addressing me. The dressing room's only other occupant was Mahogany, on the floor massaging her feet.

"Here." I separated six twenties and thrust them toward him.

They disappeared into his fist. Mose Junior's hands reminded me of puppy paws, splayed and overgrown.

Mahogany was his next stop. She fished some bills out of her bra and counted out her contribution to our boss's wealth.

He left us.

I snuggled my cash into the pocket of my leather jacket, bodyslammed the locker door closed, spun the combination lock, dosed myself from the bottle of Pear Froth body spray that someone had left out, and was ready for the floor.

"You want some hairspray honey? The humidity gets to mine, too." Micki pushed past me on her way to the mirror.

"No thanks. Is that guy in the blue jacket still out there?"

"He went with Plantagena."

Damn. I fought a niggle of irritation with my abundance of co-workers. Plantagena had to make a living, too. But in the zero sum game of Naughtyland, we all competed for the finite amount of money that slunk through the black curtains, those few twenties squeezed between the Visa cards and the pictures of the kids. We competed for it with the flatness of our stomachs, the radiance of our hair, the color of our skins. It was a competition worthy of Roman gladiators. It was a validation or an invalidation of your very being.

And it wasn't. Kindergarten taught us it's what's on the inside that counts. Right?

With stakes like those, the temptation for dancers to be jealous, to be nasty to each other, was understandable. I'd long since determined not to feel that way. Or at least not to show it. I fluffed up my breasts before I left the dressing room. But I didn't resort to hairspray.

An hour later, I was picking my cuticles at one of the back tables. Four other dancers sitting there made a tangle of elbows and calves. More clustered around us, standing.

"I haven't seen it this slow since Veteran's Day."

"Must be a game on."

"Yeah, the guys are all in sports mode."

"I think there's something down at the stadium. Isn't it baseball season?"

"I knew I should have auditioned at NastyNest. They charge you more, but it's boom, boom, boom, you're working your ass off all night."

"How much they charge?"

"Ten a dance. They got guys watching you, keeping track of how many dances you do."

"They take ten out of every dance? That's too much."

"You earn it though. It's not like this place."

Every slow night was made even more dreary with conversations like this. Normally I joined right in. With my life at stake for ten thousand dollars, however, I kept my attention on the three customers, looking for the nonverbal signs that one of them might want a lapdance.

After fifteen more minutes of watching, none of the three men had made a quick glance back at us, or gotten up to check out the cubicles, or gone to the bar for a non-alcoholic beverage of their choice. There was a fourth customer, too, one that all of the dancers had left alone, one whom I'd discounted before. He was a regular, known for his fetish for Asian women and for proselytizing Christianity. We called him The Converter. I was so desperate I got up to approach him.

The Converter smiled widely when I sat next to him. He was old and soft, and smelled like baby powder. Suspenders strapped down his belly.

"Hello," I said.

"Hello. Have you heard the voice of the Lord?"

I couldn't go through with it. I half-rose, then thought of Marilyn's gun-toting extortionist;. He was probably the kind of guy who aimed his Ruger sideways. Palm-down, I sat.

"Jesus gives every one of us a vocation, a calling. Have you let him call to you?" The Converter leaned his pink head toward me. His hair was as sparse and fine as a bathroom rug.

I smiled, prettily, I hoped. The best tactic seemed to be silence.

A half-hour later, I was twenty dollars richer. But how I had martyred myself for it. I left The Converter in one of the cubicles, mopping his brow with an ancient linen handkerchief that someone had lovingly embroidered "RW." I rejoined the other dancers at the back tables.

Some of them turned from their conversations to look at me in sympathy or disbelief.

"That guy is so not worth it," said Plantagena. Her white A-cup bra made a precarious toehold for her breasts.

"You're right." The twenty dollars hadn't made me feel any better. I was even more mentally exhausted than before.

"I can't believe no one showed up for Vanessa Sassy. This is her last show. Hope she made her money earlier in the week."

"Vanessa Sassy's here?"

"She's on next." Plantagena nodded toward the stage, where Salamé was doing yoga positions in front of an audience of two. She held the positions for long seconds, like an art model. Her song was "Do You Think I'm Sexy."

"That's Salamé's last song."

I was too depressed even to go backstage and let Izzy cheer me up.

The volume cranked the speakers into a crackle, then into the first over-amplified twangs of "Friends in Low Places." The features always played their music louder. It was supposed to add to the frenzy. Vanessa Sassy plunged onto the stage a moment later, did a handspring down the runway, then scurried up the pole like a lumberjack at a contest. The two baseball hats bobbed to follow her movements. I slumped deeper into my chair. What had happened to this Saturday night?

Izzy emerged from the dressing room. Instead of assuming her customary position of vigilance a discreet distance from the stage, she sat right up next to it, on one of the barstools. She smiled up at her girlfriend. Vanessa Sassy flipped into an upside-down position on the pole, held herself there with her legs, and reached to unfasten her bra. It was white and rhinestoned, like an Elvis costume. She tossed it. Izzy caught it. The bodyguard threw a bill on the stage.

The porn star began her spiral down the pole, blowing kisses in all directions. By the time she touched down, it was into a puddle of money. Following Izzy's lead, all the dancers had flocked to the stage.

A cluster of bangled arms dropped great percentages of the night's pitiful earnings at Vanessa Sassy's feet.

We hollered for her and she hollered right back. For her inspiring air guitar during Wynonna Judd's "Girls with Guitars," she earned The Converter's twenty. Money-wise, the night was a lost cause.

Backstage, Isabella was neatening a day-glo sheath dress on a hanger. "Isn't this a great color? I call it dildo pink." She grinned. I watched her smile wiggle over her molars. It really was cute. "That was fun, huh?"

"Yeah."

"Sorry it's such a bad night." Izzy hung the dress inside a fattened garment bag. Cantilevered bras add a lot of bulk to luggage. "Don't let 'em see you suffer."

"Okay."

Vanessa Sassy emerged from her private dressing room. She was dressed in blue sweatpants and a warm-up jacket that reminded me of the shell of an insect.

"Hey, Aisling, thanks again," she said. Though we were the same height, she had to bend to give me a hug. "We had a great time. Tell Geoffrey good-bye for me?"

"Sure."

"You look awfully glum. I'm sure the apartment thing will work out. Keep on Mose, he's a pussycat at heart."

"Right."

"The dogs are already in the limo. We've got to go. But listen, I was wondering if that black gown of yours is for sale?"

"What black gown?"

"You know the one with the feather boa collar and the gold stitching?"

Plushious Velvett's show-stealer. It had been in my locker at work since the day I'd come to ask Mose Junior where to forward it. Some of the dancers must have modeled it, we did that kind of thing all the time. Vanessa Sassy looked at me innocently, using a fingernail to scratch off extra mascara. She must have known that thing would never have fit me.

"Well, it's not really—"

"Look, I think it would be perfect for Reno. Our next stop. They love over-the-top stuff like that, the tourists are expecting real glamour, you know. I don't have time to get anything else custom-made. We start there on Monday."

"The thing is it's not—"

"I could give you fifteen hundred."

"You're a lifesaver." I couldn't believe it.

"I have big hopes for Reno. A hot new costume ought to pay for itself. As Dolly Parton says, it costs a lot of money to look cheap." Vanessa Sassy laughed. "Does that mean it's sold?"

"Of course." I dug it out of my locker. The porn star dipped into her

148

belly bag and peeled fifteen hundred-dollar bills from a stack of them.

"Thank you," I said. "You don't know how much this means."

"It's okay. I just can't help but spend all my money the second I get it. I don't have a dime in the bank. Besides, Izzy couldn't bear that look on your face. She's looking better, isn't she? Don't bother to hang it, Izzy. We've got to go." They planted good-bye kisses on my forehead. Isabella's felt soft. She promised to write. She chucked my chin. Vanessa Sassy's hair was clean and bright against the blue shell of her departing outerwear. Izzy tossed Plushious Velvett's embroidered robe over her shoulder in a fireman's carry. It slithered down the back of her leather motorcycle jacket. The twin feather-boa cuffs of its caftan sleeves beat against the heels of her black boots as she walked away.

Chapter Eighteen

I didn't have time to think about the immoral thing I had just done. Plushious Velvett and her mysterious fate had lost their urgency to me after I'd been presented with a bill from Marilyn's drug lord. The implant hadn't been Plushious'. I didn't have time to think about what that meant. I had fifteen hundred dollars in my fist. I hurled my clothes on, gave Mose Junior fifty for missing my final set, and hailed a cab home. It was one a.m. by the time I slammed the heavy security gate of our apartment behind me, drawing curses from the homeless people trying to get some sleep on our sidewalk. I yelled sorry. The Saturday night was young. I only hoped Geoffrey would be home.

The figure cuddled in the afghan on the couch was Hugh. Television light turned his hair green like a towheaded kid's who'd spent the summer in the pool. He was asleep, but the volume was cranked so loud that I didn't hear the distinctly sexual moans coming from his bedroom until I was a foot from the door.

I breathed relief that Geoffrey was home, and knocked.

"Robert?" said Geoffrey. The moans stopped. "We've been expecting you."

"It's me, look, I really need your help. It's life or death. Sorry."

"Aubrey," Geoffrey made a song of my name. "Not the best time. Gregor's here."

"That's good because we need his car."

"This moment?"

"I've got twenty-five hundred dollars and I need ten thousand by tomorrow night or I'll be killed. Get dressed. We're going back to Bloke's."

Geoffrey took my urgency as an excuse to go one hundred miles an hour over the Bay Bridge. Though he and Gregor had graciously emerged from his bedroom a mere ten minutes after my rude interruption, they seemed to think a transferrable death threat from a crazed drug lord was just some kind of a joke. Geoffrey was playing the rational Southern gentleman to my crazed Blanche DuBois. Gregor just seemed aloof, or maybe indifferent. Maybe a bit peeved. They were both half-drunk. I let Gregor have the passenger seat of the Renault, and squashed myself into the tiny space behind. Sideways, my hips grazed both the driver's seat back and my own.

"Don't spill that Scotch on my upholstery," said Gregor. That was his only remark as we made a meteoric flash through the fast lane, the bridge's retaining wall a gritty blur an inch to our left. The top of the convertible was down, which made me think of airplanes. With enough windrush over the top, wouldn't we take off or something? Whatever panicked comment I made was abducted by the wind.

Five minutes later, we squealed into a parking place around the corner from Bloke's. My hair was big and tangled, perhaps permanently. Thanks to gel, Geoffrey's and Gregor's hairdos were as perfect as ever.

Geoffrey offered me a hand to the curb. His other was occupied with a half-empty glass of Scotch and ice. He slurped at it.

"Is the booze sharpening your mental skills? Are you up for counting cards? I can't lose this money."

"Are you sure it's okay to leave the car here?" asked Gregor. He looked up and down the block. The Korean strip mall we had parked in front of looked deserted, the lights off in its noodle bar, grocery, and B-B-Q restaurant. A few cars prowled the drive-thru windows of the several nearby fast food joints. Street lighting was dim and no one walked the sidewalks. The Oakland night smelled like cinnamon donuts and chicken fried in rancid oil, and was aglow with fog.

"Don't you worry your pretty little head. Here, kill this cocktail." Geoffrey handed Gregor the glass. "You either, Aubrey. Don't you worry. A little drinkee only sharpens my arithmetic skills."

"You keep saying don't you worry. That worries me," I said.

Gregor drained the glass.

"Give me some of that," Geoffrey said, and began licking Gregor's lips.

"Can we please get going?" I said. They pulled apart, and Gregor resumed his customary pout.

All the bustle of the neighborhood had been pulled as if by gravity to Bloke's. The sidewalk in front of the place teemed with almost as many patrons as uniformed bouncers. Security was more sophisticated here than at Naughtyland. The bouncers were dressed in military-style black outfits, complete with a lethal-looking metal flashlight swinging off the belt. Patches that said 'Rathbone Security' were sewn over their breast pockets.

One of them took our driver's licenses and looked us all up and down. We were dressed more normally than Geoffrey and I had been the night before, and almost blended in.

"Any y'all cops?" he asked us.

"No."

"She a ho? No ho's."

Gregor pouted at me. Before Geoffrey completely collapsed with laughter, I kicked my roommate in the ankle.

"She's just a damsel in distress," said Gregor, fluttering fingertips over his temples to smooth his perfect hair.

"Thanks," I said.

"All right. We just can't have that kind of activity going on inside, understand. Go on in. Try not to cause trouble."

We all smiled sweetly at the guard as he gave us our licenses back.

We passed into the cauldron interior. The place was even more crowded and noisy than it had been the night before. The smell was a thick mix of colognes, the yeastiness of beer, and the poached nitrates from microwaved hot dogs. A crowd, layers deep, pressed toward the bar. Behind it five or six bartenders pulled Budweisers. The jukebox played something slightly off-speed and too mingled with the din to be identified. The area around the hot dog tray, I noticed, was the only spot free of activity. Geoffrey proceed to the back room without any of the nervousness he had previously shown. I tried to figure out whether that was a good sign or a bad one as I followed. Gregor had joined the riot at the bar, where he bought the first of many rounds of cocktails.

"Whiskey sours are not my drink."

"Not my drink, either, baby." Geoffrey and Gregor converged over the Renault's gear shift. Their kiss slopped drool onto its accordion base.

I was driving. It was five in the morning. Needless to say, Geoffrey had lost all my money. He was right about whiskey sours. He'd had my account up to five thousand before they'd switched to them from Manhattans.

The boys slowly melted downward in an embrace pinched by the bucket seats. Gregor had gotten stuck with the back. Both of them were too drunk to drive. It had been six months since I'd driven a car, and I didn't know my way around Oakland. So I drove aimlessly and fast on the deserted streets, hoping to find a big green sign to point the way to the Bay

Bridge. The activity suited my mood. Dawn light percolated the fog.

We were out of gas. I pulled into a station, one situated in the crook of an on-ramp to a highway that pointed west. I was suddenly quite ready to go home. The drunken make-out session that prevented me from shifting above second gear was the last straw.

"I'm getting gas," I knocked on Gregor's back, since it was topmost. "Who has money?"

Geoffrey popped up. His hair looked like it had been shuffled. Even gel has its limits. "You have money. You have ten thousand dollars, cold cash! To pay the hitman!" He patted my cheek dreamily. "Just check your back pocket, sweetheart!" His blue eyes were half-closed.

A suited man filling his Civic and no doubt on his way to early Mass swiveled his head toward us.

"No, I needed ten thousand dollars. You, Geoffrey, gambled away my ten thousand dollars. That could quite possibly have cost me my life. Now, I need ten dollars for gas. Who has it?"

Gregor slumped, passed out, in danger of impalement on the gearshift. I pushed him into the back seat. Geoffrey turned him over and extracted his wallet.

"Did that happen? I'm sorry." I looked up from pawing through Gregor's twenties to see my roommate's eyes magnified even bigger with tears. "I'm sorry, honey, I'm sorry I lost your money." The tears fell. More followed. He grabbed my hand and kissed it.

"Look, I've got to get gas." I took my hand away from him and went to pay before I pumped.

I had no idea how to put the convertible's top up. Therefore myself, fellow tank-fillers, and passing motorists were treated to the warm-up yodels of Geoffrey's sob symphony. I fought the temptation to tell him it was all right. It wasn't all right. But I should have known better than to have handed Geoffrey my life savings and let him proceed in that state. It was my fault, I'd been desperate, and acted desperately. I'd have to think of another way to raise the money fast, that was all.

I've never been good around crying people. Geoffrey was in full jag by the time I finished filling the tank. When I climbed back in to drive us home and he teetered against my shoulder in contrite sobs, I didn't push him off. Halfway home he fell asleep and I drove into the city with my right arm freezing inside a sleeve soaked in tears and drool.

Half an hour later, I found a parking place. It was a good ten blocks from home. I turned off the ignition and sat. The absence of the sting of wind on my face was almost a numbing sensation in itself. I rubbed my eyes. The fog was sticky and cool and seemed to have invaded my brain.

I was now eligible for bankruptcy. I owed ten grand. What was I going to do? I could run. But then Marilyn would probably be killed and I would feel guilty for the rest of my life. No, I couldn't ditch Marilyn.

I could plead with the gun-toting heroin dealer for my life. I probably would, and it probably wouldn't do any good.

I could beg for money from my boss. Mose Junior was the most miserly man I'd ever met. He'd never loan out ten grand, even to save the life of one of his favorite busty brunettes.

I could grovel to Cash.

I could get Geoffrey's father's number off one of the old phone bills, tell him some story about how there was trouble and Geoffrey needed ten grand. Trouble, like a big sale at Macy's. But "that B-movie actor who fucked my mother in 1970," as his biological son referred to him, had been incommunicado lately.

I could blackmail Todd. Unfortunately, I'd already blown his cover to his wife and I wasn't sure anyone else cared that he went to strip clubs.

I looked over the Renault. A convertible, sure, but not fancy. No leather seats. No CD player. Gregor may have had money, but it seemed he spent it on clothes. Besides, he didn't seem to like me. We'd only just met, but I'd already interrupted his Saturday night sex and stolen his date.

As someone who valued my financial independence to the point that my career choice departed from polite society to achieve it, and as someone who cherished that independence precisely because it meant I didn't have to be dependent on some man, grovelling for money from Cash would be excruciating. But so far it seemed like the best option.

Didn't I know any women with money? I thought. No, I didn't know a single woman with access to ten grand. Except maybe Sue.

The back seat of the Renault crumpled Gregor. His feet hooked the side, scratching the red paint, and a yard opposite his face jammed into the passenger side's upholstery. I turned his head enough so he could breathe through a corner of his mouth like a swimmer. He'd lost a shoe.

Geoffrey slept curled like a cat over the bucket seat and gear shift. He was smiling softly. Neither woke up when I slammed the door of the Renault.

"What's the matter? You look like you've been up all night," said Doña Rosa. The fat on her upper arms simmered as she slid a plate of huevos rancheros across the counter for me. The bean smell of El Quake-

O was momentarily overcome by the prickle of steaming red salsa from the egg dish. "Cheer up. With a handsome blond boyfriend keeping you awake, you should be smiling."

I shook pepper over the layer cake of eggs, tortillas, and red sauce. Doña Rosa's cooking always came already heavily salted.

"You sent him down here already this morning. You want more, eh? Finished with the four orders of huevos con tocino? You make each other very hungry, eh?"

I couldn't work up a smile for her. I didn't have the energy to shatter Doña Rosa's fantasy that Hugh and I had a voracious sex life happening just twelve feet above her steam trays. I don't know where she'd gotten the idea, but she got such vicarious pleasure out of it. She winked me over to the window seats. Fatigue made my stomach queasy and gave me the feeling that I was moving my arms through water. I figured breakfast would help. I cut a giant bite of the huevos. If this was to be one of my last meals, I wanted it to be good.

What, I thought as I chewed, had Hugh been doing buying four big breakfasts? Geoffrey and I were accounted for, that left only him and Zan and Vivian, three, in the apartment. Maybe he had gotten lucky. Not that he shouldn't. Not that he met a lot of women, though. Suddenly I had the urge to see him. I needed him to help me get Geoffrey out of the car and into a bed. Gregor, I'd leave to fate. I finished the plate of eggs faster than I should have.

"Come back when you're ready for lunch. I'm making platanos. Big ones, eh?" Doña Rosa laughed as she waved me out the door.

The consumers of three of the orders of bacon and eggs were lined up on the living room couch when I hauled myself up the stairs. They were two women and one man, all blond, all with the same overprocessed shoulder-length hairdo. Their heads reminded me of dandelions gone to seed. The women were petite and zipped into shapeless warm-up suits. Their faces were also identical. As if on some silent cue, they smiled at me at the same time. The man wore black jeans and a thin leather jacket cracked with age. He held a baseball cap by its brim, and tapped it over his other fist. Styrofoam clamshells veined with red grease lay open at their feet.

"Hi," said the man.

I said hi back. Hugh pushed backwards out of the kitchen, two mugs of coffee in each hand.

"Here you go. Hi, Aubrey." He put the mugs on the floor next to the styrofoam containers. "Your guests are here."

The identical twins with the hula hoop act. I'd forgotten.

I introduced myself. They were Shy Anne on the left, Shy Honey in the middle, and Barry, their road manager, on the right. They all smiled sweet and talked slow, but maybe that was a perception created by my fatigue.

I went to get them some cream. Hugh followed me into the kitchen.

"I'm sorry, Hugh, I had no idea they'd be coming so early. Thank you for taking care of them."

"They took the red eye from Pittsburgh. They arrived at three a.m. I wasn't quite sure where to put all of them, bed-wise. Fortunately they don't seem tired. Which I can't say for you. Where have you been?"

I rummaged through our refrigerator, a model so old that the door was rounded like a soft white belly. I'd grown up with one like it, and whenever I pulled its handle the pneumatic sigh of its opening was coupled, Pavlovian-style, with Momma's voice telling me to stay away from that fridge or did I want to end up fat as my aunt Arkadelphia. Momma bought refrigerator magnets for the sole purpose of posting photographs of herself taken in fat years to that appliance. Profiles of her rounded belly under print mini-dresses were stuck on with fat plastic magnetized Oreos. The photos were warnings to me as well as to her. I got fat genes from both sides, she said.

Momma. Though she seemed to take pleasure in irritating me, I knew that she also loved me fiercely. If anything happened to me, she wouldn't want to go on.

In our refrigerator, I pushed around the tupperware filled with molding crock pot leftovers and a dish of margarine mixed with toast crumbs, but found no milk.

"Are we out of milk?" I asked Hugh.

"It's quite possible."

I stood up and slammed the fridge closed. I'd risen too fast and I suddenly felt a buzz of faintness. I was really tired.

"Aubrey, are you okay? Maybe you should get some sleep. I'll go to Safeway for the milk."

"Thank you. That's very sweet." I thought of telling him about my predicament, but I didn't want him to worry. Hugh was as poor as a monk. There was nothing he could do.

"Something's wrong?" Hugh began jiggling one of his Nikes.

"I'm just tired."

"One of those coffees is for you," he said. "I was just going to drink it to be social. Unless you want to go to bed."

"I can't. I need your help with Geoffrey. He's passed out in a car, about ten blocks away."

Hugh shook his head as he turned to leave. "Sometime, you're going to have to tell me what you all did last night. It sounds like a good story."

I hoped the ending would be happy. I went to get my black coffee.

Shy Anne and Shy Honey were worthy of their names. We chatted sparsely. I warned them about Mose Junior, and they said he'd seemed very nice on the phone. They were from a town near Pittsburgh, not too long out of high school, where they'd been voted, as a unit, most likely to succeed. The entire hamlet of Heinousburg knew about their rising porn-stardom and supported their hometown girls all the way. Barry was a neighbor; they'd grown up with him; he'd used their parents' garage as practice space for his metal band. Barry nodded politely throughout our exchange, then excused himself to go to the can. When he came back we moved the twins' luggage sets from behind the television to my bedroom. I saw when they popped open a suitcase that they'd brought little more than baroque lingerie and a collection of toys. Real toys, children's toys: teddy bears, deflated beach balls, plastic pails, yo-yos, swimming rings with duck heads, even a yellow Tonka truck. Behind me, Barry excused himself politely so that he could roll two pink hula hoops past. They made their maraca noise. He leaned them against the futon, spent a few seconds rearranging them to where they wouldn't roll away.

Hugh finally came back with the milk. There'd been a line. He offered his bed to Barry with a warning that we'd be returning shortly with the occupant of the room's other single bed who was in an inebriated state. Barry said it was cool and man, he knew that feeling.

When Hugh and I got to the small parking space where I'd managed to wedge the Renault, a ten-minute walk from our apartment, the car and its passengers were gone. I hadn't noticed before that the curb alongside where I'd pulled in was painted yellow.

"Think they got towed?" I joked.

"Should we be worried?"

"About Geoffrey? Are you kidding? I'm sure they just woke up and went over to Gregor's. They fell asleep in the middle of things. Or maybe they went for food. It's Sunday, the whole Castro's brunching."

"I suppose," said Hugh, looking worried. He didn't like it when his roommates were unaccounted for or out of sorts, so his day was going badly all around. For some reason I couldn't bear to see sweet Hugh's day go badly.

"Remember in *Gone With the Wind*," was my attempt to cheer him up, "when Rhett says to Scarlett I'm sorry for the man who ever really loves you?"

"'God help the man who ever really loves you, Scarlett. You'd break his heart.'"

I'd yet to discover any scene in any novel, even a girly novel, that Hugh couldn't recall with perfect clarity.

"Right. Well, god help the man who ever worries about Geoffrey."

Hugh thought about it for a moment. He didn't seem reassured. "In my estimation," he finally said, "that quote applies more precisely to you."

I trudged back to The Tender Arms, refusing Hugh's offer to help me move out my things. I had so few things there, only a small cache of clothing, some milk and Earl Grey. Under the circumstances I had no interest in retrieving them. For all I cared, they could hit the sidewalk as fast as Sue and Todd could hurl them there. But I had to have some excuse for returning to Mose Junior's former apartment. I couldn't tell Hugh that my real mission at The Tender Arms was to grovel for money.

The familiar cabbage smell of the lobby had been replaced with the artificial tang of CarpetFresh. The red rug had taken on a new, brighter shade, and the dead insects had been wiped from the insides of the glass lamps. Somehow the lessening of the physical gloom seemed ominous, like cosmetics applied after death.

I dragged myself up the stairs. I knocked on Cash's door, then again, louder. No answer from him, but on my third try his neighbor's door opened.

"It's you." Todd looked tousled. Stubble raised a gray shadow across the lower half of his face and his blow-dry bouffant had collapsed. His ring hand held together the gray wool blanket that served as his covering. The blanket began inches above his nipples, like a prom gown. His shoulders were bare above it.

"Just getting up?"

He glanced behind him. With a quick step he was in the hall and his apartment door softly shut in his wake.

"For your information, I slept on the couch last night. Badly, too. Thanks for ruining my marriage with your big mouth." By the time he got to 'big mouth,' Todd's voice had decomposed.

"Is that what's ruining it?"

"Yes!"

"Where's Cash?"

"I don't know. How should I know? That's the last thing on my mind. Look, you've got to put this right." Todd's faced squinched, I couldn't decide whether with anger or pain.

"Sorry, no. Your failing marriage is the last thing on my mind. Got any paper? I've got to leave Cash a note."

"You've got to go in there and tell her it isn't true. I can't go on without Sue."

"I'm sure. The financial entanglement alone would take a team of lawyers years to sort out."

"No, of course we signed a pre-nup. You don't understand, we were high school sweethearts in Danville, then we went different ways for college but the separations never worked out and when it came time for grad school we—"

"God. Save it for the couples' counselor." Where was Cash? It was nine in the morning, Sunday. He was either out for lattes, in bed with a girl, or on his way to the wine country for a tasting tour, in which case he wouldn't be back in time to supply me with payoff money. I pounded on his door again.

"Did you know you're cruel? Look," Todd grabbed my shoulder with the hand that wasn't pinning his blanket. "I love Sue. You might not understand that or think it compatible with how you see me. I know you think I'm an asshole. I can deal with that. I just can't deal with her thinking that. And it's not true. You see one side of me and judge. She knows me, and I know she loves me, and we're in this for the long haul. I want you to go in there and tell her what you said to us yesterday was just out of spite, and it wasn't true."

"You seem to make a practice of lying to your wife." I turned from Cash's door to look at Todd. Nighttime crust still glued the corners of his eyes and mouth. He didn't blink as he met my gaze. Moments passed before he dropped his eyes, flung his hand off my shoulder and opened his door.

"Wait," I said. "How much is it worth to you?"

I found Sue in her kitchen, making cappucino at her gleaming espresso machine. She wore a Madras print robe that skimmed her ankles as she moved the small distance between refrigerator, counter, cupboard. Her skin was a pale contrast to the dark ovals of her glasses' frames and the sleek brown darts of her hair. Unmoussed, it fell in points aimed just below her chin.

Todd had warned her I'd be coming. Then he'd dressed and left, passing me a thousand dollar check on his way out. It was a start. Sue didn't say anything as she frothed a pitcher of milk. I sat at their table—even in their remodeled kitchen there was no room for it so it was stationed against the living room wall. The table was rough wood, antiquish, laid with a linen runner lengthwise, set with glowing silverware, linen napkins cinched into wooden holders, and yellow plates. The plates weren't the cheery breakfast yellow my mother favored as an optimistic backdrop to her war against food. Sue's plates were more of a mustard.

Sue handed me a tall latte mug brimming with frothy milk.

"You have something to say?" She sat across from me with her coffee. Sue looked like a hot compress had been held to her face. It was alternately swollen and sunken, pink across the swells and mauve in the hollows.

"Yes. Do you know anything about the whereabouts of the woman who was in 301 before me? She's missing. That wouldn't have anything to do with your gentrification plan, would it?"

"What? What are you implying? I don't know anything about her. If you want to know more about that lady, you'd be better off asking Cash." She looked sad.

Her petty jealousy humanized Sue. I didn't know if it was more pathetic that someone else had gotten her man or that the object of her jealousy was Cash. At any rate, she seemed to be telling the truth. I decided to believe her and to get this interview over with.

"Todd asked me to lie to you and say he's not visiting strippers. That I made it up." I got up to go.

"Wait." She fiddled with her double-tall mug, clicking its handle with her fingernails. "Sit down." Her tone was neutral, drained. Nothing like the uproar I'd expected. I sat. "I already knew about Todd's little indiscretions. He just didn't know that I knew."

"You knew?"

She went from fiddling with her mug to fiddling with the feathered points of her hair. "For years, of course I knew. It's not hard to tell."

"I'd imagine not."

"If you keep any kind of track of the money, you know a lot goes missing somewhere. Then there's the usual, clichéd stuff, lipstick on the collars, smelling like cheap perfume, all that."

"Right." Lots of Naughtyland's customers refused to lapdance with girls who wore perfume for fear of bringing the strange scent home to their sharp-nosed wives. "So that's why you hate us." I watched Sue take a small sip of her cappucino.

"How much did he spend on you?"

160

"Sixty or eighty. I don't remember. Another time he spent a hundred on a blonde from Chico with a phony French accent."

"I didn't know blondes were his type."

"You're going to stay with this guy?" It was none of my business, and I barely knew Sue. But it somehow felt like we were having a heartfelt chat.

"Yes. You can't imagine that?"

I watched her rub her smooth forehead with her fingertips. We were the same age, I realized, though our lives had taken different routes. Her forehead-rubbing was the gesture of a grandmother smoothing away accumulated wrinkles.

"Do you know anything about love?" Sue continued.

"Well, I was married once. But it was mostly for financial aid."

"Love takes work. Todd has a lot of good qualities, and we have a lot in common. We have common goals, a good working partnership. He's supportive of my career and doesn't expect me to pump out kids. I'm not a romantic. I don't expect things to be one hundred percent perfect. I don't expect to find my prince or my soulmate. I'm under no illusions that our relationship is something special, nor that it should be. In fact it seems to me quite ordinary. That's comfortable, that's good enough."

"Why are you telling me all this?"

"Confronting my fears, I guess."

"I'm not your confessor."

"Right. Thanks for listening. I just want you to see another point of view. At this point in my life I'm just too busy to provide daily blow jobs. If Todd gets them from another source, well, it saves me the trouble." Sue rose, arranged her robe, and returned to the kitchen.

Lapdancing, I'd often wondered about the wife of the customer, the woman who'd married the man such as the one underneath me, who had his hands clapped securely onto the bare ass cheeks of a hired stranger. I realized at that moment, watching Sue's retreating Madras above her bare, tanned feet, that she was right. I'd felt unconnected to the wives. Arrogantly, I'd thought I was different, that somehow I was able to sniff out a customer-type and would certainly never stoop to dating one. Perhaps I'd even seen the wives, for a moment, as contemptuously as their husbands saw them.

The wives were a strong absence in Naughtyland, implied by wedding rings and well-fed bellies, rarely mentioned except by old men with sad stories of loss. I'd been a wife briefly, but long enough to know that while a wife is expected to bear ageing and sagging and bullying and lack of desire from her partner, a man needn't. He may even be expected not to.

Their husbands' presences at Naughtyland implied the wives' perceived inadequacies: too old, too saggy, too fleshy, too demanding. Above all, it implied that the wives were guilty of the gravest marital sin: Not Putting Out.

I rose and left.

Chapter Nineteen

I knocked on Cash's door again. Still no answer. I found some eye-liner in my purse. Lacking paper, I scrawled a Cleopatra Kohl message in one of the square indentations on the Victorian-era panel. 'Come see Aubrey, urgent', it read, the last two words made faint by the swift erosion of the soft black powder. I went upstairs to wait.

Although I wouldn't have thought it possible for someone in my agitated state, I must have fallen asleep. A rap on the door jerked me against the scratchy discomfort of the love seat. I was still trying to orient myself when the knocks were followed by DeeDee's voice.

"Anyone home? Yoo hoo."

"Coming, hold on." I slogged my way over to the door. I was barefoot, though I had no memory of removing my chunky clogs.

"You have a very dirty face," DeeDee said in greeting as he scooted past me. "If I were my Momma, I'd give you a spit bath right now. But I'll spare you that indignity. Momma never got used to having running water."

"Sorry." I went to the kitchen, stuck my face under the tap. The smell of rot from the drain did as much to revive me as the blast of tepid water. DeeDee handed me a towel. "What time is it?" I asked him.

"Two, two-thirty."

"Shit."

"I know. Sundays go by the fastest of all."

"Is Cash home?" The towel smelled like sour milk.

"I don't keep track of the hours of the class enemy. I'm here to advise you that it would be best to move your things out today. You are here to move out, right?"

"I was just going to leave this stuff. Most of it's Vivian's."

"That clothes pile?"

"Vivian's."

"What about that laptop?"

"Hers. She's writing her thesis on it."

163

"Well if she can't come for it today, I suggest you remove it for her. Anything you care about, take. Now, today."

"Okay. Why? Is something happening?"

"Oh I wouldn't know about that. I'm just saying, landlords give you a notice but they don't always abide by its terms. You're a fool to leave anything lying around after they've given you a notice. They're vultures and they've got the law on their side, right?"

"I suppose."

"So you'll be out of here by tonight?"

"That's the plan. What are you going to do? Do you still think you'll have to move?"

"Oh definitely. After this, I'm going to have to move." DeeDee kissed me on my scrubbed forehead without complaint of the sour smell it had acquired from the towel. "Don't furrow your brow. That's my parting advice, cookie. That and drink aloe vera juice."

"Well, let me know where you go. It would be a shame to lose touch." In my heightened emotional state, I felt like I was saying goodbye forever to an old friend.

"Don't hug me so hard, honey, I'm losing my breath. Better. Of course. Listen, all I know is I'm going to Oakland. I've heard the apartments are big enough for real parties. And if anyone can singlehandedly give it some culture, well, not to toot my own horn. And if you don't come to my parties, and bring your wonderful stripper friends, I'm going to take revenge."

"Guess I better figure out how to get across the bay."

"I'll let you know how as soon as I figure it out for myself."

After DeeDee left I went to fix myself a cup of Earl Grey. I figured the pain in my stomach wasn't due only to anxiety but also to hunger. Without food in the apartment, a strong cup of tea would have to fill it. I waited for the water to boil, bracing myself against the sink.

I gulped the tea at the sink as well. When I leaned to rinse my cup, I noticed Comfortable Shoes.

She was prying apart her Venetian blinds and staring at me. When I met her gaze, she made no move to snap the blinds shut, as she had before. Our eyes held each other across our kitchen sinks. Then, after long moments, her blinds winked her out.

Well, her life would perhaps be less entertaining when I was gone, I thought. Though if spying on my mugging and my dishwashing was her current standard of fun, there wasn't much further for it to sink.

When the knock came on the door a few seconds later, I was half-convinced it was her. I moved as silently as I could through the living room and put an ear to the door. I kept quiet and didn't open it.

"Anyone home? It's Cash."

The opening door sucked the smell of his cologne into the apartment. His usual attire had been replaced by neat dark khakis and a sportcoat. His hair was sleek with gel. He even had shoes on.

"You said it was urgent?" A smile flirted over his giant teeth.

"It is. Sit down."

He did, on the love seat. He pushed the flannel shirt that I'd been using as a pillow aside, and stretched an arm leisurely along the sofa's back.

"What's up?"

"I need nine-thousand dollars by sundown. Believe me, it's life or death or I wouldn't be asking you."

Cash blew out a breath. He seemed deflated in more ways than one. "Wow."

"I'll pay you back."

"It's not that. It's, well, for one thing it's Sunday." He ran a thumbnail along a furrow of his hair.

"Right."

"Banks are closed."

"You don't have cash?"

"Some. Maybe about four grand in various hiding spots. You're welcome to use it."

"That's not enough."

"Are you in some kind of trouble?"

"Good guess."

"Okay," Cash pushed up a sleeve. "I've got this watch." He unclasped it and held it out to me. "Might get you something on the street."

The watch was heavy and golden, with a square face, and felt solid as a nugget in my hand.

"It's a Rolex. Could get you a couple thousand," Cash said. "If it was a weekday—"

"You're a life saver. I'll pay you back."

"No rush. What's the trouble, if I may ask?"

"Just a debt coming due."

"At sundown? What is this, the wild west?"

"Probably a little after sundown."

The Rolex read three-fifteen.

The pawnshops that lined several blocks of Mission Street appeared to all be closed on Sundays. I pushed my way to the final one through sidewalk throngs squeezed into bottlenecks by the stores' overflow of produce, underwear, flip-flops, and extruded plastic shapes. Mission Street shoppers were faced with the duel tasks of laying in supplies for the week while simultaneously conducting a kid rodeo. Most of San Francisco's children appeared to live in this neighborhood. A stratum of activity scurried at knee level, yelling, stumbling, running, and causing near-accidents among the bloated seventies models prowling up and down the street.

I stopped to look into the dark window of Salud Dinero Amor Pawn. A row of guitars hung over a stack of bongo drums, a computer of a type I hadn't seen since the lab in my first year of college, and a saxophone dipped at a jaunty angle. Further in the back, cases displayed a jumble of cameras. A shallow tray above them could only have been reserved for jewelry.

But the sign said it all. Cerrado.

Damn. I wrapped my fingers around the heavy watch, which I'd stashed in a front pocket of my pants for protection. Pickpockets seldom went for the front ones. Where did they take their stolen goods to sell them?

A small girl banged a proportionally smaller stroller against my calf. A blond doll fell out of it and cracked its head against the sidewalk. The girl glared at me.

"Carmela, dile lo siento." Carmela's mother had a stroller of her own to push, filled with a chubby-cheeked baby dressed in blue. She seemed impossibly slim for someone who'd just had a baby. She leaned over to pick up the doll, smoothing its blond curly do. "Dilelo!" She tucked the doll back into the neon pink fabric of the play stroller.

Carmela shot me a look of pure hatred and would have plowed her stroller right into my leg again, potential dolly concussion be damned, if I hadn't made way by pressing myself against the glass. As it was, her path was cleared and she took off down the street.

"Sorry," her mother said. "You just can't do anything with them."

"It's okay," I gave a wide berth to the children as I made my way the eight blocks back to Sixteenth and Mission. It was the drug supermarket, I reasoned, perhaps it was the Rolex supermarket too.

I got many propositions while trying to sell Cash's Rolex on the corner of Sixteenth and Mission, but a serious offer for the watch wasn't one of them. I learned the business from a few minutes of observing my competition: a short man in a cowboy hat who wore ladders of gold bracelets and watches underneath the long sleeves of his snapped-up, pointy collared western shirt. His technique was to stare straight into the middle of the street, presumably to scout out approachers from both sides. On finding a target, usually a white man or a youngish woman, he'd mosey next to him or her for a few steps, unsnapping his cuffs to display his merch, until brushed off.

I couldn't quite match his subtlety. Running up to passersby and asking did they want to buy a Rolex for two thousand was perhaps ineffective technique. But at the time I didn't see this clearly and decided Cowboy Hat was undercutting me. However, he didn't seem to be making any sales either. After watching him urinate against the Walgreen's dumpster for the second time, I began the walk home. Dusk was falling. I'd just have to give Marilyn what I had.

Cash had scared up two thousand five hundred dollars from various hiding places, which included underneath his laptop and scrolled into the four latte mugs of his Crate & Barrel baby blue set. Sue, he said, had contributed two thousand more to the loan. She felt bad for evicting me, he said. It was customary for landlords to compensate evictees with cash. I didn't remind him that Mose Junior was the evictee. I had Todd's check for a grand which I could sign over. And I had the Rolex. Perhaps my hit man was lacking a watch.

Altogether it was worth maybe seven thousand five hundred. It would have to do.

Back at 301 The Tender Arms, I made a small bundle of the money and the check, and wrapped it with the watch. The clasp closed around the stack of hundreds at its widest setting. I said goodbye to Mose Junior's apartment. Vivian's stuff was still strewn around, including her laptop, winked out on the floor. Why hadn't she come for it? She knew we were getting evicted. My plan was to hightail it for home after dropping off Marilyn's money. I'd see Vivian, who was sticking close to Zan lately, and Zan always stuck close to home. I could remind her to pry herself off her girlfriend and come and retrieve it.

Comfortable Shoes—I still couldn't think of her as Bay or, as DeeDee insisted, "a charming woman,"—was watching me blatantly now. I was aware of her face in her window, following my movements. She must have gotten the message that I was in debt to her boss. To reassure her, I waved the packet of bills for her to see and pointed vigorously in the direction of the Lotus Leaf, then waved goodbye. She must have understood my sign language. To my surprise, she lifted a hand in an almost-wave and let her blinds fall shut.

My leather jacket was flung open-armed on the Murphy bed. I put it on. Even in August, cold clamped onto the city after sundown. I took one last look around the room for anything I'd left. I smoothed the bedcovers over the inadequate mattress, uselessly, I thought. Whatever yuppie turned the place into a co-op would certainly be trading in the Murphy bed for a loft or, if scared of heights, a bedstead of refurbished cast iron that had been broken in by an authentic Southern Hillbilly, refitted with a quilt-top mattress and dressed with two hundred and fifty thread-count Egyptian cotton. I left the blankets in their tangle and flipped up the bed hard enough to jar the mattress a bit further from the rusty coils that stamped a pattern to its underside.

The handgun I'd stashed between mattress and coils clattered to the floor. I spun away, afraid that it would go off. It didn't. I wasn't even sure it was loaded. For a nanosecond, I considered taking it with me. But I realized that would turn my potentially dangerous encounter with the heroin dealer into a definitely dangerous one. So I left the gun where it was, on the bedroom floor.

I didn't consider that it might even the odds.

Jones Street was dark. Streetlighting was occasional in the Tenderloin, and night had fallen completely by the time I left The Tender Arms for good. Cash's Rolex read seven-fifty. I walked the few yards toward the Lotus Leaf's door slowly, to allow plenty of time for the short man in Dockers and a baseball jacket who stood in front of it to be let in. The man wiggled with anxiety, tapping a foot, drumming fingers against the door. The security light made a full moon of his face. The door opened, he scuttled through it, and the light went off.

I took a breath and took the man's place at the door. The security light winked on. It felt strange that it gave no heat. I rang the bell. No one answered. After a moment, the light clicked off.

"Hey," I rang the bell again. "I'm here to see Marilyn."

A heavily accented female voice spoke. "You got for her money?" it said.

"Yes," I answered, speaking the word in a few directions so it wouldn't miss the invisible intercom.

The door opened in front of me. A short, middle-aged Asian woman with a graying permanent looked me over. She was underdressed in a sleeveless silk shirt, black pedal-pushers and open-toed heels. Peppermint pink dotted her fingernails, toenails, and lips. "Show me money," said the woman.

I dug the wad out of my leather jacket pocket and presented it to her. "Marilyn with customer."

"It's okay, I'll wait." The woman retreated but made no welcoming gesture, so I pushed past her inside. The Lotus Leaf's foyer was barely lit. One votive candle struggled to shine through layers of red glass and white netting. A small television blared blue from an endtable between two facing loveseats, the room's only seating. The areas without the cold shine of the television acquired a bloody glow. My hostess went to sit in front of the television. The room was hot enough for her to be comfortable in summer clothes, and I felt sweat crinkle from my forehead and armpits. A corridor led off to the left without drafting away the thick scents of incense and body odor.

I sat opposite Silk Shirt. Between us, a coffee table held a shrine to Buddha. The small ceramic figure was sculpted in an arms-wide gesture. The Buddha smiled while several sticks of incense, held aloft in small brass urns, pumped curls of smoke around him. Scattered store-bought cookies encircled his feet. My human companion was silent. We both listened to the chirpy banter between the hosts of *Entertainment Tonight*. I hoped Marilyn wouldn't be long.

"How long has she been in there?" I asked, but the woman just shook her head. It seemed that prostitutes were typically hired by the hour, but an experienced one like Marilyn would surely orchestrate things to come to an end well before the hour was up. I picked my cuticles and tried not to breathe too heavily. The musky incense percolated down my throat.

Entertainment Tonight ended and *The Simpsons* began. The short man who'd preceded me inside emerged from the hallway, smoothing his shirt with his small hands. He gave a jerky nod to the TV watcher, who didn't look at him as she buzzed him out. That hadn't taken long. Maybe twenty minutes had passed since I'd been let in.

It wasn't Marilyn but another slim, well-endowed young Asian woman who followed the short man into the waiting room a few minutes later. This newcomer looked at me curiously, but without really breaking her focus from a car commercial. She passed a roll of money to Silk Shirt as she sat to watch the television, adjusting her neon tube dress over her bosom. I could see that she was young enough for braces. Her neck was still wet from the shower.

The Simpsons was over before Marilyn emerged. An aging hippie in tooled leather boots and a fringe jacket had preceded her by several minutes, nodded to our hostess, and received the customary silent treatment as he was buzzed out. Marilyn gave me a strafing look, then went over to Silk Shirt and passed her some money. Marilyn spoke near her ear, in a language I assumed to be Thai. The woman nodded.

"You got the money you owe me?" Marilyn had turned around, but didn't bother to come closer. Her hair had lost its frenzied look.

"Yes," I stood up.

"Don't give it to me here. Come in back." Stilettos didn't slow her down. I followed her down the dark corridor, keeping my bearings by focusing on her minidress. It was the color and consistency of bubble gum.

We passed a doorway on the right and one on the left before she turned to unlock a door with a key rubber-banded to her wrist. The hallway went on, I noticed, to lead to several more doors. Maybe eight or ten in all. Nevertheless it was quiet, no sounds of pleasure. Perhaps business was slow. At the end of the hallway, a small table covered with a red tasseled cloth served as a second shrine to Buddha. A stick of incense smoldered on it, giving the hall a musky overlay to the mildew and body splash blend. All but one of the candles that surrounded the plump figurine had gone out.

The room was as utilitarian as a urinal. There were no windows. The bed was a single and dressed in a gray sheet, the wattage was dim, and the furnishing consisted of two boxes of Kleenex and a basket on a plastic nightstand. The basket had a pink ribbon around its handle and gave the room its only accent. The basket was filled with packaged condoms. A door led to a bathroom. Neither of us sat on the bed.

"Hand it over."

I did.

"What's this? I don't want a watch." She unclasped Cash's Rolex and threw it onto the mussed sheet. Her fingers began to flick though the bills. "This isn't ten thousand." She stopped counting the hundreds and looked at me with the same fierce expression as the little girl whose dolly I'd concussed.

"Look, I didn't have time to come up with that much. It's seven thousand five. Or will be, once you pawn that Rolex."

She held the bills in her hand like a dirty diaper. I thought she was going to throw them at me.

"Who do you think we work with here?" she asked me, pacing her words for a child.

"I don't know exactly. You didn't go into detail."

"Well we can't pay only part. This guy doesn't play around!" Marilyn

170

cursed and spun for a while. I made a move to leave, mumbling sorry I did the best I could, and I really should be going, but she was between me and the door.

"Where are you going? You stay."

"What do you mean? I kept my part of the bargain. Well most of it. You can't get blood from a stone. What's your spy going to do, threaten one-quarter of me?"

"Forget spy. You trapped now. When Johnny comes, I'll tell him you stole the heroin."

"Great. Thank you very much. That's not exactly what happened, you know." Marilyn just looked at me, then sat down next to where she'd flung the Rolex. She obviously and typically had no plan. Other than to rudely change mine. Perhaps I'd been shortsighted, but I certainly hadn't anticipated being held hostage. "What time's he coming?"

"Ten."

"What, so I'm going to sit around and wait for him? I don't think so." I felt the first stirrings of real panic as my situation started to sink in. Marilyn had the key to the door, and had already proven she could overpower me.

"Yes."

"You might want to give a girl more than twenty-four hours notice when she's about to owe a hit man ten grand." I had a vision of myself working off the rest of 'my' debt in indentured servitude to Johnny, the newest latch-key kid at the Lotus Leaf, my cubicle key rubber-banded to my wrist. I'd prove the mysterious white slavery Momma had always warned me about was more than a myth.

Marilyn looked toward the door. We heard low tones, a man's, then a woman's. Footsteps passed. "We're in this together now." She wiped her nose with the back of her hand. I realized then that she was crying.

"Look," the bed creaked when I sat next to her. I decided to try a good cop approach. "Why don't we be in this together by running away from here right now? You can get pretty far with that money I just gave you."

She shook her head slowly. "Johnny's spies everywhere. They know me. I can pay them not to tell some things but not that. A girl missing is too big deal. There's no way out. Except to pay."

I couldn't think of anything to say. I felt helpless.

"That was my plan. To pay Johnny ten thousand and run. Run and hide before he learned I sell Big Brother's heroin to get the money."

"A good plan."

"But now he'll learn I stole it. He'll learn and leave us for the—"

"How will he know it's you who stole the implant?"

"No one else here has the balls."

Something buzzed. Marilyn ignored the sound the first three times, then slid off the bed to press a button on an intercom beside the door.

"What."

"Timothy here for you."

Without taking time to smooth her bubble-gum dress or to do something about her tear-streaks, Marilyn opened the door, stepped into the hall, and slammed it behind her. I listened to the slide of the bolt as she locked me in.

I spent my time alone first trying to pick the lock, then examining the tiny bathroom for an escape route, then sitting on the bed thinking about my situation. Occasionally I heard murmurs and footsteps in the hall.

It seemed unbelievable that I was about to die. I pictured Momma and Eb picking through the shit stains on the Tenderloin sidewalks and then the musky, dark hallway of the Lotus Leaf, dodging teenaged prostitutes held in slavery to retrieve my body. It would be kitchen gossip among the family for centuries, repeated to enliven dishwashing, quilting, wood-splitting, or any other tedious chore:

"She died where?" "In a cathouse." "Mmm, mmm, I always thought Darylynn should never of had children. On account of the pills. And that husband a hers, didn't he die drunk? And he was that child's daddy. How's her kidney trouble?" "Oh, it lays her up now and again. Now that new man a hers, I reckon he's got some fine younguns. His boy's an accountant up in Dayton." "Mmm, mmm." And lips would be pursed over hands snapping green beans.

I should have told someone what I was up to. I should have told Vivian, or Zan, or Geoffrey, or DeeDee, or especially Hugh, who had even asked. No one knew where I was. No one knew I was this deep in trouble. If I lived through this, I'd have to give people the opportunity to worry about me a little. I was independent and I despised fuss. Fuss, I decided in those moments, was preferable to a lonely death in a flophouse.

There was someone who knew where I was, I remembered. Not that it would do me any good. I'd informed Bay, the ultimate nosy neighbor, of my pay-off plans.

My thoughts turned to Marilyn. At least I'd had a chance at life. I was twenty-six. I'd been married and gone to college and then had a taste of independence, a chance to create a life that I wanted instead of the one I'd gotten stuck with. I'd done that successfully. Maybe that was all one could ask of life.

172

Marilyn had never had those choices. Her jadedness marked her as someone who'd been in the business for a while. She couldn't have been more than eighteen. Maybe not even sixteen. To get out of this situation, I realized, I'd have to help Marilyn make a good choice. I'd have to convince her that her life, and incidentally mine, was worth saving. I'd have to convince her to run despite the risks to herself. I consulted the Rolex. I had fifteen minutes in which to do this, before the clock struck ten.

I heard a key in the lock. She pushed open the door. She'd washed her face. I'd been half-expecting her to be followed by Timothy, but she was alone. They must have used a different room.

"How'd it go?" Any comment seemed better than the tense silence.

"Same as one hundred times before. He's a regular."

"Did you try asking him for money?" Sometimes regulars were quite generous. One of my coworkers had gotten a brand new Isuzu Trooper from a devoted fan.

"No one come here with thousands. And why would he buy me out?"

"Right, then he wouldn't have his professional virgin girlfriend anymore. Marilyn, I'm telling you, you can get out of this life. Do your customers know you're an indentured servant?"

She shrugged. "Sure. No one's that stupid to believe that a bunch of Asian girls volunteered to come over here and suck on old white dicks."

"Right."

I didn't tell Marilyn what I was thinking. That was exactly what the customers had to make themselves believe. If these teenagers didn't come halfway around the world to willingly pleasure them, what did that make them? Not a single one of the Lotus Leaf's customers, not the fringe-wearing hippie, not the moon-faced jittery guy, not the dependable Timothy, wanted to see themselves as rapists, criminals, enslavers.

Marilyn glared at me. "I take only what I earn. No extras. Not anymore."

"That's smart, not to get into a customer's debt. You don't want to owe them anything."

"I had a good plan."

"You did. I have another good plan. Let's try to leave. I know you can't just walk out the front door but we can wait in the lobby and slip out when someone gets buzzed in. I'll help you get far away. We'll get in a cab and we're gone. Straight to the airport, you buy a ticket, you can get right on a plane. You're going to LA first, right? There's a shuttle flight every half-hour. You could be there two hours from now."

"Won't work."

"Why not?"

"You never get past Angela."

"I might not be as quick as you but I can run. Believe me, I'm motivated."

"I told Angela not to let you out."

"You what?"

"I told her not to let you out. You think I trusted you to stay here?"

"Apparently not."

"The only way out is through."

At least Marilyn had her religion. I'd been clutching Cash's Rolex in my hand and suddenly I felt its waistband etching my palm. The watch read ten-fifteen.

Johnny knocked on the door at ten-forty-five. I froze. Marilyn slumped.

He unlocked the door and entered. He was smaller than I remembered from Massimo's. His scrawny chest was further deflated by the giant geometry of his silk shirt. The shirt had quadrants of black and purple, streaked through with red. It would have clashed horribly with anything, but did especially with his pale yellow tailored trousers. He closed the door softly.

"Marilyn!" He looked glad to see her. His outfit flowed behind him like a muu-muu as he walked over to chuck her on the chin.

"Who she?" Johnny's English was basic, and I wondered why he was using it with Marilyn.

"Customer."

"Show her good time okay?" he laughed.

"Sure."

Johnny extracted a wad of cash from the front pocket of the trousers and chunked off a quarter-inch. He handed the quarter-inch to Marilyn. When he stretched his arm to give it to her, I noted that he wore a watch almost identical to Cash's. Johnny's had diamonds inserted where the numbers should be.

Then he slithered out.

"God. What just happened?"

"He paid me for the week."

"I thought he was supposed to kill us."

"He hasn't gone for the implants yet. He'll go just before Big Brother comes. Then he'll see one missing. That's when we get killed. Hopefully just you."

"Aren't you being overdramatic?" I remembered the feeling from my teenage years. Marilyn counted her money and didn't answer me. She wasn't exactly a typical teenager. "Well how does it work? Do they take inventory or something? How will this Big Brother guy know there's one missing?"

Marilyn looked at me scornfully. "They come in twos."

Of course. After a moment I asked her why Johnny had spoken to her in English. He's Vietnamese, she said. English was their common language of commerce.

"Are most of the girls here Thai?"

"Most. Some Vietnamese. Like Johnny."

"So how did you happen to get involved?"

"I wanted to come to America."

"Why?"

"Make more money."

"Were you in this line of work in Thailand?"

She nodded. "Father sold my virginity when I was twelve." She was playing with her fingernails. One snapped off. "Made money for him."

And I thought my father had been a bad deal. Early Lyle had had little to offer as a parent and even less as a husband, but he hadn't sold me. Perhaps he wouldn't have even had the opportunity presented itself. When I got old enough to figure out that I didn't have to put up with his abuse and threatened him with one of the weapons from his hunting collection, he'd ungraciously left. Momma begged him to come back, of course, and he did—for a while, but the crossbow incident was the beginning of the end of his tenure in the family. It seemed I'd gotten off easy in the father department.

"Who did your father sell it—you—to?"

"A man who took me to Bangkok. Then I work for him on Patpong."

"What's Patpong?"

"Sex area. Many girls from my town work there. Some boys, too. We sent money home. No work in the country."

"Did you want to go to Bangkok?"

She shrugged. "Make a lot more money there. There I work in pussy clubs. The first English word I learned was pussy. Pussy tricks, open can with pussy, throw ping-pong ball with pussy. Write with pussy, smoke cigarettes. Razors in pussy, needles in pussy. Shower Shows. Fucking shows. Customers pay more for hand jobs and blow job."

"You did those right there in the clubs? With everyone watching?"

She nodded.

"The men didn't mind having their dick sucked in public?"

"Cheaper that way. They could take us away for more money. They had to pay house to take us out."

"God. So how did you end up here?"

"Someone came into the club, said lots of work in United States. You won't have do it on a stage, and there's no hustle. They send customers to you."

"That does make it easier." The worst part of working at Naughtyland was the hustle. The fake smile, the humiliating cajoling. The competition. The feeling that your body wasn't good enough, that you weren't pretty enough. And if cajoling and body and hair didn't come together that night and you didn't make your stage fee, you'd go home owing money.

"Besides, I wanted to come to America," Marilyn continued.

"Why?"

She shook her head at me. She must have given up on bothering with her incredulous glare at my frequent stupidity. "Nothing for me there."

"But it's your home."

"I had American boyfriend. He was six months with me in Bangkok. He lived on Kao San road. I lived with him there. He paid for me to leave the club most nights. He cried when he left and sent money. He wanted to get married but I said no. He's too young. He wanted me to come. He's from near here. Mill Valley. I wrote him to tell him I'm coming. I told him where, so he could come and get me. He came and saw me once here. He never came back."

"That stupid fuck."

Marilyn shrugged. "I was stupid too. Too trusting."

"Did a lot of the dancers over there have foreign boyfriends?"

She snuffled. I realized it was her laugh. I hadn't heard her laugh before. The noise was short. "That's why we work Patpong. To meet a farang man for a boyfriend. A white man. It's only way out of the clubs."

"Looks like you found another way."

"Yes." She didn't add her ticket out came at the expense of two operations and a lengthy period of indentured servitude.

"At least he taught me good English. Most girls on Patpong say. 'You holiday? You buy drink? Want make love?' Anthony taught me to speak good English to the farang, but they like the girls who can't."

"Probably because it makes you seem dumber." My coworkers with accents were never at a loss for customers, a phenomenon that had led several women to adopt fake lilts and drawls during working hours. Marilyn shrugged.

"So he was the reason you decided to come here? What was his

176

name? Anthony?"

She didn't answer.

"When he came to see you, did you ask him for money to get you out?" Marilyn started to cry. "He said he already cashed his trust fund for me in Thailand and he didn't have anything left." I was afraid Marilyn would swing into full crying jag as she had the day before in Vivian's clothes pile. She didn't seem to be losing control, however. The tears for that particular disappointment must have already been shed.

"You were counting on him to buy you out when you signed on to come over here."

She nodded. Her head was bent forward, and hairs stuck to her cheeks.

"I'm sorry. He sounds like an asshole." What kind of person would leave his girlfriend to this life? My surge of hatred for Anthony gave me a new determination to live through this and to take Marilyn with me. And if public transportation ever made its sordid way out to the pleasant Marin exurb of Mill Valley, where the houses were all mansions blasted into cliffs and the millionaire residents hoarded their privacy and their views, by god I'd be the first one on it, and I'd hunt down the scoundrel. The mental image I had of myself disembarking a bus and looking to the left and to the right as I patted a pistol tucked in over my butt reminded me of guns.

Why hadn't I brought that gun?

Marilyn's sob caught. Someone was knocking at the door.

Chapter Twenty

I'd been holding her hand, I didn't know for how long. We both seized up at the sound. I felt the bones underneath my palm fan out between her fingers, like cards in the hand of a poker player.

A screech in Vietnamese followed. The door was kicked. It hiccuped in its frame.

Marilyn caught her breath. She reached over me to one of the boxes of Kleenex, extracted a pink tissue and applied it to her face. Hysterics continued in the hall, but Marilyn's expression had stilled. She stood and went to answer the door.

Johnny ricocheted into the room.

"Implant gone!" he screamed. He was waving his arms like a conductor. The motions gave him volume. "One gone!" he repeated, directly to Marilyn, who had recoiled and stood in the bathroom doorway to avoid her pimp's whirlwind entrance. Johnny did a one-eighty to look at me. His mouth and his forehead were tight as guitar strings, but even panic and fury spared his plump baby cheeks.

He snatched his hair and seemed to pull himself back around headfirst to face Marilyn. He returned to shouting what I assumed were accusation in Vietnamese. Not that Marilyn could understand him either, but the gist was clear. His gold rings and his wristwatch glinted through the fine black strands of his hair.

"She took it," Marilyn pointed to me.

And we'd been getting so close.

Sticking around at that point would have pushed the limit of sisterly solidarity beyond all reason. I bolted through the open door and charged down the corridor, sidestepping two astonished teenage girls who'd poked their heads out of their rooms. I made for the lobby. My legs were longer than Johnny's, and I was far ahead of him when I reached the waiting room of the Lotus Leaf. The incense had thickened the air so that I coughed as I assaulted the front door.

Of course it didn't open.

My clawing and cursing at the door continued to startle the two men in the waiting area. They'd been examining a photo album, probably of the Lotus Leaf's offerings. Each was dressed in a regular-guy uniform of crewnecked sweaters and jeans. Between the pewter television light and the candle, the men were lit like a 3-D movie.

"Let me out!" Silk Shirt, who now had a name, Angela, stared at me impassively. I repeated my request. She returned her gaze to the *David Letterman Show*.

The two customers were still looking at me, eyes wide. Then they were looking behind me. Then I felt a body collide into my back with the ferocity of a rat terrier. My wrists were grabbed. I fought the hold, straining my upper back and shoulders to open my arms out. I got one arm free. Johnny barked at the woman in front of the television while I kicked at his crotch. She hastened out of television stupor and bustled to some kind of activity. Out of the corner of my eye I saw the two customers jump to attention and hold up their hands, bleating.

Sure enough, Angela the housemother had pulled a gun.

"Okay, okay," I said.

"Come back," said Johnny. I assumed he was talking to me and referring to the back rooms and not to his two customers and referring to come again. They surely wouldn't, after a scene like tonight's.

"You know these women are held in indentured servitude, right?" I addressed the two men, who still had their hands raised and looked in bewilderment at me, Johnny, Angela. "They're kidnapped from Thailand. They're just girls." Johnny pulled me around the corner before I could say more. On the trip back we met no curious faces in the corridor.

Marilyn wasn't in her room. "Where's Marilyn?" I asked. Not that she'd done me any favors, but I didn't like to think about what they'd do with her now. Anyway, it wasn't like she'd betrayed me. She'd told me all along that the whole incident was my fault and that it was her intention to blame me fully for the missing heroin. And she'd been honest. "What'd you do with her?"

"Where implant?" Johnny steered me into a sitting position, back on the bed.

"It's gone. Look, I didn't know what it was. It was a mistake."

"You sold to cops?"

"No, no. I gave it to a cop only because I thought it was a body part of a missing friend of mine."

Johnny looked at me with an expression that mixed panic, disbelief, and contempt. He lifted a trembling finger like a schoolmarm. Then he whirled away from me and started pacing. "Forty thousand dollars… Forty my part! Forty per cent! Best quality! From Burma!"

He'd come up against the wall by the bathroom. He threw a tantrum against it, kicked and punched the plaster like a spoiled child. After a few moments he slowed, hung his head, and stopped the kicking. His hands stilled against the wall, formed into claws. White powder from the drywall dusted his loafers and made a little smattering around him on the linoleum floor.

He turned his head to look at me over his shoulder. "You no steal again," he said, and grinned at me fiercely. Then he left the room, slammed the door, and locked me in.

It was more than a schoolmarm's admonition, and I had what seemed like an eternity of time to ponder Johnny's parting words as I sat on the stiff, sheeted bed, waiting for whatever was to come. It's strange what thoughts come to you in what promises to be the final hour of your life. Mostly I felt the whole thing was surreal, wasn't happening. Then I thought about summer nights on Momma's front porch swing, in her time between husbands when she was alert enough to stir up pitchers of lemonade. She made it from real lemons and dozens of little pink packets of Sweet-n-Low. It was sweet as candy the way she liked it, and we'd pump the swing and listen to its joints creak and pop, and listen to the insects sing. Those were uncomplicated nights, the air smelled like the honeysuckle that weeded the property line. I thought of Momma wrestling with my hair each morning before school, and the time she'd been so dazed while trying to fix a meatloaf that she peeled away an entire onion into the compost bucket. Her dazed condition brought its cause to mind. I pushed away thoughts of Early Lyle.

I thought of Hugh and the way he put his hands on his hips sometimes, like a girl. Then I thought of Vivian, picking away the top layer of herself, at fingernails, cuticles, toes, eyebrows, while willing her thesis into creation. I hadn't told her to fetch her laptop. I envisioned it cracked open and sliding down the pile of her clothes once Todd and Sue threw them at the mercy of Taylor Street. That would probably be first thing in the morning. If it remained there five seconds without getting stolen then the neighborhood was getting either overpoliced or hopelessly soft. Shit. Viv's process for writing the thing had involved more break time than work time, but this particular break might cost her the laptop. Not that she'd seemed to have much content on there anyway. Mostly I felt bad about it because I'd failed her.

I'd failed Marilyn, too. And Plushious Velvett. And by walking right into this crazy situation, I'd failed myself. Why had I thought that Marilyn would be able to work with the seven thousand five? I'd just assumed she really had some money stashed away somewhere. She'd assumed the same of me.

I pressed cold fingers to my eyes until I saw reeling bronze strobes.

There had to be a way out of this.

I heard keys in the lock. Involuntarily, my knees came up to my chest and I hugged them. Pains crisscrossed my gut.

Marilyn was pushed through the door.

Her jewelry was missing, the gold necklace with a charm that she wore and her rings. The rubber band that had fastened her key to her wrist was also gone. Her face looked no different, not bruised, nothing any more swollen than it already had been. She looked away from me and stayed near the door, which had slammed behind her, its quick motion inhaling flyaway strands of her hair.

"What happened?"

"He fined me the twenty thousand." She smudged at a nostril, careful to avoid stabbing herself with her fingernails. Then she looked back at the wall.

"He really did just want his money, huh? Marilyn, I'm sorry."

"He's left us here for Big Brother. He wants me to live, to give him his money, but he can't tell Big Brother what to do. If I live that means another three years here."

"No. No. We're going to get you out. We'll work out some deal with this Big Brother guy and then I'll think of some way to get you out."

She just shook her head.

"Come and sit down."

She came and she sat. When I reached an arm around her shoulder and squeezed, she didn't resist. My hand wrapped easily around her thin upper arm. I felt the outline of its bone as I pulled her towards me. I tried not to think about the hard nudge of her breasts.

Marilyn's uncharacteristic malleability unnerved me as much as anything had that night. I had to think of a plan, fast.

I checked the time on Cash's watch. Midnight. My grip on that watch had never loosened. It was frozen in my fist. I let my fingers close around it again, and asked Marilyn a question. "When you came to see me yesterday, you said you paid someone to say they saw you here, and someone else to say they didn't. Can you pay them again to help us?"

She looked up at me with a blank expression. Perhaps what I'd said hadn't registered.

"Can we bribe our way out of here? What happened to your money?"

Marilyn sat up. My hand fell from her back. A moment passed and she still hadn't said anything.

"Did Johnny get it off you?"

"No. I have it. He was too crazy to remember about it."

"Great. And I still have the watch. So all we need is someone who wants them. Who do we give them to?"

Marilyn looked toward the door and I remembered the absence of the room key from her wrist.

"But he took your key to the room," I said. We couldn't get out the door to reach potential bribees, and I doubted they'd come moseying in to see us. Fraternization among the girls seemed to be frowned upon. I could feel my chest deflate. I rubbed my forehead. Okay, plan B. Had to be a plan B.

"Yeah but I have another one."

"You do?" She grabbed the second box of Kleenex and began ripping out pink tufts. The tissues pattered down onto the bed and the floor. A moment later she had the room key pinched between two fingers.

"Great! So, you let us out, we pay someone off and we're gone." My enthusiasm died when I saw the dismayed look on Marilyn's face. At least she'd gotten some of her zest back.

"Angela won't take my money now. They'll kill her if she lets us go."

"And the other person was my neighbor, Bay. We can't exactly reach her. Okay then. If Angela won't take money, we're just going to have to get her gun and shoot the front door open. She got to it pretty fast, she keeps it close by. Do you know where she keeps it hidden?"

"In the TV Guide. Last week's, always."

"And you know how to shoot it, right?"

She looked at me with some of the old disdain.

"Okay. So I'll create a distraction, meanwhile you go for the gun. Shoot out the door or the lock on the door or something and run like hell. Just don't shoot me."

"Where are we running to?"

"Away. I don't know, anywhere. Try to get a cab. We might get separated, so go to this address." I made her memorize my address on Church Street and hoped that, in the event that she actually got that far, someone would be home to let her in. She was repeating it back to me a second time when we heard the rhythmic thuds of someone running down the hall. We jumped to press our ears to the door. A female voice accompanied the thuds. The voice was screaming a Vietnamese word.

"Angela," said Marilyn. She was already keying the door open.

"What's she saying?"

Marilyn unstrapped and slipped off her high-heeled shoes. "I don't know. I don't speak Vietnamese."

She opened the door into a cluster of panicky girls, some half-wrapped in sheets, some naked, whipping up the thick incense smoke. I charged through them.They seemed to be going in every direction possible in the dim, narrow hallway, colliding with the walls, random as electrons. A middle-aged man appeared directly in front of me, bare chested and holding a shoe. His face was clouded by the smoke. I ducked around him, noticed the distinct tang of carbonization in the air. Something was burning. With my next breath I inhaled a lungful of the acrid air and clutched my chest, coughing. The coughing fit slowed me, and Marilyn passed on my left. I staggered after her to the waiting room.

When I got there her small body was braced around a handgun. Her finger was the only part of her that moved, wiggling for the trigger. Oddly, the inner door was already open. She was taking aim at the metal cube on the prison-like grille of the security door.

"Don't shoot!" I hollered and ran to stop her.

Chapter Twenty-One

Her shot zinged low, shattering the ceramic Buddha on the coffee table and whumping into the upholstery of one of the loveseats.

"What the fuck are you doing? Did you want to hit him? Come on!" I pulled her up out of the crumple she'd fallen into when I'd broadsided her. "Come on!" We pushed past two preteen girls who stood clenched together in front of the television. I released Marilyn's hand when we were up against the security grate and I was face-to-face with DeeDee. He appeared frozen.

"Come on, DeeDee, let go," I had no idea what he was doing there, but I'd never been so glad to see anyone. I tried to be soothing, but my voice was tuned sharp. I pulled at DeeDee's fingers. He was silent and staring at me in mute panic. He'd seized two of the security gate's bars. His face looked as though he'd been sprayed with a strawberry glaze. A drop of sweat followed the furrow between his eyebrows, moving slowly. His chin shuddered. The heat off his body was making me sweat as well.

"DeeDee, you're going to hear another noise, okay? Another gunshot. You'll be okay. You're not in Vietnam, you're in the Tenderloin, in San Francisco. It's Aubrey. You with me? Can you let go and take a step back? Marilyn, don't shoot him!" DeeDee remained paralyzed. I wrapped my hand around his for a reassuring squeeze. His fingers were cold and pulseless as the metal bar in their grip.

I took a step back. Marilyn shot, aiming through the lock down into the ground. The door reverberated and whistled in painful high pitch. She swung it open. DeeDee had dropped and rolled on hearing the gunshot and was blocking the sidewalk in front of us, curled up like a boll weevil.

The heat outside was more like an Ohio front porch night than like the wet chill of San Francisco in August. As I bent down to DeeDee I felt sweat bloom in my underarms and a dry blush ignite my face.

Then I realized the roar in my head wasn't only emotional. I turned from shaking his shoulder to look at The Tender Arms, and saw that the old tenement was on fire.

Flames wicked up the sides of the building from shattered windows. The brick had already blackened on the corner nearest us. As I watched, a fireball curled around a shred of curtain, rose, then evaporated, showering flakes of ash. An upturned audience crowded in the middle of Taylor Street. Three policemen were shepherding them, the swirling lights from their cop cars delighting two kids that Sheila was trying to keep together. I picked out Todd's tousled hair in the crowd, and followed him down to Sue.

He had his arm around her. Cash was in the crowd too, standing beside a thin blonde that I'd never seen before. For clothing, they shared a sheet. A downdraft blasted their blunt cuts back from their faces.

The flames from the window of 301 were tall and thin, flitting above then below the line of the roof. The most vigorous flames came from the apartments beneath Mose Junior's. Other windows spat black smoke. It was obvious the fire was spreading rapidly. No fire truck had arrived. City services were notoriously slow to enter the Tenderloin. I was surprised to see two cop cars already on the scene. All I could think of was that their drivers had been looking for streetwalkers to harass, or that the yuppie quotient in the neighborhood had finally reached a critical mass. Perhaps their premature presence was a success of Sue and Todd's Neighborhood Watch.

At my feet, DeeDee unrolled. "I'm okay. Big breath, big breath. I'm a grounded, steady object. I'm exiting my victim stance." He rocked to a sitting position, cooing to himself.

"When did this start?" was all I could think of to ask.

"Okay. There'll be a new star in my nightmares featuring the Viet Cong. That hooker was aiming at me!"

"No she wasn't. She's not a hooker, she's a slave. And she was trying to shoot out the lock on the door so we could get out."

"Well that wasn't obvious. Nearly scared me to death." DeeDee clutched a hand to his heart. "Help me up." He wrung the hand I offered.

"Sorry. We had to get out of there. Are you okay?"

"Oh, I suppose I'll live. I'll consider it aversion therapy."

"The building's on fire," I told him. My left side was cooking, my eyes drying out from the nearby heat. We were raising our voices in proportion to the screaming hiss, like rock concert feedback, of the flames.

"I know. I was looking for you. When I arrived I warned the lady behind the desk about the fire. Calmly, mind you. Evidently she panicked, at any rate she ran off screaming. You're okay?" He squeezed my arms, feeling down their lengths as though inspecting a fryer.

"What was she screaming?"

"Fire."

"How did you find me?"

"Bay told me you were here when I was evacuating her from The Tender Arms. Don't worry, everyone got out okay."

"She told you I was here?" Bay had possibly saved my life. I hadn't gone to the Lotus Leaf without informing a friend after all.

"She trumps your average nosy neighbor. She knows everything. You just have to speak her language to get it out of her."

I looked up to her kitchen window. Bay would have had a clear line of sight not only to the spot where I'd found a valuable breast implant, but also to the Lotus Leaf's front door. Her window exploded outward as I watched, the blinds flailing in the tortured air. Two floors beneath it and to the right, DeeDee's windows pumped fire with the ferocity of a Cold War-era weapon. A familiar sweet smell enriched the bonfire scent. The flames must have gotten Clem's crop.

"But your apartment!"

DeeDee's expression was strangely serene. "I warned you before about what anxiety does to your face. It's worse than ten years under the ozone hole." DeeDee was practically shouting by the end of his sentence. The noise of the fire was escalating. We gave up trying to have a conversation.

Someone must have finally translated Angela's cries, because teenage girls wearing little other than high heels clustered on the short space of sidewalk between us and the Lotus Leaf's doorway. Whatever men had been flushed out of the place must have crept away.

No one resembling Johnny or Big Brother seemed to be hanging around. The crowd was dotted with American officials. I was safe for the moment.

I remembered Marilyn and looked for her, but she was gone.

Cop cars squatted at either end of the block. Maybe that was why Big Brother hadn't shown up. He couldn't exactly plow the limo, or whatever his wheels were, right through them. What kind of car did gangsters favor these days? Probably one of those big SUVs that could pass for tanks.

"Shall we take a closer look? Everyone likes a fire. Besides, I want to hear what it's like in there," DeeDee was looking over the frightened, huddled girls. "Looks like kindergarten recess."

"And I don't want to meet the principal."

"Let's go blend in," DeeDee reached for my hand and we walked

186

toward the street crowd, both of us staring at The Tender Arms. The heat was violent but the fire's primary assault on the senses was its noise. It boomed. It found things to burst, to crackle, and to weld, and it belched their demise out of the building's windows. I thought of DeeDee's personal effects: the spiderweb curtains, powdery books, wicker, shellac. No wonder the flames bloomed biggest from his windows. I squeezed him with a hug as we walked, but a firestorm liquifying his beloved ghetto rooms seemed to be one trauma that didn't aggravate DeeDee's vapors. He seemed entranced, almost joyful. At the time I attributed his odd mood to an unexpected permutation of his shell shock.

In fact, the fire also mesmerized the rest of its audience. The permanently mesmerized Clem stood off to one side, hands jammed in his pockets. He didn't seem to be registering much of the event. Cash, I noticed as DeeDee and I approached The Tender Arms evacuees, a process made slow by DeeDee's weight on my arm, looked awed. His blonde accessory pulled the sheet tighter under her arms. Her expression combined thrill and embarrassment.

"I got my notice today," DeeDee was saying. He leaned into my ear so I could hear. We headed toward the back of the crowd, skirting the shell of the most intense heat. "Thirty days. Isn't it precious?"

"You're kidding? Eviction? On what grounds?"

"Shhht! Tell you in a minute." We passed Gloria, whom I'd first met as Cowboy Boots, and whose rayon eveningwear slithered behind her in the downdrafts. She wailed to a silent, pale boy in black stovepipe pants hemmed inches above his white ankles. The boy appeared to have been recently shocked one notch above utterly bored. Nico, the artistic neighbor I'd yet to meet, I thought.

"None," DeeDee finished.

"What?"

"None needed." He stopped. We faced the fire from the back of the crowd. Black-red firelight wavered the hollows of his face. Crisp shadows knifed between the pleats of his reflective hair. "It was the perfect capitalist crime. Our clever class enemies used the Ellis Act."

"What's the Ellis Act?"

"The Ellis Act is a tool of rich landlords who went whining to the Board of Supervisors that they weren't making money fast enough from their overpriced slum property. They wanted the option to evict all tenants and get out of the rental business. Our scum-sucking Board gave them the Ellis Act."

"So they can sell the building?"

"They can let it go condo and make a few million bucks."

"Exactly what happened here."

"Oh, it'll happen all over the Tenderloin now. Us non-Yuppies are history now that the richie riches have decided to make real estate out of the slum. I should have seen the buy-out coming. Sue and Todd are such condo people, really."

I blinked against the dry scorch in my eyes. When I opened them, I found Sue, watching the fire from in front of us. She stood motionless, pinching herself into her thick robe, brown hair melted down her neck. Todd reached around her shoulders to hold her against his side with one hand, and held his other to his forehead.

"Well their condos are turning to ash now."

"Oh, they've no doubt got insurance. You can't get rid of the bad element in the neighborhood that easily, but this ought to slow them down."

The fire seemed to have reached a plateau, the noise now steady and loud, but the heat waning. Flames inched incrementally higher, creeping to fill the gap between floors. Would fire trucks never come? We watched five minutes longer, the crowd still silent, before I heard the first whisper of an approaching siren.

"In this neighborhood, they'd just as soon let it burn," DeeDee said. A few moments later he clawed my shoulder. "Isn't that someone you know?" he swiveled me to look down the block.

Approaching the onlookers, the cops, and the flames, in long strides down the middle of the blocked-off street, was Plushious Velvett. A shoulder bag beat against her hip.

"God." I shrugged DeeDee's hand off my collarbone.

She wore blue jeans and, I guessed from her quick gait, comfortable shoes. She came toward us, aiming her cigarette and her gaze at the windows of 301.

I called her name and pushed toward her through the crowd. She looked thinner, her features deprived of makeup's primary-color trim. Her hair was caught in two scrawny bleached pigtails. She stopped fifty feet or so from the perimeter of the crowd, and blinked away from the fire for a moment to look at me as I agitated my way towards her.

Finally she said, "Do I know you?" she asked.

"Hi. We worked together at Naughtyland. Then I was living here," I gestured to the burning building. Then I noticed her shoes—white Keds tied with a thick, glitter-gunned lace. "I can't believe you're here! You'd gone missing and, well, I saw your, poetry and I found—" An orange V-neck netted her breasts, the pair just as incredibly large as before. I shut up.

"Oh god. The poetry. You saw it?"

I nodded. She shook her head, the movement quick, like a terrier breaking a neck. Her pigtails were thin as antennae.

"My anger management counselor suggested that shit." She then imitated the tranquil cadence of a cult leader: "'I'm hearing that you feel like you might want to murder somebody? How wonderfully strong. How about channeling those feelings into a poem?'" In her own cigarette rasp she said, "No shit Sherlock, that wasn't going to work. You ever take anger management?" She put her Camel to her lips.

"No."

"Well it's a load of shit. I'm telling that to the judge next time I run into him." Camel smoke leaked out her nostrils while she spoke. "Which I hope is never."

"I thought—"

"I meant to burn those things, but I got out of there pretty quick. After that terrible night at Naughtyland—you work in a terrible place by the way— I never wanted to see this town again. Anyway, nothing happened. I didn't do anything to the creep. Not like I didn't have the chance." I had no idea what she was talking about. Plushious Velvett indicated the blackening hull around 301's windows. "Came back for my stuff. But here it is burning down. It's just my typical luck. My robe's in there. Cost me ten grand."

"Your robe—"

"Custom made don't come cheap. And my new thigh-highs, left them too. There goes another four hundred. Poof." She snapped her fingers. "More money this old girl has to earn back." She patted the crotch of her curve-hugging jeans. "I can't wait for the day I retire my pussy."

"You could always look for other work."

"Nah. You know, you love it, you hate it. It's a job."

"About your robe—" I considered just letting her think it had actually been vaporized by the fire, especially after hearing she'd flunked anger management class.

"Forget it. It's gone." She paused for another hit off her Camel. "Too bad too. The guys in the midwest really went for that one. Next week, Fort Wayne Indiana." She blew a final exhale and stomped the butt with the sole of her Ked.

I decided to take her advice and forget that I'd stolen and hocked her midwest-acclaimed robe. I'd repay her for it someday. "So, you're still working? I heard you didn't show up for your gig after Naughtyland."

She met my eyes. "You found the poetry. Talk to me straight here; you find a gun?"

"Yes."

"What did you do with it?"

"Put it under the mattress. Now it's burning up with everything else."

"Well that's something good come out of this fire."

We watched it for awhile. The siren sound was closing in. It wouldn't be more than a minute before the fire truck arrived. I didn't push Plushious Velvett to explain herself.

In a moment she continued anyway. "I left here ready to go to LA, to stalk and kill my plastic surgeon." She found her Camels in her purse and spanked the pack until one poked out. "I was really going to do it." The small flare of her lighting the cigarette was lost in the general glare. "Know where he lives, fancy house in one of those canyons." She whipped the match away and it extinguished itself on the pavement. "Had to drown my gun to make sure I didn't act on the impulse. You ever act on impulse?"

God. I had. But I'd yet to have an impulse of the caliber of Plushious Velvett's. I answered, "Yeah."

"Well it ain't worth a lifetime in jail. I spent the past week stalking him. Just made sure I didn't kill him."

"You followed him around?"

"Made his life difficult for a week." She shrugged. "It's nothing compared to the pain he caused me. Mine'll last a lifetime."

The fire truck had reached us. Echoes of the siren wail shuddered the block. The cops herded us to the far sidewalk. The pack's movement separated Plushious Velvett and myself. I got shunted to the far left, opposite the Lotus Leaf. The fire truck pulled up to The Tender Arms, its siren creating painful riptides in my eardrums. Then the siren stopped.

In my eardrums' recovery period I was deaf. The background hiss of the fire came back first. Then I heard someone yelling my name.

I froze, momentarily panicked. Then I recognized the yeller as Geoffrey. There he stood at the end of the block, grinning wildly and waving me over.

I ran for him. His inexplicable laughter gave me ample access to his breath, but it didn't smell like he'd been drinking.

"You should have seen the look on your face!" His words were slurred.

"What are you doing here? Nevermind. Tell me later. Let's just get out of here. You got a car?"

"Yes, in fact I have Gregor's car. I have Gregor, too, in the palm of my hand, have you noticed? There he is." Geoffrey pointed down Turk, where the Renault was parked about half a block away, its top down. Gregor sat perched on its trunk, legs hanging into the back seat. Vivian sat beside him. She provided the animation for the two of them, shaking her head, biting her nails. Gregor slowly tipped a flask into his mouth.

"I've got to get out of here. Let's go." I grabbed Geoffrey's arm and tucked it under my own.

"What! We can't leave. We still haven't gotten Vivian's laptop. She needs it for her thesis, you know."

"Geoffrey, do you see that giant fire?"

"Oh the fire, the fire. It's so lovely. Gregor is so brave, even after I warned him about your new neighborhood he agreed to drive her over here to get her little laptop. He had to take some ludes first to calm him down. That's what took us so long, waiting for them to go into effect and all." Geoffrey was moving as well as talking at the pace of a whiny child, and I had to pull him along.

"Well, you came too late. Her laptop is feeding that fire. The building we were living in is burning down. Come on, we're almost there."

We reached the car and its passengers overheard the last of what I'd said. Vivian didn't look as upset as I'd anticipated.

"I'm sorry about your thesis, Viv," I said. In my opinion, Vivian over-reacted to most events. To be fair, in her opinion I underreacted. The loss of several month's work, however unproductive, would have upset even me. Vivian surprised me with what she said next.

"Yeah well. I've been sitting here thinking maybe it was for the best. What a great excuse to get my advisor off my back. The building burned down! Better than my dog ate it. Where were you? I was worried you'd gotten caught in that thing when I couldn't spot you in the crowd. They said there was no one inside, though."

"I'm fine. I was in a building next door. Long story. Let's get out of here." I looked up and down Turk. The street appeared deserted except for a lone hooker, standing between two parked cars near the Taylor intersection, smoking a cigarette and watching the fire. She didn't appear to be looking at me. Still, for all I knew she was another of Johnny's spies.

"I want to drive," slurred Geoffrey.

"No." Vivian and I answered him together.

He got behind the wheel anyway, bouncing like a kid. The keys dangled from the ignition, but he seemed to have forgotten they were necessary.

"Nobody drives my car but me." Gregor's eyelids wobbled over his pupils. His eyes were bloodshot and his movement sluggish but his speech was up to tempo.

"I don't think that's—"said Vivian.

Gregor interrupted her, "You saying I can't drive my own car? Is that what you mean? Some people can't just say what's on their minds, can they? Can't say it to my face?"

He didn't know Vivian.

"Okay, dopehead," she began, "you're a mess from those barbs you're on. It's a miracle that you haven't totalled Daddy's little mid-life crisis sports car already. Your driving sucks in the best of circumstances—"

"Vivian—"

"Why don't you just say what you really think?"

"Oh Christ. Why don't you hear what I really think?"

A car approached from the direction of Market. It was an old car, wide and low, its headlights enfeebled. Hiphop music gave it a heartbeat. The streetwalker switched from looking at the fire to looking toward the old low-rider. She stepped from the protection of the parked cars.

"I'm driving," Vivian concluded.

"Not my car," said Gregor. "Not even if it was as decrepit a relic as this approaching jalopy."

The approaching jalopy slowed in front of the whore. She stuck out her chest. The car crept past her. She gave it the bird. Moments later the car rolled up to us. The driver was an Asian man, heavyset and tall enough for his head to almost bump the car's ceiling. His grub-like fingers were in the perfect ten-and-two positions on the steering wheel. His driver's-ed teacher would have been proud.

He was the chauffeur. Two men sat in the back seat. One of them was Johnny.

Chapter Twenty-Two

The car moored beside us. Johnny lunged forward. He pointed at me and shouted. Johnny's backseat companion played it cooler. He reached around the colored silk of Johnny's shirt to roll down the window.

I whirled and sprang into the driver's seat of the Renault, banging Geoffrey into the passenger's. I yelled something, kicked the clutch to the floor, spun the key, revved. We were blocked from street access by Johnny's pimpmobile, so I aimed the car for the sidewalk. The Renault heaved up onto it. A parking meter paddled by inches from my ear.

"What are you doing?" shouted Vivian. Somehow she and Gregor had made it safely into the Renault's back seat. We heard a gunshot. Close. The sidewalk was wide but I had to steer between the looming metal stalks of parking meters on my left and a chain-link fence that bordered a car park on the right. A parking place two slots ahead was empty. We jounced off the curb through it and I bore a hard right. The Renault just missed hitting a middle-aged woman who choked a fifth of booze in a brown paper bag. She was dressed in her bedroom slippers and a housecoat.

"Hey fuck you!" she said. "Bringing crime to my neighborhood! I'm calling the cops! Stop!"

I heard the jalopy's brakes and assumed it was trying to avoid running over this community activist. That should buy us some time.

"He's shooting at us. Any more questions?" I accelerated toward the intersection with Market.

"Wow," said Geoffrey. "Are we going fast?" He had a hand out in the airstream. He studied his fingers as he spread them apart then fit them back together.

Vivian snatched his sleeve to pull the hand back into the car. "Yes more questions!" She yelled near my ear. "Why is he shooting at us!?" The Renault bucked as I ground it through the intersection with Mason Street. The clutch caught high. I'd have to get used to that. Market would be next, and it had better be a green light. I didn't want to stall this thing out.

"Just get down!" The light ahead was green, then yellow. I checked the rear view. The feeble lights of Johnny's ride warbled half a block behind us.

I put the Renault in fourth and gunned through Market just as the light turned red.

"That oughta hold them." Streets south of Market were wider and in a grid, a practical layout designed to give access to the industrial plants and warehouses that had once flourished in that old flat part of town. I got up to sixty by the donut shop in the middle of the block. I knocked the gearshift around, looking for fifth. "Don't ride my clutch," said Gregor.

"They're shooting at us," Vivian screamed. "I'm sure they'll respect the law and stop for a red light. Where are you going?"

"I don't know, I'm getting away!" Vivian was right about our pursuers. A glance in the rearview mirror proved that we were being gained on. I pulled the car left onto Mission Street. The big car swung around behind me. Someone squeezed off another shot.

"Shit!" I said.

"Okay, that guy in the back seat is leaning out his window with a gun."

"Which guy? Crazy looking shirt?"

"No, it looks pretty plain. Who is he? Who are these people?"

"I think his name's Big Brother."

"You're fucking kidding."

"Don't think so."

I took the left at Fourth Street, cutting off the struggle for momentum of a 14 Mission bus, and steered us back across Market. The Renault scrambled over the four steel rails of the inset trolley car lines that striped the intersection with San Francisco's main street. The wheels spun. We fishtailed as I searched for a gear. I settled for second and the little car leapt back into the Tenderloin.

As I swerved up Stockton Street I heard a retching from the back.

"Jesus Christ. Are these people you met at that strip club of yours? How do you get into these things? You've got to lose them somehow," Vivian was saying.

"Okay. How?"

"Whatever you do, don't take Grant."

Union Square, a small block of concrete and greenery that tourists crossed to get to the theater from Macy's, flitted past on our left. The homeless people who lived there must have been stilled by the cold, or by whatever else numbed them. Scarcely a yelp acknowledged our meteoric passage. The slight incline of the street would soon bubble upward. We were headed for the small, close hills and the small, close streets of Chinatown.

The Renault wailed as I dropped it into a lower gear for the approaching hill. Geoffrey fell forward until acceleration clapped him to the seat back. I risked a look from the symmetrical canyon of low rises and parked cars and signs lit with Chinese characters that bore down on us in fast-forward, to take a peek at my roommate.

Geoffrey was asleep.

"God. Vivian, can you belt him in?"

"Look out!"

I didn't have time to swerve and narrowly missed a young white couple who'd been staring at each other and holding hands instead of getting about the business of crossing the street. Vivian fumbled with Geoffrey's seatbelt. Our roommate's head lolled over a collarbone. A sparkle of drool glossed Geoffrey's lower lip.

"Are they still behind us?"

"I saw them when we were back at Union Square. A few blocks behind. Why don't you put the top up on this thing?"

"If I knew how, I would have."

"Figure out how. Make that college degree worth something."

"I'm trying to drive. Look at all the fucking buttons on this dash."

"I'm trying to help Geoffrey."

Screams from behind us prompted Vivian to swivel. She hadn't gotten Geoffrey's belt on, but kept an arm around his neck to tether him to the seat.

"I think they hit that couple."

"Are they okay?" The last thing I needed was two deaths on my conscience.

"They're standing. I think they just got scared. Forget the stupid top. It's not like a piece of canvas is going to stop a bullet." Vivian finally clipped in Geoffrey's seat belt.

To our left, all the roads went up into a residential neighborhood of stairstepped Victorians and sidewalks pinned with saplings. The streets climbed at an angle that would throw the Renault's engine far above our heads. It looked scary. I took a right.

I slammed on the brakes. The Renault stopped, off-kilter, its front left bumper tapping the nose of the cab of a giant white truck.

"This is a one-way street!" Vivian's voice was far too loud in the sudden relative silence. The car idled mockingly and the truck made loud electronic beeps that indicated to those underfoot that it was backing up, apparently onto the sidewalk in front of a produce store. It was doing so slowly in order to maneuver between the two rows of parked cars that hedged the street. They left room for only one lane.

"We're dead," I said. Something brushed my shoulder and Gregor's face followed his arm until it was next to mine. I smelled his strong cologne and, fainter, vomit. He punched a button near an airvent and a whirr indicated the roof was beginning to unfold.

"That'll help," I said.

"Great driving." I couldn't tell from his whisper if he was being sarcastic.

The truck in front of us crunched backward into and over stacks of waxed cardboard boxes on the sidewalk, then sighed a gradual, airbrake halt and chunked into a forward gear. The beeping stopped and it rolled slowly toward our right headlight.

Vivian was looking out the back, through the oval plastic that served as the rear window. "Where are they?" She bit her nails.

"Good question." No traffic at all went past behind us on Stockton. "Maybe that woman in her nightgown really did call the cops."

Vivian shook her head. I picked a cuticle. The roof snuck over my head, met the windshield and stopped. I stared at the small dark windows of a store in front of us. The name of the store was pressed onto its windows in shiny gold Chinese characters. Old brick framed the windows and their display: a basket of gnarled roots. The door set into the middle was old and wooden. Old-fashioned apothecary jars were stationed in the window on the other side of it, big bellied and filled with powders. I could tell what that store would smell like, sun-stoked dust and the sweetish odor of ginseng. I went to a similar place from time to time to buy ant chalk.

Geoffrey sighed beside me and smiled lovingly in his sleep. Another good dream.

"You can go," said Vivian. The truck had moved.

I nudged the Renault between the cab of the truck, which now faced across the street, and a Volkswagen Bug rusting in its probably unofficial parking place. No cars were coming the right way down the street. I went slowly anyway, down a slight incline past other produce stands boarded up for the night and thin dark rowhouses, tufted with iron security grilles, and in some cases, with pagoda roofs. The street became two-way at the next intersection, at Portsmouth Square. Several young Asian men loitered underneath the marquee of the KungFu Theater on our left. The theater was the only place on the block open for business at that late hour.

"Well, no sign of them." I couldn't believe I'd lost Johnny, Big Brother and their thick-fingered chauffeur so easily. We'd been going straight up Stockton, and they'd been a block behind us. My only evasive maneuver since then had been the one right turn. "I guess we can go home."

"Just be careful," Vivian said. "Those guys in front of the theater are totally staring at us."

"Well, look at us. I'm sure I look as freaked out as you do, our boyfriends here are both nodding out, and there's vomit dripping off the side of our car. Of course they're staring at us."

"One's talking into a cellphone or something."

"So they have a cellphone. I hear everyone does." At Kearny, I stopped and prepared to take a right. I actually turned on the blinker. Then I noticed the street was one way and flipped the blinker to indicate left. Geoffrey was still sleeping peacefully, his ribbed t-shirt and jacket shirred around the two straps of his seat belt.

"You don't think it means—"

"Stop being paranoid." I made the left turn. Smooth, slow. There was no other traffic. It must have been between one and two a.m., and the party had moved from Chinatown's cheap restaurants to North Beach's cheap sex shows. I took a left onto Columbus, a diagonal street that divided Chinatown from Little Italy. North Beach was straight ahead. I headed up the slight hill toward a twenty-foot tall sign of a neon girl whose nipples and lasso blinked red. We paused for the intersection with Broadway. Bands of buddies helped each other across the street, some clutching each other's shirts in mirth or nausea. Many of them had shorts on, baggy ones that dripped past their knees. They were uniformly young white males. Out-of-towners who'd dressed for the weather long before nightfall. A last bunch of them wagged past against their light.

No menacing jalopies in sight.

I turned left on Broadway to head for the tunnel. We were approaching one of the hilliest parts of the city, and frustrated engineers had blasted a hole through one of them rather than try to stretch Broadway over it. It was for these steep hills that the cable cars had been invented by an animal-lover sickened from watching horses fall in their tracings and injure themselves as they scrambled for footing. I accelerated towards the tunnel's concrete mouth, flipping through the gears. We were back in Chinatown and a cluster of black-lacquer-fronted restaurants jostled up to the street.

I was watching the light at Powell Street, the last intersection before the mouth of the tunnel. It had just popped up to yellow, and I planned to gun the Renault underneath it when a behemoth of an SUV made a right-on-red onto Broadway, angled itself in such a way as to hog all lanes and bounced to a stop. The thing was large as a HumVee and the color of a capped tooth.

I punched the brakes. We skidded for a moment. The Renault stopped under the streetlight, close enough for me to see the logo that was affixed to the SUV's pearly white rump. "Cadillac," it read, prettily, in golden script.

A young Asian man leaned out of the Cadillac's front window, calmly assessing us. His bowl cut angled across the mouthpiece of the cell phone he was talking into. Before I could analyze the situation further, I found myself cranking the steering wheel to aim the car down Powell, hitting that street at a rate that prickled my hair even with the top up.

"Bloody hell!" Gregor spoke.

"It's not following us," said Vivian.

I gave a nanosecond glance at the rearview mirror. We weren't being followed. The street was also free of cars in front of us.

"Feeling better?" I asked Gregor.

"Change gears! Change gears!"

"We're going downhill."

"And don't ride the clutch. You'll be the utter death of my car. You get a car, you can ride your own clutch. You're paying for an oil change and a tune-up." His words came out at Chipmunk speed. It appeared that Quaaludes had delightfully chaotic effects on Gregor's nervous system.

"No problem. Next time I'm wanted by a Vietnamese sex and drug ring, you can drive." A slight incline slowed me before the intersection with Clay Street, which was fortunate. The Renault was twenty feet from the intersection when a black limousine prowled into the juncture from the right, just as the Cadillac had, and blocked the road in a similar manner. I didn't slow much, just hauled the car around to the left.

"They're trying to trap us!" Vivian said.

"Well what do you suggest I do? This isn't the easiest neighborhood to get out of."

Clay Street was leading us back into the overburdened alleys of Chinatown's heart. I was forced into another left on Grant by a strategically-placed sedan that hunkered like a linebacker in the intersection. The blocks were tiled so closely together in that old neighborhood that the sedan stretched across both crosswalks.

I'd been directed into a roadblock. A triptych of cars fanned across the upcoming intersection with Washington Street. Their headlights crossed like a musketeer pledge of friendship. It was impossible to see the drivers or the vehicles clearly behind the bars of light.

I ducked and hit the brakes. The Renault stalled. The car's abrupt stop jerked Geoffrey downward. At least he was headed toward the protection of the floor.

"Here we go," I said. But no bullets shattered the windshield or tore through the canvas top.

"Why doesn't somebody think of something?" said Gregor, and "What do these people want from you?" said Vivian.

"Heroin or else about a hundred thou."

"Great. Just explain later. Do cops come to this part of town?"

"No way. It's gangland. He wants me. I think you three should run."

"Unless you have a syringe of adrenaline handy to inject into Geoffrey's heart, he's not running. What's Plan B?"

We were silent then and the night outside was, too. I looked up and through the Renault's windshield at the rollicking fog. City lights charged the fog's underbelly. Narrow buildings, several topped with the silhouette of Chinese pagodas, framed the lighter sky. I didn't really see any reason why Johnny's boss would want to keep me alive. I picked a cuticle and waited for bullets to rent the ghostly scene.

Someone knocked on the window. My conscious passengers and I jumped.

Chapter Twenty-Three

He was a thin Asian man, more the age of a treasured protégé than of a don. His innerwear, polished-cotton shirt, shiny belt, black trousers, appeared shrinkwrapped to his body but his black suit jacket was loose enough to swing. The jacket's hem threatened to sully itself against the Renault as he leaned toward the window. Delicately, he parted its halves then pocketed his hands, pinning the jacket back.

He looked at us expectantly, like a waitress over an order pad. His black hair was layered and beautifully gelled. It darted toward the back of his head with the precision and the glint of a fish's scales.

"You guys are in big trouble," he said.

"No, not them. I'm in big trouble," I said. He didn't seem to be armed, though that loose jacket could have hidden a handgun.

"Johnny's gunning for you hard," the young man replied, rather politely. He'd finished looking me over, and nodded to Gregor and Vivian in the back. "Your friend okay there?" With a flick of his head and a flash of those gleaming fish scales he indicated Geoffrey. My roommate was sagging toward the floorboards, basted to his seat by the seat belt. The shoulder strap had snatched up his jacket and shirt so that their hems were at the level of his nipples. His right arm hung hoisted above his head. He looked like a small boy stuck and gone to Mommy for help getting into his PJs. Vivian tipped his head backward against the seat. His mouth fell further open and he snorted lightly.

"Seems to be okay, thanks for your concern. Look, I'm sure we can be reasonable. I can definitely pay Johnny back. Or Big Brother or whoever. I didn't know that implant was filled with heroin when I gave it to the cop—"

The young man stopped me with a gentle raising of his hand. "No need to go on," he said. "Your business with Johnny is none of my concern."

"Really?"

He shook his head.

"Then what is, exactly, your concern?"

He was looking past us down the street. I turned to look as well. Nothing there except the dark sedan and winked out shop signs behind it, stair-stepping down the hill. When I turned back he'd extracted a cigarette from a shirt pocket.

"Smoke?" he asked.

"No, thanks," I said.

"Yes, I'll take one." Vivian rarely smoked.

"Oh thank Christ, that's the only utterly sensible thing I've heard in hours. I'm so over this tension thing." Gregor uncrumpled enough to reach toward the offer.

The Asian man handed Viv and Gregor each a cigarette. A lighter got passed around and an instant later I was gagging on three separate smoke-streams.

"Can we just get this over with? What do you want?"

He slowly exhaled then answered me. "Whatever you did, it pissed Johnny off good. He's hopping mad."

"This is not news. Gregor, can you put the roof down? I can't breathe." Gregor reached over me with his cigarette hand to punch the button. The roof uncoupled from the windshield. "If you're not with Johnny, how do you know all this stuff about him being mad at me?"

"We hear everything he says over the cell phone. Whoever he's got running electronic security is failing him. Smoke bothering you?" He stood to exhale over the retracting roof. I examined the apprentice's jacket for gun-shaped bulkiness. It fell around him like a tablecloth, overdramatic, but smooth. "Johnny and his boss aren't coming in here," he said, dipping into a squat. He held onto my windowsill for support.

"They're not?"

He shook his head. "Not their territory. Ours."

"Great. So as long as I stay in Chinatown the rest of my life I'm safe. What are rents around here?" No wonder we hadn't seen the old jalopy lately.

He laughed. "Sense of humor."

"Look, what do you want again?"

"Johnny wants you bad. Soon as you're out of here, he's got ten, twenty guys going to be on your ass. You'll never make it."

"Thanks for the warning. So, you're keeping us prisoners to help us out."

The don-in-training stood to blow out another lungful. He moved his

201

cigarette daintily to the side as he leaned forward once again to speak into my window, the other hand still in the pants pocket. "We've got an old dispute with Johnny's boss but he doesn't get out much, know what I mean? You're going to lead us to him. Then we let you go, and you don't have to worry about Johnny and his boss no more because they're going to be dead. You saw nothing and you don't know nothing. No worries?"

"I'm going to lead you to him? I see. I'm rolling bait. No, that doesn't worry me at all." The interlocking headlights blocked progress and the dark sedan blocked flight. I wasn't looking forward to being in the middle of a gang shootout, and I certainly balked at leading Johnny and Big Brother to their deaths, even though they were scoundrels. But most likely they'd figure out what was going on and sensibly flee. And I couldn't live in Chinatown forever. "Do I have a choice?"

"Doesn't seem like it." He stood and walked to the curb, where he ground his cigarette out on a mailbox and reached into his pocket. When the pocket hid his hand I tensed and Viv sucked in a breath. The man extracted a handkerchief, shook it out, and wrapped the cigarette butt inside it as he walked back over to us. "The worst problem in this city," he said, "cigarette butts everywhere. Makes it ugly. You got an ashtray in there?"

Gregor said no the smell would be appalling. The apprentice collected Gregor's dwindled cigarette and Vivian's, walked to the mailbox, extinguished them on it, and returned, wrapping the two filters in the handkerchief along with his.

"Got to bury them, they say that's least polluting. Now. We want you to go up to Broadway and turn right," he said, "back the way you came. Go down the hill toward the Embarcadero. The last thing we want is to get caught up in the Tenderloin. They know everybody out there and got half of them on some kind of kickback. They'll probably intercept you either on Battery or on Sansome. They got people cruising both. With you as distraction, we'll move in. That's the plan." He repocketed the handkerchief and stuck a hand in to the car to shake Vivian's, Gregor's, mine. "I don't know what you did and I don't want to know, but you're giving us an opportunity we've waited for for years. They never leave their neighborhood. Take care." He gave the Renault a thump as he straightened, as though sending a horse off to graze. He headed toward the three cars, jacket flapping like a flag, his shoes and hair getting shinier with each step towards the crossed beacons of their headlights.

"Damn, that was weird," said Vivian. "Are you going to do it?"

"I want you guys to get out and go home."

"What? No way," said Vivian, but I felt Gregor's arm slink beside me. He grabbed the door release. He started to pull it, then relaxed. "Oh I can't do it. I just can't abandon my Renault. And just how is a person supposed to get home without a car, hmm?"

"Go up to Stockton and get the night bus. You're crazy. Go. Why endanger yourselves for no reason?" The three cars ahead of us had broken their molecular bonds and were moving, backing into side streets, executing three-point turns. They were all late model sedans like the one behind us, all in dark colors. They looked government-issue.

"And I'm driving," said Gregor. "You've ground my gears to dust."

"You are not driving," said Vivian. "You are high, or low, on Quaaludes."

"I drive better on them. They dull the edge of road rage. There's just no courtesy anymore on the streets."

The sedans vanished, quietly as civil servants. The narrow street darkened with their absence, and the empty rows of parked cars and the winked-out Chinese signs and the unfamiliar silhouettes made me just as uneasy as the encounter with the don's apprentice had. I started the car. Viv and Gregor quarreled down Grant, up Columbus, past the turn onto Broadway. We followed Broadway along the base of the rocky crag of Telegraph Hill. One of the dark blue sedans idled below the florescent marquee of a porno video store: 'Just in See John WaYne BobbiTt unCut', it read. The car faced downhill. Its driver revved the engine. The driver's cigarette twinkled at the car's window.

"Hop out here," I said, stopping the car. My passengers had become silent.

"We're not leaving you. Let's just get this over with." I turned around to look at Viv. I read her expression: don't make me argue. Then she looked worried. "Just go," she finally said.

Geoffrey grunted as we gathered speed down the long, sloping hill. A strut of the Bay Bridge soared in front of us, pile-driving confidently into silt, chest out, displaying its nighttime crust of little light bulbs along suspension-cable arms. We'd left lively North Beach and the sidewalks were empty. Low brick warehouses dominated by loading docks fit together across these dockland blocks. I whizzed past Sansome.

Nothing. We passed Battery.

Suddenly as if the Renault had been magnetized, metal rushed us on the short flat stretch between Battery and Front Street. Several jalopies converged on the Renault's trunk, and a couple more aimed for its front end, though they swerved before risking bent fenders. On the block ahead, four cars were charging us. They were arranged abreast in a fighter formation made silly by wall-eyed headlights.

I hadn't had time to slow down. When I saw the cars preparing to collide with us head-on I braked hard and the Renault bucked then stalled.

"Crimeny," said Gregor. I plunged the clutch and turned the key but got nothing. Geoffrey must have woken up. He started screaming. Or maybe it was still me. I heard a gunshot and ducked. A few more shots followed, clapping echoes against the low brick buildings. We had to get out of there before they swelled into a round of applause. I found myself cowered in the well of the Renault, down by the pedals.

Long squeals accompanied a smell of burning rubber.

"Get down! Are you crazy?" That was me to Gregor, who loomed above me, a dark upright shape against a background of yellow fog, large from below.

"What are you trying to imply? Why don't you just say it to my face?" He put his hands on his hips and looked up from me around into the night. Gregor was slightly built and made a small target, but I still expected a volley of bullets to punch through him at any second.

"You're nuts! Don't you hear that shooting going on? You're standing in crossfire!"

"For your information I'm not quite nuts but I am driving. You can't seem to treat my clutch with the respect it deserves."

"Would you just get down?" The Quaaludes had obviously oiled his nerves. In our current situation, driving did seem best left to him.

I crawled over the gearshift and over Geoffrey's heaving ribcage and into Vivian. She tugged me into the backseat. The squeals and gunshots seemed to have moved to our right, but it was hard to pinpoint the source of their echoes. I wedged first one hip, then the other, into the small space and huddled my head into the seat.

"Haha!" The engine caught. The car moved. Geoffrey seemed to be trying to soothe his screams into words.

"Just stay down!" Viv told him. She hugged him around the seat, staying low. Gregor sped off.

My stomach was the barometer of the Renault's path. I couldn't see where we were going, but our route had lots of turns. Gunshots speckled in the distance, then nearer, then away again. Perhaps they only seemed further, their noise drowned out by Geoffrey's hysterics. I didn't blame him, waking from a coma to find four pairs of headlights nearing his face. He probably thought he'd died and gone to hell. Vivian was trying to comfort him.

I smelled salt and putrid old death. We were at the edge of the Bay.

"Whoo hoo!" said Gregor.

"Are we away?" I had to yell.

"And it was a fine test of my driving skill." Gregor's voice boomed like a candidate's. I sat upright in the seat and the wind took possession of my hair. The bay lapped off to our left behind poorly-lit boatsheds and concrete docks. Condos rose on our right. We were speeding along the Embarcadero. I reached forward to pat Geoffrey.

"Just don't do a victory lap," Vivian said. "They forgot all about us when that other gang showed up. Have you ever seen such fast U-turns? Don't take too much credit. Listen. We've got to calm Geoffrey down somehow. Can you think of anything?" Vivian's arms were still wrapped around our male roommate, just under his armpits, clamping him to the bucket seat. She couldn't see that he was looking down at her grip, his face tight with terror, and that his yells were directed at her hands.

We passed between the inky bay and the steel truss—the same size as a tower block of condominiums—that fastened the Bay Bridge to land.

Geoffrey sucked in a long breath, and after that his screams shimmied into words. "I've got four arms! I've got four arms! I've got four arms!"

Chapter Twenty-Four

The air at the top of Twin Peaks sagged into our lungs. Gregor had driven us up into the atmosphere, to San Francisco's highest point, because it would calm Geoffrey, he said. They'd had some previous good trips there and those pleasant memories would take the edge off. Sure enough, as soon as the Renault had passed into the cloud, cold and wet as a dog's nose, that began halfway up the mountain Geoffrey stopped yelping and stuck his hands up like a roller coaster rider. Perhaps he'd worked out his misunderstanding about his arms. Perhaps the fog was inducing sensory deprivation.

By the time we reached the top we were well snuggled into the swirling whiteness, so that our faces and hands were scoured with cold. We parked. The fog exorcised Geoffrey. He and Gregor went for a walk disappearing into the cloud.

I had some explaining to do to Vivian, and I did it. I tried to keep the thread of the story coherent though I'd come down off an adrenaline high and was feeling as though I was on ludes myself.

"Why didn't you tell me this was happening?" Her head was propped on the tented fingers of her right hand. She'd been looking at me intently throughout my account of finding the implant, handing it over to Will, discovering I'd been in possession of twenty grand, wholesale, one hundred grand retail, worth of heroin, then meeting its previous thief and having to raise the cash to make it up.

"Well, I didn't know myself until yesterday. Didn't know the last part, anyway, the part where I pay off the drug lord or die. You weren't around. I had to act fast."

"True," she bit a nail and looked away from me. "Zan and I have been having problems. I've spent most of my time lately holed up with her. But I shouldn't have been so insular."

"Don't blame yourself. I'm sorry." I took her nailbitten hand. "Sorry about you and Zan."

"Thanks. I think I might have really finished it off this time."

"Zan's pretty forgiving."

"She's stubborn as hell. She never forgives a fault and she'll never bring it up again but you can tell she's remembering it next time you screw up. But back to you. I should have noticed something was up. Of course you'd never say anything. You don't need anybody, right? You're always in such a frenzy of independence."

We'd rocked the front seats forward to make breathing room and she picked at the tan vinyl of the seatback. We were both flopping forward against them in exhaustion. "What if the fire hadn't started and this Big Brother—could that really be his name?—had gotten to you?" She shook her head.

"Thanks for the vote of confidence. That didn't happen. We got out of there."

"And what if the boys and I hadn't come looking for my laptop?"

"I don't know. Okay, I'm glad you were there. Happy now?"

"Say you needed us."

"Forget it."

She smiled. "I'll be working on you even longer than on this damn thesis."

I imagined her laptop in a wave of purple flames, buckling like cellophane, *A Penetration of the Male Gaze,* or whatever it was, still burned into its screen. "Your thesis. It's my fault. DeeDee told me to make sure—" DeeDee.

DeeDee had warned me explicitly, earlier that day, to be gone from Mose Junior's and to have that computer out too, and to do those things by nightfall.

"Your fault? Who's this DeeDee person? Why are you internalizing whatever she told you? Give me a break. If I'd really wanted it, I would have taken it with me when I left. Right? Some Freudian thing kept me from it. Some part of me wanted to be rid of it. The whole thing is sickeningly transparent. Almost embarrassingly transparent."

DeeDee had warned me. I couldn't believe I had been so slow. DeeDee was The Tender Arms' arsonist. He'd warned me to be out of apartment 301. The fire had clearly started in his place. He told me he'd been the one to evacuate everybody. He'd been evicted. But that didn't matter. His hatred for Sue and Todd and what they stood for was motivation enough. He'd struck against the ruling class. He'd practically confessed his act to me, and probably thought he had confessed it, not counting on me to be too dim a bulb to catch on. But I'd been so preoccupied, these past twenty four hours, with Johnny, with Marilyn—

Marilyn. "We've got to get home. Geoffrey! Where are you? Let's go!"

No answer. Vivian said, "I know, that's the longest bathroom break. They're probably lost somewhere, or making out. We'll never get out of here."

"Yes we will. I've got to get home." I found the door release and wiggled out of the sports car.

"Where are you going?"

"Gregor?" Visibility was such that my hands fuzzed like television snow. "Come on!"

A figure that I approached turned out to be a visored telescope swivelled in the direction of the Bay. The view from Twin Peaks was inspirational in clear weather. I kept calling the boys, jogging the curve of the retaining wall.

I found them where the wall ended at the roadway. They were cross-legged on the pavement in a spot chosen for no particular reason: it was not sheltered from the cold, nor did it provide something to lean against, nor was it padded and comfortable. Vivian's guess about their activity had been right.

"We've got to go."

"Oh, surprise it's you. Always breaking apart our little rendezvous. I think someone is jealous," Gregor said.

"I swear I'll never interrupt again. But I've got to get home. I'm meeting someone there and I forgot all about her."

"I'm sleepy," said Geoffrey. "Sleepy. Kiss me again."

"Would you come on? Sorry." I was, too. They'd rightly had enough of me for the night. But I had to make sure Marilyn was at my house and get her out of town and tell her that her captors had run across some trouble of their own. I wondered how she'd feel about that, but doubted she'd show any gratitude. Gratitude isn't felt by those with no expectations of life.

Without speaking to me Gregor hoisted himself, then Geoffrey up. He dusted them off. He pinched his jeans at the knees and snapped their creases back. He led Geoffrey to the Renault.

"I called a cab an hour ago."

"I'm surprised you didn't go down to Market and hail one."

"Do I have chump written on my forehead?" She inclined her head for my inspection, looking up.

The striking feature on her forehead was a small constellation of pimples travelling up the hairline from her left temple.

"No."

"I'm not standing on Market for everyone to see me."

I'd found Marilyn. She was at the apartment on Church Street, tense and upright on the couch, glaring at the stairwell. She'd watched Geoffrey's and Gregor's stumbly ascent without changing her basic scowl, and she'd watched Vivian check her over from a distance with the same expression, showing some restraint, I thought, in not telling off my ogling roommate who'd never seen a sex slave before. The boys went to Geoffrey's room and Viv went into the kitchen.

Marilyn had no luggage and was still in her bubble-gum outfit. She sat feet apart, knees knocked together. The latex tube of her skirt didn't give her many options for knee positions. She smoothed a chunk of hair behind an ear with the opposite hand.

"Well I'm glad someone was here to let you in."

"I had to ring the bell for ten minutes before someone came down. Blonde lady said she was a porn star in the movies."

Shy Anne. Or maybe Shy Honey. What must the twins from Heinousburg think of this crazy household?

"Look, you want to borrow some clothes? Or just keep them?"

She raised her eyebrows at my hips then looked back up at me.

"I know, they'll be too big. What cab company did you call?"

"Blue and Green."

"They'll be another half hour, at least. Hold on."

Zan was smaller than I, shorter and with slimmer hips, though she still had probably thirty pounds on Marilyn, if you didn't count the teenager's breasts. I clicked open the door to her and Vivian's room, stepped softly inside. Their futon was occupied by more than one form. Had Zan—but tufts of blonde didn't need much illumination. I counted three frizzled hairdos against the pillows. Barry and the twins. Where did that leave Zan?

I heard the faint bleat of a car horn. The Blue and Green must have arrived ahead of schedule. I quickly found a pair of dark Levis but no t-shirt that would fit around Marilyn, so I grabbed one of Vivian's gigantic flannel shirts from the floor. Marilyn was halfway down the stairs by the time I got back to the living room. I threw the clothes at her and pounded down the stairs to tell the honking driver to be quiet and she'll be down in two minutes. The night was in its darkest hour, and its coldest.

Marilyn was buttoning herself into the shirt, a green and black tartan thin with wear, when I returned. Her bubble-gum dress was wadded on the floor by the television. I was startled by how short she looked without the high heel shoes. She left the shirt untucked and the straight slope of it off her breasts made her look somewhat less busty and a little less skinny.

"Shoes." I sped back to my room. There was a sleeping figure in my futon, too, but I didn't pause to try to figure out who it was. I grabbed a pair of thick socks from my basket of them and a pair of Georgia boots that my step-father had gotten me for Christmas. They were sturdy and not my style. Eb did all his holiday shopping at the Farmer's Co-op. I raced the socks and boots back to Marilyn.

"These okay for Thailand?"

She snorted and pulled on a sock, balancing on the other foot. "Thailand. I'm not going there."

"I thought that was the whole point!"

She shoved her foot into the left boot. It slid in easily. The boots were sizes too big. "Then you missed the whole point."

"But it's your home."

"Is San Francisco your home? You talk with accent from somewhere else. Home is not so great."

I couldn't argue with that.

Marilyn jammed on the other boot. Her fingers flew as she laddered the laces through the eyelets. "I bought my family a house. They have the nice place in their village, all wood. I did enough for them. Here or in Bangkok, I'm dead for them. It's okay. That way we're all better off."

Marilyn tugged the boot laces into a loopy bow. The fact that Vivian dressed like a twelve-year-old boy had finally found its point. In her over-large flannels and Zan's jeans, facial features theatrical under disintegrating blotches of make-up, Marilyn looked like any other student at Suburban California High. "Where are you going, then?" I asked her. "If you don't mind my asking."

"New York City." She started down the stairs.

"New York. Tough town."

She ignored me, pounding the stairs faster as she neared the bottom.

"Wait," I said, but she didn't and I had to run after her. "You think San Francisco summers are cold. It gets even colder in New York." I wiggled out of my leather jacket and tossed it as Marilyn swung open the front door. By reflex, she turned and caught it. She pushed open the security grate, and I followed to stop its closing clang from waking the neighbors. Its bars were cold, its force backwards surprisingly fierce. Marilyn punched her hands through my leather jacket's sleeves, flipped her black hair out over the collar, stomped to the cab, and hauled its passenger door open.

She didn't thank me. The cab took off before she had a chance to slam its door.

Chapter Twenty-Five

Sleep that night felt like work. I ground through a few hours, aware of commotion—rustles in the hallway, the mumbles of buses, the toilet flushing more often than seemed necessary, the melodies of roommate conversations. Despite my exhaustion it was a relief to open my eyes and give up trying to sleep. My room offered no time cues. My night job meant I didn't need an alarm clock and sunlight didn't make it through the tenement-spacing, tight as orthodonture, that separated our building from the building next door.

I was lying on my back. Neither the futon underneath me nor the quilt on top of me, a polyester creation of my Granny Leann's, was particularly comfortable. Rather than cuddling in a cloud of comfort, my nightly experience was more like crawling into a manila envelope. Normally it didn't bother me.

Were Big Brother and Johnny dead? I'd have no way of knowing. It wouldn't make the papers. But it wouldn't matter; I'd brought their rivals to them, leading the charge. Even if Johnny and Big Brother had survived the shoot-out, they wouldn't threaten me again. Chinatown had my back.

I turned my head to look at Hugh. He'd been the rumple in the quilt that I'd noticed the night before. He seemed to be a tense sleeper as well, though I suspected that with him it was a regular trait. He'd curled himself against the wall, a frozen cringe slapped up to the plaster. His hair stuck out, the color and stiffness of well-used corn brooms; golden stubble grew across his jaw. At least a foot of space separated us, room for another roommate or guest, I thought, cynically. God. How long would it be until Mose Junior solved our housing crisis? Where were we all going to fit?

I turned my head back to look at the ceiling of my small room. Since I didn't share it, normally, I'd taken the smallest of the three bedrooms. It wasn't much bigger than an Ohio walk-in closet. Furniture wasn't an option even if I had any to put in there. I kept my clothes in baskets on the floor, a line of them fit against the wall opposite the futon. The edges of them grazed the mattress's other edge.

I raised my hands to my eyes and pressed until I saw beige diamonds.

"What?" said Hugh. The quilt gathered a bit with his acceleration to a waking tension level.

"I didn't say anything."

"Aubrey?" He didn't move.

"Yes. What's wrong with you?"

"You got home late," he said, speaking over his shoulder. "You have quite a lot of guests."

"Right. Well, the latest one already left. Do you always sleep with your glasses on?" The black frames were flattened close to his face and pressed the lenses almost to his eyes.

He reached up to pull his glasses a centimeter down his nose. "No. I was waiting up for you. Last thing I remember is the *Dr. Who* marathon ending, so I must have fallen asleep around two."

"I didn't get home until something like four."

"I offered my room to your latest guest. The one in the um, pink dress? Janie?"

"Janie? You mean Marilyn."

"She introduced herself to me as Janie."

"Huh. Maybe that's her real name." It didn't seem very Thai. Perhaps her Mill Valley boyfriend had renamed her, as one does a shelter pet, something sweet and girl-next-door and pronounceable. Janie. But maybe she'd picked a new name for her new, New York City life.

"At any rate, Barry and the twins were already in Zan's room and Zan was in mine. I thought she might feel more comfortable if it was all girls."

"Thanks Hugh. I don't think she was planning to go to sleep, though. Thanks for looking after them. It's fine that you slept in here."

"I didn't mean to fall asleep. I was waiting up. You seemed to be in some sort of trouble." Hugh pushed himself into a sitting position and shook his head so his bangs fell into place, skimmed across the top bar of his glasses. His straight hair was cut to one length, a blond skirt with a V of darker stubble climbing up underneath it in the back. It was the haircut of a four-year-old, but it worked well on Hugh. Zan cut it for him, smoking in the kitchen, always failing to even it out.

Hugh folded his hands around his quilted knees. Then he looked at me. His brown eyes had highlights the same gold color as his hair.

"It's good to see you," I said. He hadn't gotten any closer, and he had to reach over pretty far to give my shoulder an awkward pat. "What have you been up to lately?" I had a sudden need to hear about a lifestyle that wasn't caught up in gang activity, prostitution rings, or the dim lights of pornography. A life that made the happy rounds of meals, work, television, reading, sleep.

"Me? You're just changing the subject." He pushed his glasses up his nose.

"No, really, I'm interested. How's work? How's the thrift store?" I reached over to hold his hand.

He gave me a strange look then took a breath. "Well, it's proceeding. We get most of our books during spring cleaning and at the end of the year when yuppies are looking for tax breaks. I haven't been terribly busy this summer."

"Prices going up?"

"No. Inflation hasn't been significant since the seventies."

"Okay. How's life been here at home? Catch me up."

"Vivian and Zan have been fighting. Most of our dishes are broken. I'll get us more from the store, but might as well wait until the two of them have made up. I haven't seen Geoffrey much. Vanessa Sassy kept him busy, then he's been spending time with Gregor."

"It's been okay having the houseguests?"

"Well, now that there are four of them I think there might be a problem with the bathroom."

"Three. Marilyn left last night. You're right though. I'm going to have it out with Mose Junior. He can't just expect me to host his precious features forever, just to save him a thousand something in rent. That guy is rolling in it." I kissed Hugh's hand. He never complained, so when he did I took it seriously and felt terribly bad. "I'll talk to him today."

"It's not like I dislike Barry and the twins, but the extra people do strain to the facilities, now that you're back as well."

"Right. I'm back. Oh god, Hugh, the place I was staying caught on fire." I rubbed my forehead at the memory of heat, the rotten smell of pot smoke, sirens that screamed red. DeeDee.

"The Tender Arms?"

"Yes, last night. Everyone's fine, everyone got out, but the whole thing went up in flames."

"Those old buildings are real tinderboxes sometimes. In 1906, it was fire that destroyed this city, not the earthquake. Your temporary home was brick on the outside, but those built-ins, moldings, doorframes, floors, everything inside was wooden. And that disintegrating wallpaper in the hallway." Hugh shook his head at the memory of the rancid velveteen with its regal fleur-de-lys pattern that had hung in the lobby and stairwell of the old tenement. "I'm sorry but the place was a firetrap. You had vacated, right?"

"Right." Hugh's palm pressed sweat into mine. "Let's get up and go to El Quake-O. I'm starving." I suddenly was. Thirst began in some internal core and radiated. When had I last eaten?

He was looking at our hands, then opened his abruptly so that mine slid off onto the quilt. "Me too," said Hugh. "I'm hungry, too."